A SEASON FOR VIOLENCE

A SEASON FOR VIOLENCE

THOMAS B. DEWEY

WILDSIDE PRESS

Published by Wildside Press LLC.
www.wildsidebooks.com

PROLOGUE

IN THE MONTH OF JUNE

LONNIE KIRK

He was pushing the Stingray down the South River Highway, coming into town about three in the morning, when his lights picked up the girl, stumbling across the road a hundred feet ahead. He was hitting about seventy, and in the time it took him to bang the brake and decide whether to take his chances with the row of trees on his left or the guardrail on the river bluff she had stopped, turned back, changed her mind, and started to run. She ran diagonally toward the bluff into his path, and the rear end of the Stingray screamed as he swerved; the tires held up all right, but he felt the brakes going and had to twist the wheel as he passed her. He wound up broadside to the driving lanes, with the stink of rubber in his nose and all the words he could remember in his mouth and the taut sickness in the pit of his belly.

After ten seconds he noted that the engine was still running, and he eased off to the right side of the road, scraped his front fender against the guardrail, and stopped. Looking back in the rearview mirror, he could make out the girl, walking away with her left hand out and held low, as if to catch herself. He mouthed a few more words, got out, walked toward the girl, and stopped several feet short of her.

"Hey," he called.

She stopped but didn't turn.

"You all right?" he said. "Need any help?"

She didn't answer.

Goddam it, he thought, what is it to me?

After a few seconds he walked on up to where she was standing, her feet slightly apart. A red purse dangled from her right hand. She had long black hair that had been done up high on her head, but it was now disarranged and fallen around her face. Her dress was twisted awry, and she was wearing a white sweater with the sleeves pushed up to the elbows.

"Listen—" he said.

She looked at him, and he saw she was only a kid, maybe sixteen, seventeen, Italian, with those big black eyes in a round face.

"You sick or something?" he said. "You need a lift somewhere?"

"I—don't know," she said.

"Where you going, walking?"

"Home."

"Crudsville?"

"Yeah."

"You're going the wrong way. The bridge is back there."

She looked beyond him along the dark road toward the lighted bridge and the straggling lights of the opposite shore of the river. "Oh," she said. She turned with a vague gesture, switched her purse to the other hand, and started off the other way, leaning toward the guardrail. He watched her for a minute, then went after her. She reached his car and started out around it.

"Come on," he said, "I'll give you a lift home. I live over there too."

She looked at the car and at his face. "You do?" she said.

"Come on, get in."

She hesitated and looked away, then looked at him again. "You a cop or what?" she asked.

"I'm a bartender, just getting off work. You want the ride?"

"I guess so," she said.

He opened the door, and she got in. She moved as if in pain, sliding carefully under the wheel and all the way over to the far door. He got in and started it. He eased away, tried the brakes, and found they were all the way gone.

"You sure stripped my linings," he said.

"What?"

"My brakes—running down the goddam road—"

"I'm sorry," she said.

Oh Christ, he thought.

She sat with her big eyes wide open, staring ahead through the windshield. He drove slowly, hugging the right side of the road, one hand on the emergency brake.

Forty bucks for new linings, he was thinking. And something sure as hell cracked in the rear end. Goddam punk kids—I thought there was a curfew.

"What's your name?" he asked.

"Betty," she said. "Elizabeth Petrucelli."

"Mine's Kirk. Lonnie Kirk."

"Okay," she said. "Thanks for the ride."

He turned onto the bridge. There was no traffic in either direction, so he opened it up some, hanging onto the hand brake.

"What happened?" he asked. "You walking home from a date?"

It was some time before she answered. "I guess you could say that," she said.

"You look sick."

"I'm sorry. I'll be all right."

The hell with it, he thought. He drove off the bridge on the Crudsville side and turned left on River Street. "What street do you live on?" he asked.

"It's all right," she said. "You can drop me off anywhere—"

"I asked you what street? I'm not asking for your goddam telephone number."

She winced and said, "Garibaldi Street, corner of Elm."

He turned out of the warehouse district to get away from the smell of the riverside. It would be ten blocks out of his way to take the girl to Garibaldi and Elm. I guess I asked for it, he thought.

The girl shifted carefully on the seat, put her hand on her belly, and leaned back, closing her eyes. Her skirt hiked up, and for the first time he saw the blood on her thigh.

Oh no, he thought, not to me. By God, no! He pulled to the curb abruptly, and the car lurched under the fast braking. The girl straightened and looked at him.

"All right, what happened?" he said. "Just so I know what to expect."

She was scared. She put her hand on the door.

"Just tell me what happened," he said.

"You said you weren't a cop."

"I'm not a cop. I got you in the car, and you were wandering around on the road and you got blood on your legs. I got to know the facts."

"Listen, leave me alone—I'll get out here—"

He caught her arm as she pushed the handle. "Talk to me," he said.

She didn't struggle, but she didn't say anything either.

"Some guy got to you," he said, "and threw you out of the car, right?"

"No—he didn't—I mean, he didn't throw me out. I got away—I got out by myself. That's why I was walking."

"Where did he pick you up?"

"He didn't."

"You had a date with him."

"Yes."

"Some Italian kid?"

"No."

"He wanted to and you didn't and he did it anyway, is that right?"

"Well—oh, leave me alone—"

"What was his name?"

"I don't remember—"

"You had a date with him and you don't remember his name?"

"It doesn't make any difference."

"It makes a hell of a big difference to me."

"Why?" she asked.

He rubbed his face roughly. "Oh, Jesus," he said, "you're too damn young to understand. Just tell me what his name was."

"What will you do?"

"Nothing. For my own protection I have to know."

She stared out the window for a long time, then, in a voice so low he had to bend close to catch it, she said, "Dexter. Robin Dexter."

"Is he from over here in Crudsville?"

"No."

"Other side of the river, huh?"

"Yes."

"Rich kid?"

"I don't know."

"Robin Dexter," he said.

"What are you going to do?"

"I don't know. Nothing. I just had to have the true facts, just in case."

"I wouldn't say it was you," she said.

He thought about that for a minute, then put the car in gear and left the curb. "Okay," he said. "I'm sorry it happened. You want to see a doctor, anything?"

"No, I just want to go home."

He made his way over the broad, rough streets, lined with old frame houses converted to rooming houses and brick faced apartment buildings. At Elm Street he turned left and made the six blocks to Garibaldi. The girl had the door open and one foot out of the car before he could come to a stop. He took it as easy as he could with the hand brake, but the car jerked enough to throw her forward against the open door, and her head struck the window.

"Watch it!" he yelled.

She got her balance and moved clear of the car. "I'm all right," she said. "Thanks for the ride."

"Listen, you better tell somebody about this."

She shook her head firmly. "Not me," she said. "Not me."

She gave the door a push. It didn't quite make the latch, and he had to reach over, open it, and slam it shut. By then the girl was walking away rapidly. He sat for half a minute watching her, then made a U-turn and headed back toward his own neighborhood, where he had an apartment in a converted house, a higher class section than Garibaldi near Elm. He passed within a block of the police station on Twelfth Street between River and Elm, drove a block and a half, then stopped.

Better go tell them, he thought, and then, *The hell with them. Let them do their own work.*

He drummed with his fingers on the wheel. The girl will sneak in the house and maybe get cleaned up and in bed safe. Or maybe her old lady will look in and see the blood and start yelling in Italian and wake up the old man and the kid will be scared and maybe she'll think she ought to keep the damn rich kid out of trouble, so they'll keep yelling at her and she'll say the first thing comes into her mind. Some guy—Kirk—Lonnie Kirk, she'll say.

He lit a cigarette, sat there till it was smoked out, and tossed it in the street. So I guess there's only one thing to do, he thought.

He made a slow U-turn and drove carefully back to Twelfth Street to the police station.

CHAPTER 1

IN THE MONTH OF AUGUST

GINO BLANCO

Gino backed his pickup into the nursery loading zone, jumped down, and began lifting sacks of mulch into the truckbed. It was not yet six-thirty in the morning, and the sacks were still damp from the night moisture. The sun was up, but it was hazy, and there was a chill bite in the air. Gino didn't mind. The tingle of cold on his ears and neck was bracing. The light, rich stench of the stacked planting mixes and manures had an edge of pungency that would dull as the day warmed.

Two boys, gardener's helpers, lounged against the wall of the nursery shack, watching without offering to help.

"Hey, Gino!" one called. "Take it easy with the muscle."

"Save yourself," the other said.

"For college," the first one said. "Hey, Gino you gonna go to college, no crap?"

Gino tossed another sack into the truck, ignoring them.

"How much they pay you to go to college?" the first one asked.

"By the game they pay," the other said. "If you win—huh, Gino?"

"Nah," the first one said, "just play. No win, no lose."

"Look at him with that heavy stuff. You gonna rupture yourself, Gino."

Gino pulled an order form from the hip pocket of his jeans, counted the sacks in the truck, made a note on the invoice, and scrawled his name under it. Then he took it to the door of the nursery shack and pushed it through the mail slot. He walked back to the truck, opened the door, then turned briefly toward the two boys and cupped himself in derision. As he climbed into the cab one of the two shouted obscenely at him. Gino paid no attention.

He drove south on River Street toward the Fifth Street Bridge. The sun was warm now through the early haze, and he rolled down the window and rested his bare arm on the sill. On his right the river, nearly a mile wide, flowed almost imperceptibly southward, more slowly than his truck moved. The wide, roughly surfaced street was indented by loading ramps and laced with angled railroad spurs. Truck trailers were backed up to some of the ramps, and some were beginning to load. A few coal barges had pushed off their riverside moorings and were moving downstream with the current.

Across the river rose the high gray bluffs of the West Side, topped by a thick fringe of green parkways. A few church spires showed above the trees. Except for a few old estates near the north edge of the city, which clung like fortresses to the rim of the bluff, the living and business buildings of Gilesport were hidden from the lower bank. But Gino knew they were there. Several homes and business buildings he knew well because he worked there and took care of them. But they were just places to go and to work in. He lived here on the east side of the river, in Crudsville, because he had been born here and knew it and, knowing it, liked it. And because he had played football here, and because Lewkie lived here, too.

Lucrezia Delfino. Gino liked to roll her classic name over his mind's tongue. It gave his image of Lewkie a special grandeur when he linked her with that historical Lucrezia or the great Bori, the opera singer, whose records he used to listen to in the high school library, sitting in the close booth that reeked of sweat, with the volume turned low so nobody else would hear. He would think about the similarity between Borgia and Bori, and about Lewkie, and with the lush melodies of Verdi and Puccini soaring to crescendo in his ears the three Lucrezias would blend into one heroic figure of feminine sound and glory, and he would feel Lewkie in his chest and groin. And after the music stopped, he would have to sit there for a while and think about something else before he could leave the booth.

Of course, Lewkie would never poison anybody and she wasn't much of a singer except for a few folk songs and rock 'n' roll tunes that everybody was always singing. She had a light, not quite true voice and sang on the top of her breath as if she wanted to keep it a secret. Even now, driving in the moist morning without music, bouncing in the truck seat, he could call up the feeling of Lewkie in his arms, warm and light against him, her mouth part of his mouth, and her tiny tongue against his, and his hands on her small, tightly bound breasts and wherever else she would let him put them. He felt the swelling ache and relived the eternal, savage quarrel:

"Listen—"

"No, Gino, not there—"

"Why not?"

"Because."

"Everybody does it."

"Not me—not yet."

"When?"

"I don't know—"

"Lewkie—"

"Maybe if you go to college—"

"College! What difference does that make?"

"I don't know."

"Lewkie, for God's sake!"

"Gino—be good to me."

College, he thought. All right to play football. But to study, to have to be eligible—not like high school—all strangers—

Making the turn onto the high bridge, he ground his teeth and the truck's gears in savage concert.

Business was going good all summer. Fifteen regular customers and some extras. Like today, all day for Mrs. Forester, setting those new beds—landscape work. Seventy-five bucks for one day. I could take care of Lewkie all right, right now.

Then, straightened out on the bridge, heading for the green parkways on the far side of the river, he began going over in his mind the planting and bedding he would be doing that day for Mrs. Forester because it was futile and disturbing to think about Lewkie.

DONNA FORESTER

She had been awake for some time, but Carl hadn't known it. She lay still and heavy in the bed, listening while he bathed, then listening to the whirring of his razor and the sounds he made in the next room, dressing and packing.

A wave of nausea twisted through her stomach, and she put her hand there, pressing hard, squeezing her eyes shut till she felt a few tears start under the meshed lids.

Son of a bitch, she thought. She opened her eyes, looked at the ceiling, and felt the nausea fade. "Son of a goddam bitch," she said aloud. Good thing my big brothers taught me about words, she thought. She thought of some other things to say, and her lips moved, but she didn't speak them. The nausea returned, and she thought about getting up for a glass of water, then thought better of it. Just lie here and die, she thought.

She smiled, feeling the skin crack at the corners of her mouth. That would give him something to think about, she thought. At least he'd have to stay long enough to make the funeral arrangements. He wouldn't want to come home to a stinking corpse.

The nausea struck again, and she pressed her naked stomach with both hands. I wonder what it's like? she thought. The smell. Do male and female corpses smell different?

Oh, God, let's not get into that, she thought. He'll be sticking his head in here any minute, hoping I'll be asleep so he can sneak out easy. I wish I had the guts to hit him with something lethal.

She pushed herself up, lay on her elbows, and let her head fall back limply. It made her eyes go out of focus, and she blinked them rapidly and fixed them, so that she was gazing upside down at a framed needle-point sampler that hung above the headboards on her side of the bed. It had come down to her through her mother's family. It had been made, as she remembered, by her great-grandmother, who had lived in Massachusetts, and the faded letters of the motto read:

BLESS THIS HOUSE

"Amen," she said aloud.

She heard Carl's step outside the door, sank down on the pillow, and closed her eyes. The door opened, and there was a silence. She could visualize him in the doorway, studying her, trying to decide whether she was asleep or awake, uncertain whether to speak.

"Donna—?" he said quietly.

"Yes, what?" she said.

"Taxi will be here in a couple of minutes."

"Oh? Well, say hello to it for me."

He hesitated, then came into the room a few steps. "Anything wrong?" he asked.

Oh, God! she thought. "No," she said. "What could be wrong?"

"I've got to go," he said. "I'll be back next Wednesday, maybe Thursday."

"Have a good time," she said. "Have a ball."

A pause.

"This is a business trip," he said.

"I know. They're all business trips."

"That's right."

Another pause.

"Well," he said, "good-bye now. Take care of yourself."

"Yeh, I guess that's it," she said.

Outside, a horn blew. "What do you mean by that?" Carl said.

"I don't know. There's your taxi. You wouldn't want to miss the plane."

"Look, if you're not feeling well—"

She turned suddenly onto her side, away from him, and put her face in her arms. "Oh, for Christ's sake, go!" she said.

"Listen, Donna—"

She heard him take a step toward the bed, then stop. If he touches me, she thought, I'll slug him, I swear to God—

But he turned and walked away. She heard the bedroom door close and his angry bustle, gathering up his things. The horn blew again. She heard the front door slam, and a few moments later the taxi pulled away. Then it was quiet. It was so quiet she could hear the faint buzz of the electric clock beside the bed. She opened one eye, saw that it was seven-fifteen, and closed the eye.

He'll be in San Francisco in time for breakfast California time, she thought. I wonder, Does she meet him at the airport? Or does she have things all ready at her goddam apartment for when he comes in? Do they eat first or—?

Stop that now! she thought.

She turned again, bouncing hard on the bed, as if turning her body could turn her thoughts. Outside there was the roar of a truck, the groan of its springs turning onto the drive.

The gardener, she thought. Oh, boy, I got to do that today—plant all my lovely flowers! No, the gardener will plant them. But I got to be out there, bright and smiling, showing him. What's his name? Gino. Gino what?

The sun through the drawn curtains was warm gold. Hot, she thought. A hot, steamy day. If I go to the club for lunch, I can sit in the garden room and—sweat!

She pushed the sheet off and lay still for a moment on her back, feeling the screened warmth of the sun. In the back yard there was the sound of wood and metal banging as Gino unloaded tools from the truck.

Donna got up and went to the bathroom. Returning through the dressing room, she caught sight of herself in the three-paneled mirror and stopped. "Thirty-eight," she said aloud to her own image. "Not old—not old."

She put her hands on her breasts, lifting, and watched the firm thrust of her nipples. I remember when he couldn't get enough, she thought.

She tightened her stomach muscles and looked at the flat, firm sweep of tanned flesh below her diaphragm and the gently convex, still taut belly.

"No fat," she said. "See? See how good care I take?" Exercise, she thought, and the right food.

She raised her arms high overhead and stretched, rising slowly to the tips of her toes, inhaled deeply, then exhaled slowly and settled down on her heels. The slight exertion caused her face and neck to flush pink.

She adjusted the panels of the mirror and slapped vigorously at her buttocks. "No fat there, either. See?" She stretched upward again, then bent with her knees locked, her feet only slightly spread, and touched the floor with her fingertips. There! she thought. Not old, damn it. Thirty-eight and the best lay in River County.

She straightened with a weary shrug, picked a housecoat from a hanger, stepped into it, then zipped it up over her breasts and went to the kitchen. After she got the percolator plugged in and had poured a glass of orange juice, she went to the window and looked out to where Gino was working at the back of the deep yard. He worked, she noticed, with great economy of effort. His movements seemed leisurely, but the accumulation of cuttings and other detritus was already immense.

Coordination, she thought It must be coordination. It's more than sheer strength. Athlete, she thought. Football player.

The coffee was ready, and she was pouring her first cup when he knocked at the kitchen door. She zipped the housecoat the rest of the way up before opening the door. He stood there in his heavy work shoes, large and diffident on the service porch. His blue denim shirt was wet with sweat, and there were smudges of garden soil on his thick brown arms.

"Good morning," she said. "Come in and have a cup of coffee."

"Well, I—"

"If you don't like coffee, I've got—"

"Oh, I like coffee fine."

She stood back, and he wiped his feet carefully on the mat before entering. "I wanted to check with you," he said, "before I start digging up the old stuff—I mean those bulbs and—"

"I know. Old stuff is right. Here, Gino, sit down." She set out a cup for him and filled it. "Cream and sugar?"

"Well, if you—"

"Sure. Go ahead, sit down. There's nothing precious about the furniture."

He squeezed himself into the booth in the breakfast nook, and she sat across from him, aware suddenly that the housecoat was not a conventionally adequate covering under the circumstances.

"You certainly cleaned out a lot in a hurry," she said.

He looked at her, then quickly at his coffee. She moved briskly.

"I thought we would make the border all around three sides," she said, "and a little deeper—I guess I mean wider—than it was, and with kind of scallops. Then we can put the new bulbs along the back and change the roses and those other perennials where we have to. They're all pruned?"

"Yes, ma'am. I did that last week."

"Of course. Did you bring plenty of mulch?"

"A whole truckload. I can take back what we don't need."

"Oh, let's go ahead and use it up. All the richer."

"Whatever you say, Mrs. Forester. I better be getting back to work."

"It's hot out there today. Don't you have a hat?"

"Yeah, but I don't like to wear it. Gets in the way."

"Well, watch out for sunstroke."

He was on his feet now, towering over her like a tree. The telephone rang in the other room, and she jumped, then frowned at herself, settled deliberately, and drank the rest of her coffee.

"Thanks for the coffee," Gino said, as he went out.

The phone had rung eight times when she reached it in the bedroom. She snatched it from the cradle, and her voice had a harsh edge when she answered.

"This is Donna Forester."

"Hi, Donna—Peg Farrell."

"Yes, Peg, how are you?"

"Oh, all right. Listen, I thought we might have lunch today at the club. It's—"

"I don't know. I don't think so today."

"Oh—well, I just thought—Jack is having lunch downtown, and—"

"I'd love to," Donna said, "but today—"

"And Carl's gone again, isn't he? I mean—"

"Yes, he's gone."

"So I thought we might—"

"I'd really love to, Peg, but I have the gardener here for all day, and I'll have to be around to supervise."

"I see. Naturally. Well, maybe tomorrow."

"Yes. Give me a ring tomorrow."

"Okay. Good-bye now."

Donna hung up and sat on the bed with one hand resting on the phone. But what will I do if I don't go to the goddam club? she thought. I'll sit here and think up something. Something what? But not with Peg. Not at that stupid, stuffy club, with everybody looking at me and thinking about Carl being gone—again—again—

In an anguished flurry she rose, reached out blindly for support, then made her way into the bathroom. She sprinkled bath salts into the tub and turned on the water, then pulled the zipper of her housecoat down and stepped out of it. Suddenly she was cold, shivering, but when she put her toes into the tub, it was a burning agony.

"Oh, God!" she said, "what will I do? How do you—?" She began to cry and sat down on the edge of the tub, feeling the steam rise around her naked back. She sat with her face in her hands till she heard the water begin to run out the overflow drain. Then she adjusted the taps and sat paddling with one hand till the temperature was right.

When she got into the tub, she had stopped crying, but she was still cold and she sank down till the water was at her chin. The enveloping warmth soothed her. The tight twist of pain in her stomach began to dissolve, and she stretched her legs luxuriously, looking down at them. They were foreshortened under the surface of the salt-clouded water. She giggled. Like something in a funhouse mirror, she thought.

The telephone rang. No, she thought. It rang again. "Shut up!" she said.

But after the fifth ring she climbed out of the tub, threw her house-coat around her, and ran dripping to the bedroom to answer.

"Donna?" a woman's voice said. "This is Liz Dexter. Listen—"

Oh, my great God, Donna thought. She started to hang up, then clamped her mouth shut and hung onto the phone.

"Listen," Liz was saying, "I'm going crazy. I've got to talk to some-body."

Why me? Donna thought. Why, why, why?

"This thing about poor Robin has me frantic, and I don't know where to turn. Please, Donna—"

"Yes, Liz," Donna said, forcing herself to be calm. She had begun to shiver. She crawled under the bedclothes, wet as she was, and pulled them around her shoulders. She had to fight to keep her teeth from chattering.

Liz's voice lowered. "Pete isn't down for breakfast yet," she said. "I don't know what to do—he's promised to talk to Dick Kramer again—"

"I'm sure," Donna said, "everything will be worked out. Just hang on, Liz—"

"But we haven't been able to get anywhere with anybody," Liz said. "It's unbelievable. I thought—you know Evelyn Kramer pretty well. If you could talk to her—"

Evelyn Kramer, Donna thought, cringing. Like trying to slice a marshmallow. "I'm not sure," Donna said. "What could I say?"

"I don't know, but Donna—if you had ever been a mother—"

Oh, Christ! "Look Liz," Donna said firmly, "I've got an appointment at the beauty parlor in forty-five minutes. I'm about to get dressed. If I can find a minute, I'll call Evelyn Kramer. Will that—?"

"Oh, thank you, Donna. I have to go now. Pete's coming down—"

"All right, Liz, I'll see what I can do." She hung up, climbed out of bed, and ran back to the tub. The water had cooled some, and she ran more hot into it and made herself lie quietly, awaiting the warmth.

Call Evelyn Kramer, she thought. What an idea. "Hello, Evelyn? This is Donna Forester. About this unbelievable case of Robin Dexter—"

What's unbelievable about it? she thought savagely. He did it. He got this little Italian girl in the back seat of his car and got his damn thing out and into her and she didn't want to and she got hurt some and—he raped her, for God's sake! And that's a crime. So what the hell can Evelyn Kramer or anybody else do about the precious boy? Especially me?

She pushed Liz Dexter out of her mind, slid deeper in the tub, and began slowly to wash herself, listening to the sounds Gino Blanco made working outside in the garden.

CHAPTER 2

LIZ AND PETE DEXTER

Liz Dexter sat across from her husband, Pete, in the breakfast room and twirled her empty coffee cup with long, compulsive fingers. Now and then her fingers shook, and she would let go of the cup and clench her fist, open it and stretch her fingers till they ached, then begin again to twirl the cup.

Pete was hidden behind the morning paper, but she could see him as through a one-way glass of memory and association: the big, square face with the thick brows, gray now, once reddish brown; the gray crew-cut hair, the sharp—needle-sharp—penetrating green eyes; the loud, impatient voice. Military. She had thought of him for years as military, erect, in command. But he had never been a real professional soldier—only that stint in Washington during the war, behind a desk. Colonel Dexter—honorary title so that the Army could make use of his business experience and contacts. Business—Robin—Her stomach cramped violently, and she gasped.

"What is it?" Pete said from behind the paper.

"Nothing. I think I'm getting the ulcers back."

"Better go on your diet," he said.

She felt a sudden urge to tear the paper out of his hands and slap him with it in his square, smug face. She actually reached out but drew her hand back. She was afraid of him, always had been afraid. Why? How had it happened to her? With most of the couples she knew, it was the other way around.

Thank God she had tried to bring Robin up to have some tenderness, affection—But how had he got into that awful thing with that little—

"Listen, Pete," she said.

Pete lowered the paper but didn't answer. He turned three more pages, and she saw his sharp, gray-browed eyes run down the columns of the financial page. Then he folded the paper neatly, laid it beside him on the table, poured himself another cup of coffee, and looked at her. "Yes, Liz?" he said.

"About Robin's case—"

"Now, just take it easy," Pete said, "and listen." His voice had that insulting, icy authority she had grown to fear and hate. He tapped on the newspaper with a firm, square finger. "There's nothing in the paper about it today. That's one good break. But they probably wouldn't run anything till tomorrow, anyway, when the trial's scheduled to start.

"You know very well I haven't sat around and let things go. I offered the girl's father five thousand; I had it in my pocket in cash. I had ten in my pocket and I would have gone that high. It would have been all right with the old man, but that Jewish lawyer from Dick Kramer's office had been around, and the girl and her mother were afraid."

Liz clenched and opened her hands. "I know, I know—you told me—"

"I'm just repeating the history to show you I'm on top of it."

On top, she thought.

"So next I fired that stuffed-shirt lawyer, Henley, who knows all about taxes and property titles but nothing about criminal law, and I got me a scrappy, hungry criminal man—"

"I know," Liz said. "I know you fired Henley, but—"

"—and he's on top of the case."

Liz leaned far over the table, her breasts on her clenched fists. "But the trial—the publicity—"

"Remember your ulcers," he said.

"I was talking to Donna Forester a few minutes ago," Liz said, "and she said she'd call Evelyn Kramer and talk to her—"

"Will you let me finish, please?" Pete said. "I said this lawyer—Gideon, Harry Gideon—was on top of the case"—he paused dramatically—"if the case comes to trial at all."

Why can't he tell me these things? she thought. Why does he have to be so damn big shot! "You mean there won't be a trial?" she said.

"I mean I'm working on it and I'm working hard."

"But it's tomorrow!"

"You've heard of continuances, my dear?"

"Of course, but it's already been postponed—"

"Now just listen carefully. Dick Kramer is the District Attorney. He's one of us. But he can't just throw the case out the window and let it go. Not after the publicity. It would be political suicide, and I happen to know that Dick Kramer has political ambitions. I know he's having lunch with Senator Morris today and I know Senator Morris is very shortly going to announce his retirement from public office.

"It also happens that I have some influence around the courthouse—and even in Washington, as you may be aware. I've been using it. I'm going to use it some more today. First, I'm going to call on Dick Kramer at home, before he leaves for the office." He looked at the watch on his hairy wrist. "It is now ten minutes to nine, and if I may be excused from this family discussion, I can get to Dick's house by nine o'clock."

Liz could no longer suppress her rage. For the first time in her life, afraid or not, she lashed back at him. "Certainly you may be excused," she said. "When did you ever have to ask to be excused? You can be excused to hell and back!" She pushed herself away from the table, her tears blinding her to his shocked face, turned, and ran from the room and halfway up the stairs. There she stopped, gripping the handrail with one hand, her stomach churning. She waited for Pete to leave the house. She heard his military footsteps going away toward the back door. She wiped her eyes with the palm of her hand and listened to the roar of the Jaguar and the angry sound the tires made on the drive, and heard it roar off down the quiet street. Then, hauling herself by one hand, she climbed the stairs.

She washed her face, dried it, and put on some fresh powder and lipstick, then walked on tiptoe down the hall to Robin's room at the back of the house. He was lying face down on the bed, nude, as he always slept, and the sheet had been pushed down, half exposing his buttocks. She looked away, her eyes taking in the old familiar room with its accumulation of souvenirs and male equipment—fishing rod, baseball gear, a few books, some sports magazines, snapshots of girlfriends pasted on the wall.

Tears welled in her eyes, and she brushed them away with her wrist and entered the room. She looked at him for a moment, long and lean on the bed, his head on his folded arm, his face turned away. She drew the sheet up to his waist, and he stirred without turning to her.

"Robin?" she whispered. Then louder. "Robin, dear—are you awake?"

He stirred again, lifted his head, and turned it slowly to look at her.

"Oh," he said.

"Listen, would you like some breakfast? I'll bring it up."

"Nah, I'm not even awake yet."

"I'm sorry."

He grunted something by way of dismissal.

"Listen, dear," she said, "everything will be all right. Your father is on his way to see Mr. Kramer. I'm sure they'll work something out."

He looked at her for a few seconds. "Okay," he said. "Good." He turned away, wriggled under the sheet, and lay still.

She lingered a moment, then left the room and went slowly down the hall to the stairs.

RICHARD KRAMER

Dick Kramer was having breakfast at the kitchen table at nine o'clock. On the table beside his plate was a small stack of letters, and beside the letters was a memo pad. From time to time as he ate he scribbled notes on the pad. The morning paper was also on the table, unopened and unread.

He ate hurriedly because it was late. Usually he would have finished breakfast before nine, would have leftover correspondence out of the way and at least half the paper read before he left for the office. But this morning he had risen later than usual and had dressed with more than usual care, and he was behind schedule.

While he ate, a tall, gray-haired woman in a white uniform worked over the kitchen sink and the stove. As Dick scribbled a note on the pad she poured him some coffee and set the pot beside him on the table.

"Thank you, Edith," he said.

Edith didn't answer. He was reading the last letter in the pile of correspondence when the doorbell rang at the front of the house. He glanced up to see the maid leaving the kitchen. He looked through the last few papers, poured himself coffee, and pushed his homework into a slender, black briefcase. He was lifting the cup to his mouth when he heard the loud, peremptory voice of Pete Dexter in the living room. In momentary panic, still holding the cup, he started up, reaching for his briefcase as if to run. Then, long schooled in the discipline of public encounter, he sat down and composed himself.

Braced though he was, he winced when he saw Colonel Pete Dexter push through the swinging kitchen door. He comes on like the whole damn Marine Corps, Dick thought.

"Morning, Dick," Pete said.

"Hello, Pete."

Edith slid into the kitchen and went to the sink.

"Edith," Dick said, "you might go up and see how Mrs. Kramer is feeling. She might want breakfast."

"Yes, Mr. Kramer," Edith said and left the room.

"Coffee?" Dick said.

"No, thanks," Pete said, pulling out a chair. "Don't want to keep you. I know you've got a busy day ahead. But, then, you always have."

"Usually," Dick said. How's he going to try it this time? Dick was thinking. He's tried everything there is. "How's business?" he asked.

Pete shrugged. "No complaints. If it weren't for taxes—"

Dick nodded neutrally and, in spite of himself, glanced at his watch.

"I had a telephone call yesterday from Vince Farrell," Pete said.

"In Washington?"

"Right."

Dick said nothing.

"Old Vince and I grew up together," Pete said. "Funny how things work out. I went one way, Vince went another."

Dick restrained a wry twist of the mouth. Talk about indirection, he thought. Pete Dexter is saying, 'Look at me. Big business all my own, and poor old Vince, working for somebody else all his life—for wages.'

"Yes," Dick said.

"Old Vince has been the Senator's right-hand man for twenty years now."

He wants me to ask what the telephone call was about, Dick thought. There was a pause.

"Vince wanted me to have a talk with Steve Carolla," Pete said. "Kind of sound him out before the Senator gets together with him."

"I see," Dick said. I see real clear, he thought. So hurry up and get it over with.

"That's another thing," Pete said. "Funny thing. A guy like Carolla—beat his way to the top. County committee in his pocket. Most powerful political guy in the state—and yet—"

Dick sat quietly, waiting.

"Even Steve Carolla," Pete said, "has got something he wants, something he hasn't got yet."

"I suppose everybody—" Dick said, reaching for his briefcase.

"And the thing Steve Carolla wants," Pete said, "I've got."

They rose at the same time. Dick slid the briefcase under his arm, and Pete Dexter put his hands in his pockets.

"I understand you're having lunch with the Senator today," Pete said.

"Yes," Dick said.

Pete nodded gravely. "You've got a future, Dick," he said. "You know how to handle yourself. Play your cards right, you can hit the top. Nothing I'd like better."

"It's a little premature," Dick said, "but thanks for the good wishes. Anything else on your mind?"

"No," Pete said, moving toward the swinging door. "Just wanted to wish you good luck with the Senator. Morris is a good man. Shrewd. I've known him for years. If there's anything I can do—"

"Thanks," Dick said. "I've got to get to the office—"

"Sure," Pete said. "So long, Dick."

Dick Kramer watched him shoulder his way out of the kitchen. Then he hitched the briefcase up high under his arm and went quickly up the back stairs. Edith was descending as he climbed.

"I'll fix Mrs. Kramer's breakfast," she said.

"Fine. Thanks," Dick said.

He went down the hall, turned into the bedroom, and found his wife, Evelyn, propped up in bed, wearing a yellow satin bed jacket, idly turning the pages of a leather-bound datebook.

"Good morning. How are you feeling?" he said.

"Oh—it's you. Better, I guess. I didn't sleep very well."

"Sorry. I'm a little late." He leaned over her. She tilted her narrow, pale face up, and he kissed her cheek. She smelled faintly of violets.

"We have a bridge date at the club for tomorrow night," Evelyn Kramer said. "It's still all right for you, isn't it?"

"I guess so," he said, "if you want to."

"I'll see how I feel," she said.

"I may be late this evening," he said. "I'm having lunch with Senator Morris—" He paused with some expectancy.

Evelyn yawned and put her hand delicately to her mouth. "That's nice," she said. "Have a good time."

"Well, good-bye for now," he said, turning away.

"Uh—Dick," she said.

He turned back. "Yes?"

"About Robin Dexter—this awful case—"

"What about it?"

"It seems so silly—all that fuss and publicity—"

"It's not exactly silly," Dick said. "The case against him is very strong. It's not something to be shrugged off."

"Well," she said petulantly, "it's—you know, kind of making a mountain out of a molehill, isn't it?"

"That depends," Dick said, "on your definitions of mountains and molehills."

Evelyn frowned. "Oh, I know—the law and all that," she said. "But after all—some wild Italian girl. They have different attitudes, you know. It isn't the same for them."

Dick felt an old, familiar tightness in his chest, an impulse to run away blindly, as he had for a moment wanted to run away from Pete Dexter. "As to their attitudes," he said, "I wouldn't know. I know about the law. I have to run now. Have a good day. Try to get some rest."

"I'll try," she said.

He went out quickly and returned along the hall to the back stairs. He had to squeeze past Edith, who was coming up with a breakfast tray. They didn't speak to each other in passing.

AL LEVY

At eleven-fifteen Al Levy, broad, thick-chested, quick on his feet, came into the office he shared with Deputy District

Attorney Blake O'Brien. He dropped a worn, well-stuffed brief bag on his desk with purposeful force. Blake swung slowly in his chair to look at him.

"Guess who I just had a conference with," Al said.

"All right—Harry Gideon, the Dexter boy's lawyer."

"Right. Guess who was with him?"

"The boy's father."

"Wrong." Al pulled papers out of his bag and slapped them down on the desk.

"Who?" Blake said.

"Steve Carolla."

"Well—" Blake said mildly. "Big Daddy Carolla."

"Didn't say a word, not one damn word, just sat there with his big face with the cigar stuck in it."

"So?" Blake said. "What was the offer? You should be President of the United States?"

"Knock off the phony dialect," Al said. "Not me, for Christ's sake. So Mr. Richard Kramer should be President of the United States."

Blake's eyebrows lifted and fell. "Gideon said so?"

"Naturally not. But we know, don't we?"

Blake O'Brien displayed curiosity against his better judgment. "What would work? I mean with the case."

"The boy would quietly plead *nolo contendere* and the girl would withdraw the charges and the case would get stuck in the drawer."

"I see. Mr. Carolla would take care of persuading the girl to withdraw."

"That is the gist of it, yeah."

"What does Carolla care about it?"

"Carolla doesn't care about the case. He cares about Carolla. He wants something from Mr. Peter Colonel Dexter. This is how he will get it."

"What does Dexter have—?"

"Come on. About nine million dollars' worth of property up the river that if he sells any of it, like to Carolla, say, it would be a bad tax bite. But for a consideration—"

"Okay. But about Gideon—I seem to remember there's a Superior Court Judge, name of Harris, would have something to say about it. You going to walk into Judge Harris's chambers and say the girl is backing out?"

"Oh, no, boy, not me. Like walking off the Fifth Street Bridge sideways. But Mr. Richard Kramer could hold a consultation with the judge, and there would have to be some phonying up, like the case isn't really too strong and blah, blah, blah, and Mr. Richard Kramer could swing it."

"Oh," Blake said.

"Oh, shit. The case is so strong it's busting out of my briefcase. Gideon knows it, and Kramer knows it. Everybody knows it."

"So it's got to be laid in Kramer's lap."

"Yeah," Al grinned. "But that won't be new to him. It's been there a long time. Ambition, boy—ambition is the killer. He can have a big, sensational case, which he will surely win and grab off a big hunk of public support, from a sociological viewpoint. Or he can quietly lay the thing to rest, and Carolla and Pete Dexter will see that he gets a chance to run for President of the United States. He would probably lose the election because he belongs to the wrong party. But he could have quite a ride and he could no doubt be a senator for many years to come."

'The way you put it, he can't lose, case or no case."

"Not quite that simple. How would you make the decision, assuming you understood the real meaning of power, which is money, boy, money?"

Blake didn't say anything.

Al Levy picked up his phone and dialed three numbers. "Hello, Ida," he said, "what time is the boss's lunch date with the Senator?... Okay, I got to see him. Urgent. Set it up for me. About five minutes from now, okay?" He hung up, picked up the papers from his desk, and turned to the door.

"What are you going to do if Kramer ducks out on the case?" Blake asked.

Al Levy looked at him for several long seconds. His broad face was serious for a change. "Resign," he said, "and go into private practice."

He left the office, walked down a corridor to the elevator, and stepped into it. Two minutes later Ida, the District Attorney's secretary, showed him into Mr. Kramer's office.

Dick Kramer leafed through the papers Al Levy had laid in front of him, looked out the window behind him, then across the desk at Al. Al Levy, Dick thought. The best lawyer in the county. If I duck out, he'll quit, as sure as we're sitting here. That's up to him, but what am I going to do? "You're sure of your case, huh?" Dick said.

"I'm positive."

Dick Kramer picked up the stack of papers, joggled them up and down on the desk till the edges were even, and handed them to Al Levy.

"There's something more," he said. "You've got something going in you over this case. You're close to being sadistic about it."

Al put the papers under his arm and got up. "No," he said, "I'm not sadistic. If I were a private attorney and Mr. Dexter would come to me with this case, I would take it. I wouldn't expect to win it, but I'd give it a good try. But I'm on the other side now and, maybe, all right, I've got something going in me. This big rich kid got his hands on this unrich, lightweight girl and banged her—against her will—till it hurt. I've got a witness, the most honest of honest men, because he will testify in his own exclusive interest. A witness named Lonnie Kirk, a bartender.

"All right. That's the case—a lot of it. But, like you say, there's more. I think it's morally wrong for a strong boy like the Dexter boy to do what he did to that girl. I know damn well it's against the law, and I know where I'm working. And that's what I've got going on in me over this case."

Dick Kramer swung slowly in his chair, looked out the window, and swung back. "Okay, Al," he said. "Go to it."

DONNA FORESTER

Donna, wearing the same housecoat she had worn on arising, looked out to where Gino was working under the noon sun. He had taken off his shirt, and his broad naked back was wedge-shaped as he squatted over the new flower beds and worked easily with his large, competent hands.

I wonder—she thought. No, she thought, no, you can't—Why not?

But what if he didn't—? Oh, God, I couldn't stand that.

She stiffened, turned from the window, started out of the kitchen, and stopped to lean on both hands on the long shelf opposite the back door. Her head moved in jerky, negative swings from side to side. No—no—no—

She pushed herself from the shelf, turned, and went to the door. Her hand on the knob hesitated, plucked, gripped, and turned it. "Gino—!" she called. "Gino Blanco! Will you come here, please?"

When he came in, she was leaning against the shelf. He hesitated before entering, wiped his feet, then came in.

There was a glass of cold orange juice on the table in the breakfast nook.

"I thought you might like a cold drink," she said.

He looked at the juice and then at his work-stained hands.

"Well—thanks, yeah. Could I wash my hands?"

"Certainly," she said, pointing to the sink.

She stood there with her buttocks planted against the hard edge of the shelf while he washed his hands, dried them, crossed to pick up the orange juice, and began to drink it, not hurrying.

"What do you do when you're not working, Gino?"

"What—?"

"I mean in your spare time? What do you do for fun?"

"Oh—just mess around, I guess."

She looked at the back of her right hand as if inspecting her recent manicure. Her fingers shook slightly. "Do you have a girl?"

He shrugged. "I go out sometimes."

He doesn't want to talk about her, Donna thought. So all right. Good.

He finished the juice, looked for a place to put the empty glass, and finally settled for returning it to the table. "Thanks very much—"

"What do you do about lunch?" she asked.

"I brought it. I've got a lunch bucket in the truck." He was looking at her as if uncertain how to leave.

She lifted her right hand, palm up, and her fingers curled. "Come here, Gino," she said.

After a moment he approached her. Her vision had gone somewhat awry, and his face was out of focus. She looked at his thick, broad chest, filigreed with fine black hairs. She put her hand on him, felt him withdraw, then return.

"Gino—" she said. With her left hand she found the zipper of her housecoat and drew it down to her waist, exposing her breasts. "Gino—listen—"

He was looking down at her breasts. She lifted his left hand with her right and drew it inside the housecoat. It was slack for a moment against her ribs, then firm, and still cool from the cold glass. She found the zipper of his jeans, toyed with it a moment, then pushed it down.

"Gino—did you ever—you know, Gino?"

"Well—I—yeah—"

"I don't care. Here—just stand still a minute." She had him in her hand. Carefully, gently, she thought. So strong—so good. No, you can still stop. No—oh, yes, oh, God, yes!

She turned at the shelf, still holding him. "Come, Gino—in here. Come with me."

She let go of him then, and walked quickly out of the kitchen, through the dining room, and into the hall. And Gino followed.

Then they were in the bedroom, and she was sliding her housecoat down from her shoulders. It wound up draped over her hips as if she'd been posing for the *Venus de Milo* or something. She paused and without looking at him," said, "Gino, listen—if you don't want to—if you have a thing against—older women—"

And he said, "No, I want to. You don't seem old to me."

"Thank you, Gino. Come here, closer, let me help you." She was cursing herself, practically mouthing the words, for being so craven, namby-pamby, fink, chicken—for trying to use him to make the decision for her.

"Gino."

"Yes, ma'am?"

"Oh, goddam it!"

"Something wrong?"

She turned to him suddenly, taking him by surprise with her arms around his neck. They both lost their balance, and she managed to fall back onto the bed, dragging at him, so that he sprawled over her. The look of concern on his face made her laugh.

"Ah, Gino—so clumsy, I'm sorry. Come, come here, let me—there."

He submitted to her caresses and directions like a good schoolboy, and she had a few moments of self-disgust, but she didn't stop. When he went into her, she cried a little, but by then Gino didn't notice.

"So good—so sweet," she murmured, "Oh, Gino, do it—love me."

Without warning, irrationally, she thought of her talk with Evelyn Kramer three hours earlier. I wonder, she thought, how long it's been since Dick did it to that paper-doll wife of his.

CHAPTER 3

The River County Courthouse had been built—according to the cornerstone—in 1897. The county had long outgrown it, and now it housed only certain administrative departments, of which the District Attorney's office was the chief. The three-story building was of native limestone and perfectly square, with a belltower on the top that resembled a somewhat elongated derby hat and might have been designed by El Greco. Twenty years before Richard Kramer's time the single old bell that had hung in the tower for two generations cracked, and experts agreed it was not repairable. There had been talk of replacing it with a genuine carillon, but the cost was outrageous in the view of the county supervisors, and they had settled for an electronic bell device that could be operated by a clock. Old-timers were fond of pointing out that with the money the taxpayers saved by foregoing a real carillon they were able to build and landscape, in its glorious entirety, the Sheriff's office and county jail, which was steel and concrete with opaque windows, and which stood with its back to the courthouse, across Chestnut Street, and fronted on the Mall. The Mall was a wide parkway dividing the city of Gilesport into two distinct parts, which were sometimes referred to as Old Town and New Town. It was two miles long and ran from the Westview Cemetery on the west to the river bluff on the east. This juxtaposition had given rise to the local proverb: "You can't get around the Mall." It was true in both a literal and a figurative sense, but the plan had been less deliberate than merely inevitable because of certain county land commitments and an embarrassing plenitude of federal money.

The courthouse was in Old Town, which suited Dick Kramer perfectly well. He had resisted for several years, through the plaintive urgings of his staff, the suggestion that the D.A.'s offices would be more comfortable and would operate more efficiently in the new county building on the Mall, the one that stood east of the Sheriff's office and which, like it, was steel and concrete and glass. More comfortable, maybe, he could admit, but operate more efficiently? No, not while I'm in office.

"I'm an Old Town boy," he had said more than once when the issue had been raised. "I was born here, right in this courthouse, twenty years ago, the day I passed the bar. All the law I know is right here in this building."

"The law is the same across the street," Al Levy had said once.

"I don't believe it," Dick Kramer had said.

Al hadn't pushed it because it didn't matter to him where the office was, as long as he could find his way to court. For Dick Kramer the "Old Town boy" concept went deep, in a way that Al Levy, a New Yorker, might accept on faith but could never really understand. Dick's actual birthplace, though not in the courthouse, had been nearby, in a small frame house on the outskirts of the business district. A cut-rate shoe store stood now where the house had been, but the memory of it stayed with him well enough. As a small boy he had played on the Civil War cannon in the southeast corner of the courthouse lawn. He had got in the way of gardeners planting elm trees along Chestnut Street, trees that now stood fifty feet high and screened, mercifully, the modern steel, concrete, and glass buildings along the Mall. When he had gone away to law school, he had done his holiday boning up in the courthouse library, and in his third year he had got a job as court clerk for Judge Whitehead, who had been District Attorney during World War I and had retired from the bench at eighty-two. The judge had put himself out hiring Dick for the summer only when he could have had a permanent clerk, which would have been a lot more convenient. But Dick was going to the judge's old school, and a letter from the dean, an old chum of the judge's, had swung the decision. They had got along all right after the first couple of weeks. The grizzled veteran was demanding and irascible, and it had been necessary for Dick to stand up to him on two or three hot occasions. He had no idea through the summer whether he was doing his job well enough to please the old man. But in the fall, as he was leaving to go back to school, the judge suddenly held out his hand, and when Dick took it, said, "Good work, Kramer. You've got guts and discipline. That's what it takes."

Still, he would think, it's not just sentiment that hooks me to this courthouse. I believe in continuity, in the chain-link progression of human affairs. When a man is looking for justice, he should have a certain place to go, not by looking it up in a book, but just because it's known, because his father told him, and his father before him.

He had never tried to explain this to anyone except once, long ago, to his wife Evelyn. She had been impressed and properly enthusiastic about his devotion to the legal tradition. But they had been young then, and in love.

* * * *

By half past twelve, Dick Kramer had cleared his desk of all the accumulated items that could be disposed of without assistance from beyond his own office. He had dictated sixteen letters to officials of the state, including two to the governor about county aspects of a proposed highway building program that could involve litigation in land acquisition procedure. He had written and revised three opinions on proposed county building ordinances, for transmissions to the supervisors. He had read and dictated replies to fourteen letters from citizens on subjects ranging from a complaint about the noxious odors emanating from the sewage disposal plant at the foot of Knox Street to a hysterical prediction of the imminent destruction of a prominent official by murder. He had directed copies of his replies and the original letters to the appropriate departments. He had conferred with the city manager of Gilesport by telephone and had explained, on somewhat shaky grounds, the county's position in regard to jail facilities, especially regarding juvenile offenders. The position was that while the county was more than willing to cooperate in providing emergency facilities, such as temporary detention, no permanent arrangement between city and county could be made without a meeting between the county supervisors and the city council, and this ought to be initially informal and, if possible, not open to the public. The city manager was quite young, a graduate of the Harvard School of Public Administration, and he had definite opinions about efficiency and the importance of cutting red tape in matters of legal hospitality. Dick had been patient and, in the end, noncommittal.

"That's something old Judge Whitehead left out," he muttered when the city manager hung up. "Patience. Guts, discipline, and a lot of sheer patience."

His secretary, Ida Fielding, who had been on the line taking notes said, "I beg your pardon, sir?"

"Nothing, Ida," Dick said. "Didn't realize you were still on. Did you get that?"

"Yes," she said. "He's a regular fireball, isn't he?"

"Yup," Dick said and hung up.

He went down the hall to the men's room, washed up carefully, and checked his shirt to make sure it was fresh enough to wear to lunch with Senator Morris. When he got back to the office, Ida was typing up her notes on the telephone conversation. There had been a call from Mr. Steve Carolla.

"What did he want?"

"He didn't say," Ida said.

"Is it urgent?"

"He didn't say that, either."

"Then I'll call him later."

After a suitable pause, Ida asked, "Do you know what time you'll get back from lunch?"

"No idea," Dick said. "I'm lunching with Senator Morris and I don't know what's on his mind."

Ida Fielding looked at the backs of her fingers on the typewriter keys. Dick looked into space. On top of the courthouse the electronic carillon sounded the three-quarter hour. Dick looked at his watch.

"Right on the button," he said. "You can't beat electronics."

"I guess not," Ida said.

"Well, I'd better get going. If Mrs. Kramer calls, will you tell her that as far as I know it's still all right about our bridge date tomorrow?"

"I'll tell her."

"Okay, see you later."

As he left the office he was thinking, I wonder why we play those little games with people we've known so long and so well. We both know what's on the Senator's mind, all right, but neither of us wants to admit it. Little games.

He took the elevator to the ground floor and started out through the covered passage at the southeast corner of the building. He had to step back to make way for a couple of sheriff's deputies with three manacled prisoners in tow. Dick stood back against the wall while they passed. Neither the deputies nor the trio of accused took any notice of him. As he went on into the passage ponderous footsteps bore down from behind, and Judge Harris caught up with him. They turned a corner and walked together down the wide ramp that led to the official parking area under the Sheriff's office.

"I heard by a roundabout route," the judge said, "that there might be some quick disposition in the Dexter boy's case."

Dick let a moment pass, hoping his timing would be as accurate as that of the electronic carillon. "Not unless he pleads guilty," he said. "I talked to Al Levy about it this morning. It's ready to go."

"I see," Judge Harris said.

"How is Mrs. Harris?" Dick asked.

"Just fine. And Evelyn?"

"A little under the weather, but she'll be all right."

"Good, good. See you later."

"Right," Dick said.

They separated, and Dick went to his car in the slot marked: DISTRICT ATTORNEY.

Driving down Bank Street, north on the river bluff, he thought about the call from Steve Carolla. He knew that Carolla had got into the Robin

Dexter case and he knew that Pete Dexter had brought this about. He also understood that Pete Dexter could lead Carolla around a little because he had something that Steve Carolla wanted. But he couldn't think of a reason for Carolla to call him personally. The big Italian boss was too powerful and too smart to do anything so straightforward as to call the D.A. himself in a personal cause. Certainly he wouldn't approach him directly on behalf of Robin Dexter, because that would put him too much in Dick's hands. That would be asking a favor from somebody who, in Carolla's eyes, was far beneath notice. Anyway, by this time, Carolla would have learned that Al Levy was going ahead with the case, and there wouldn't be any way to change its course that would have anything to do with Carolla's influence.

It could be, Dick thought, that he lost the exchange and wants off the hook, wants to get dissociated from the case altogether. He could say to me that he just happened to be in Harry Gideon's office on business and Pete Dexter and Al Levy happened to drop in and if he'd known what they wanted to talk about he would have got up and left because what difference did the Dexter kid make to him? That wouldn't mean anything except that he would be putting me on notice that whatever might happen about the case, he would now and forever deny any connection with it. And everybody would go along with Carolla all right because Steve was bigger than anybody in the downstate precincts, anybody but Senator Morris.

Impatient with himself for having dwelt so long on a distasteful subject, Dick blew his horn at a dawdling motorist, pulled out around him, and drove faster along Bank Street toward the venerable, ivy-covered Greenbriar Hotel, where the Senator had scheduled the luncheon meeting.

He probably just wanted me to say hello to the Senator for him, Dick thought, just so the name Carolla would never quite leave us, just to keep himself in view. As if anybody in politics could possibly forget him. The son of a bitch, Dick thought. Someday—someday I'll get—And he cut the thought off as he would a tape running through a recorder. Watch it, he thought.

He was well out of the riverfront business area now, winding up the old hill streets with the big estates set far back, most of them hidden by trees that had stood for a hundred years and more. There were iron gates between stone pillars, winding macadam driveways disappearing among elaborately landscaped banks. Old rose plants dropped long, thorny stems over stone walls. He drove past his mother-in-law's house, speeding up a little by reflex, wondering whether she was outside and had caught sight of him, so that in the course of the afternoon Evelyn would get a call, and Mother Stevens would say, "I saw Dick drive by about one o'clock. I wonder why he didn't stop?" Evelyn would either remember that he had a luncheon date with the Senator or forget it, in which case she would probably say, "I don't know. I'll ask him about it." And she would ask him about it.

Maybe it would be smart to stop by for a couple of minutes on the way back to the office, he thought. And then he thought, *The goddam hell with that.*

He drove into the hotel grounds and slowly around the circular drive that enclosed the gardens with the big fountain in the center.

They were rich in those days, Dick thought. So rich. And they loved it.

He happened to know that the property tax liens on at least half a dozen of the old estates were so pressing that far-off sons and daughters and grandchildren were scrimping and shuffling their own accounts in order to contribute to the family homestead where the old folks still lived. On the outside these homes were kept in good repair as a matter of neighborhood pride. He shuddered to think about what some of them must be like inside, with no servants anymore to do the chores. Not Mother Stevens' place, of course. The Stevens fortune, though it hadn't increased much, was still intact, being based on real estate. Including, he thought with discomfort, some substandard tenements in Crudsville.

He shook that thought off almost as quickly as he had cut the thread of his lethal plans for Steve Carolla. There was plenty of space in the hotel parking lot, and he found a slot and stopped, taking time to check his appearance in the rearview mirror before leaving the car.

He went in by a side entrance, got into an elevator, and rode to the third floor, to the Men's Bar in an alcove off a suite of private dining rooms.

A white-jacketed maitre d'hotel appeared out of nowhere as Dick entered the bar. "Good afternoon, Mr. Kramer," he said. "The Senator just phoned and asked me to tell you he'd be right along. He was delayed."

"Thanks," Dick said, "I'll just have a drink while I wait."

"Of course."

He had the bar to himself, and it was comforting to have the time and light fortification of a martini to change pace, to adjust to the soft old world, the mellowed elegance of the hotel and its aura of well-being, to switch from the feverish, disconnected world of the office, where everything was changing so fast, to this quiet hub of tradition, inside near the center of life, where the wheel turned more slowly.

He laid a five-dollar bill on the bar, and after a while Charley the bartender, an ageless Irishman built on the order of a tall jockey, picked it up.

"Haven't seen one of these in a long time," he said.

He rang up seventy-five cents and put down three dollars and a quarter in change. Dick didn't say anything. At length Charley, with a shrug, picked another bill out of the cash drawer and added it to the change. "Knew I couldn't get away with it," he said. "Crime doesn't pay. Right, Mr. Kramer?"

Dick smiled and felt at home. The elaborate building of a joke, even an old joke, was as comforting as the martini. But watch out, he told himself. Don't sink all the way in. We don't know for sure what's on the Senator's mind, do we? Maybe he's decided to run for one more hitch and just wants some support. But he could take that for granted.

Anyway, I hear the weather in Washington, D. C., is miserable.

He drank slowly, and he had finished the martini and was trying to decide whether to have another when Senator Morris came in. He came in silently, light and quick on his feet, a lean, gray-haired man of seventy-one who, Dick thought suddenly, could easily pass for fifty.

I hope I can last that well, Dick thought. He was glad he hadn't ordered the second drink.

"Dick," Morris said, "nice to see you. How's Evelyn?"

"She's fine, thanks. You look healthier every time I see you."

"Don't let the outer shell fool you, young man. Inside I'm turning to cottage cheese."

"May I buy you a drink?"

"Well—I reserved Room C down the hall here. Think they're setting it up now. We can have one in there if you like—or a bottle of that good *Chateau of the Ninth Pope,* or whatever they call it."

"Good."

"Hi, Charley," the Senator said, waving toward the bar as they turned from the room.

They walked down the carpeted hall. "Sorry I'm late," Morris said. "Had a last-minute phone call from Pete Dexter. I'll tell you something. That guy is a talker, a real talker."

"Uh-huh," Dick said.

At Room C Dick beat the Senator to the door and opened up, standing back to let Morris go in first. A Negro waiter in a dinner jacket was setting a small dining table from a cart bearing an intricate silver service. He acknowledged them without bowing.

"Senator," he said, "Mr. Kramer."

"Hello, Ralph," Morris said. "Looks mighty good."

"Yes, sir," Ralph said. "You going to like a little wine, Senator?"

"Yeah, bottle of that *Chateauneuf* stuff—unless the house has something special."

"All right, Senator. I'll be through here in a minute."

The white-curtained room was furnished as a sitting room, and there was a bar at one side on which were bottles and a freshly filled ice bucket.

"You want another martini?" Morris asked.

Dick declined. They sat down on an old-fashioned sofa covered with a flower-print fabric, and the Senator lit a cigar.

"Somebody was saying Evelyn hadn't been well," Morris said. "Hope she's improving."

"She's all right now. She was in the hospital a couple of days for observation. Doctors couldn't come up with much—bed rest, you know."

"I know. I'm glad she's feeling better. Mary gave us a scare couple of weeks ago. Coughed up some blood—had dizzy spells. But she got over it."

"Good. I can't imagine Mary ever being sick."

"Yeah."

Ralph wheeled the cart away from the dining table. "I'll send up the wine, Senator," he said. "You just ring when you need something, okay?"

"Okay, Ralph, and thanks."

The door closed behind Ralph, and there was a long moment of silence. The Senator's shoulders slumped, and he leaned back on the sofa, his fist on his thigh, the cigar sticking out between his fingers. "I'm tired. Beat," he said. "Here it is the middle of August, this session is still going strong, and I don't know if we'll ever get a vacation. I have to get back Monday, which gives me three days to see about eight hundred people."

"So it goes," Dick said.

"Maybe it would be smart to hire a hall," Morris said. "Just throw everybody into one big room and answer questions from the audience."

"There's plenty of room in that shiny new civic auditorium on the Mall," Dick said.

Morris chuckled. "You never did go strong for that big improvement, did you?" he said. "Taxpayers took a real beating."

"Taxpayers always take a beating. But it wasn't the money, it was—I don't know, the idea of it. This is my hometown. I guess I can't accept change."

"Know how you feel. How about some lunch?"

On the table were two fruit compotes on ice in silver bowls, a soup tureen on a chafing dish with a silver ladle beside it, and a long dish of relishes. The linen was clean and soft. They began to eat, and the Senator got down to business.

"As I say," he said, "I've been busy, and I'm a little out of touch. Fill me in. What's been going on?"

Dick was prepared. The request was serious and in line of duty. Dick had thought about it for several days and had even considered writing out a full report in detail and giving the Senator a copy of it. But he had decided against this. He knew well enough what Morris was interested in, he knew what to say and what to leave out, and he knew he would stand in a better light if he could extemporize, show that he was on top of the county administration and had things at his fingertips than if he had buried everything in a ponderous, bureaucratic memorandum. So he had marshaled the facts in his mind and had committed nothing to paper.

The last time he had talked to the Senator had been in the early spring, and he began back there, with the decision of the supervisors to go along with Governor Wrightson on a statewide overhaul of the property tax structure. This was nothing new to Morris, but he would be interested in how the decision was holding up under the pressure of time and the in-fighting in the legislature.

"So-called urban renewal up north," Morris said, "makes it rough. Every farmer from here to the Ohio River is afraid he'll have to pay for every lakefront high-rise deluxe apartment house personally, all by himself."

"That's right. I had a letter the other day from one of the Grange people. He was asking how the county government could justify raising honest, hard-working people's taxes in order to build fancy whorehouses up in the city."

"Whorehouses," Morris said, smiling. "I know. But how does it look? Is there a big fight building up?"

"I don't think so. By the time the legislature gets it worked over—"

Morris nodded. "The only taxes that will go up—that will be no-ticeable—will hit city landlords and maybe a few down here, like in Crudsville."

Like Mother Stevens, Dick thought, nodding. He went on with his report, covering the major trends in relations between county and state, bearing down on certain personalities, going light on others. Morris didn't interrupt. The maitre d'hotel came in with a bottle of *Chateauneuf-du-pape* and they went through the ritual of the opening, the tasting, and the approval. Morris said they were ready for the main course, and the maitre d' opened the door, snapped his fingers, and beckoned Ralph, who wheeled in the cart and, after removing the fruit and soup dishes, served generous helpings of sirloin tips with asparagus and mashed potatoes.

They ate for a while in silence.

"Everything seems to be holding pretty well," Morris said finally. "Anything else I should know about before I visit the supervisors?"

"I think I've covered it. They'd like inside stuff on re-apportionment if possible."

"Who wouldn't?" Morris said. "There isn't any inside stuff. It's in the grinder."

"How will it go?"

The Senator shrugged. "It'll work out. Nobody will get hurt much—maybe down south."

"It always works out," Dick said.

The Senator pushed his plate aside, poured some more wine and leaned on both arms on the table. He looked at the wine in the glass as if he were inspecting it for foreign matter.

"No," he said, "it doesn't always work out. Not always. That's why you keep going back. You can't stand the goddam climate, your legs give out, you get so confused your head aches half the time, you lose friends you've known since you were a kid, and you make enemies you never heard of before—and you keep going back."

Dick said nothing. If there was something Morris wanted to deliver, he would make the delivery in his own time.

The expression of reverie on the Senator's face changed abruptly to brisk interest. "Dessert?" he asked.

"Just coffee for me, thanks," Dick said.

Morris rang for Ralph, who appeared almost at once, bringing a silver coffee service and cups. While he cleared the table and served the coffee the Senator got out two cigars, offered one to Dick, who declined, and lit up. Ralph went out, and Morris leaned back in his chair.

"How are you getting along with Steve Carolla?" he asked.

Dick shrugged. "Nothing special," he said. "I had a call from him just before I came over here, but I was out and I didn't take the time to call back. Later, maybe."

Morris went to the bar, poured brandy into two glasses, and brought them back. Dick accepted the brandy.

"Steve Carolla," Morris said, "is a thorn in the public flesh, but he's a pretty good one. He delivers a big vote and he doesn't ask too much in return. He doesn't push too hard. I can turn him down, and he'll take it. Most of the time what he asks for is reasonable."

Dick kept quiet.

"He's got power because his own people trust him, and a lot of other people are afraid of him—without much reason. He's built up this myth about himself—Big Sinister Steve Carolla. Fact is, he's a mild-mannered fellow who likes to live well and he's figured out a way to make it. I don't know how much money he has, but it's enough. He pays his taxes and stays out of trouble. He'll put pressure on you when he needs something, but he knows where to draw the line. The thing is—never be afraid of him."

This time Dick was silent because he couldn't think of a reply.

Morris dropped the subject, his face went through one of those changeovers, and he got up and took his empty glass to the bar. "I've got an announcement to make," he said. "Just between us for the time being."

"All right," Dick said.

"This is my last term."

Dick said the proper thing. "You can't do that to us," he said.

"All right," the Senator said, "we've got through the garbage phase. It's the truth. I had three little coronaries last year and it's no fun and I'm not ready to go. With Mary's flare-up—it just looks like the time to retire."

"I'm sorry to hear about the coronaries," Dick said.

"So—" Morris said, "about six months from now we'll be into a campaign. Somebody's got to run where I used to."

"Yeah," Dick said.

"How about you?"

In spite of all the preparation, the thinking, the expectation, Dick wasn't ready for the question. It had come too fast. It was on the tip of his tongue to say, "Me?" He managed to say nothing.

"You can tell me you haven't thought about it," Morris said, "but I won't believe you."

"Sure," Dick said, "I've thought of it. I haven't done anything about it."

"I know you haven't. And I know that if you decided to do something about it, you wouldn't sit around with phony reluctance, waiting to be asked. So I'm just putting it to you now. How about you running for Senator?"

After a moment Dick said, "Yes or no, counselor?"

Morris smiled. "No, naturally not yes or no. But pretty damn soon."

"Before you go back to Washington?"

"That would be nice, but I couldn't push you that hard. Think about it, talk it over with Evelyn, try to figure out what you've got going here as D.A., and whether you'd rather stay with it for a while or go on to something else. If you've got bigger aspirations than Senator, you'd probably be better off to shoot for the statehouse first. But I'd like to see you take my place."

"Why?" Dick said.

The Senator was prepared for the question. "Because you're young—forty-seven now, right? You're honest. You've got brains and drive. And you're in the most strategic down-state office there is. What I mean is, you've got the talent and you've got a chance to make it."

"How much of a chance?"

"A real good chance, Dick. Superficially you've got the right racial and national background. You look good enough. You look straight-forward. You're a good speaker and you think on your feet. Your nose is clean. You came from humble beginnings. You worked your way through school and you made it. You've been elected District Attorney three times in a row without much trouble. Everything is going for you."

Dick helped himself to coffee.

"I'm not pretending I can choose my successor," Morris said. "I can't promise you the office. You'll have to do the running, and it's hard work. But I'd like to see you try it."

"All right, I'll think about it," Dick said. "I appreciate your confidence in me. I don't know—it seems like a giant step."

"Sure it does—it is. But once you're in, there are a lot of gratifications. There's excitement and change. And I'll be leaving a lot of unfinished business that somebody will have to pick up and go ahead with. What I was saying earlier—you keep going back to that unfinished business." The Senator looked at his watch.

Dick got on his feet. "Have you mentioned this to anyone else?" he asked. "About me making the race, I mean?"

"Oh, no. Hell no, I wouldn't do that. Of course, you're in a certain position, and people are going to be thinking about you as a logical choice. You can't keep people from guessing. Sometimes they hit it right."

"I know."

"That doesn't have to bother you. By the time anybody gets around to trying to stop you, you'll have so much momentum going—"

"I wasn't thinking about that exactly."

"Oh," Morris said. Then, "You were thinking about Pete Dexter."

"Yes. Pete Dexter and Steve Carolla."

"Let's try to keep them separate. They have different interests. I know Pete Dexter has all that land, and Carolla would like to get his hands on some of it. They might make a temporary deal on something—tell me about this trouble the Dexter boy is in."

Dick told him the facts, hurrying through it so as not to burden Morris with details of a local crime.

"Who's taking it to court for you?" the Senator asked when Dick had finished.

"Al Levy. He says it's a sure thing."

"Al Levy's a good lawyer. It's a problem for you. Can't get around that. Do you have any way out of it?"

"Nope. Not now. I told Al to go ahead and give it all we've got."

Morris nodded. "Then that's what you have to do. Assuming you win the case, you'll alienate some strong people in Pete Dexter's circles, but these things wear off. You won't lose among Carolla's people, and I don't think you'll lose Carolla. Look at it this way. If you were the defense lawyer in this case—Harry Gideon, say—and you won it, got the boy off, Dexter's people would say you only did your duty, and you'd lose a lot of Italians. You might lose Carolla. Not that Carolla has any idea of swinging to the other party, but—he might stay home. And when Steve Carolla decides to stay home, nothing much happens."

"I understand."

Morris held out his hand, and Dick took it firmly.

"A hot case is always a problem, win or lose," the Senator said. "But you know all about that. The only advice I have is to be careful about your newspaper handouts. Sensationalism, especially sex sensationalism, is a tricky issue for a conservative party leader to handle. You might talk to Al Levy about that in connection with the trial."

"I'll talk to him," Dick said. "Thanks for the lunch, and I'll give you an answer as soon as I can."

"I'll be waiting to hear from you. Give my best to Evelyn and take care of yourself."

"I will. So long now."

"Good-bye. Maybe we can get together again for a minute before I go back."

"That would be nice, but you're busy."

Morris opened the door for him. "Think it over carefully," he said as Dick went out. "As you say—it's a giant step."

Dick nodded, lifted his hand, and walked away down the hall.

* * * *

He drove carefully, not too fast, because he found himself shaken more than he would have acknowledged to anyone else. He could admit to himself that he had considered the possibility that the Senator would ask him to accept the mantle. He had even hoped for it. But the realization was more stimulating than he had anticipated. His wish had been put into words by Senator Morris himself. It had thus become a possible thing. At the same time it remained a dream that could dissolve at any time for any number of reasons—such as the trial of Robin Dexter.

Passing his mother-in-law's house, he looked straight ahead, taking no chance that if she were outside, she might catch his eye, which would make it necessary for him to stop. This was no time to talk about idle things. The hard lump of expectation was like an egg in his chest. It would take some time before he could wear it comfortably.

Should he talk to Evelyn about it right away—that evening? He couldn't decide. He thought not.

It was mid-afternoon, and traffic was not heavy on the through streets. He skirted the main business area and drove down the Mall to reach the parking lot under the Sheriff's office.

I'll have to learn to go along with changes, he thought. Lots of changes. He parked the car and walked by the underground passage to the courthouse elevator. The smell of the old wood reassured him. I made it this far, he thought, and I can make it farther.

He wondered what Carolla would say when he returned his telephone call and what he would say in reply. "Don't be afraid of him," the Senator had said.

All right, Dick thought. I won't be afraid of him—or anybody.

He looked into Ida's office, and she handed him some messages. "Mr. Levy would like to see you as soon as possible," she said. "He has his principal witness in the office, and the man has to leave for work at four."

"Will you call him and ask him to come right up?" Dick said. He sat down at his desk and started looking through the messages. His hands were shaking slightly, and after a few seconds he leaned back and gripped the arms of the chair tight.

What's the matter with me? he thought. And the answer came at once. I'm scared. I'm afraid.

CHAPTER 4

Al Levy's witness was a well-built man in his late thirties. He was groomed and dressed with the slightly oversharp precision of a waiter or a bartender, and his face was guarded and impassive.

"Mr. Kirk has to get to work," Al said, "so I thought we could give you a quick fill-in, in case there's anything I've overlooked. If you have any questions—"

Dick nodded and looked at Lonnie Kirk. "You picked up the Petrucelli girl on the road, is that right?" Dick said. "Yeah," Kirk said.

"We appreciate your cooperation," Dick said. He glanced over the summarized facts of the case, which Ida, with characteristic foresight, had got from the file and put on his desk. "That was three months ago," he said. "Is your memory of the events pretty clear?"

"Good and clear," Kirk said. "I burned out a set of brakes that night and I just got 'em paid for last week."

"I see," Dick said. "And you picked up the girl, and when she was in your car, you noticed there was blood on her legs. Is that what made you suspect she'd been attacked?"

"Well—she was kind of shaky on her feet—on the road—and kind of messed up. I put two and two together, you know."

"Uh-huh. When you asked her what had happened, she told you she'd been raped, right?"

"Finally she did, yeah. I had to work on her a little."

"How do you mean, work on her?"

"Well, she didn't want to talk about it, so I kept after her with the questions, and finally she told me."

"I see. And that's the only way you learned she'd been raped. You don't have any other facts—of your own knowledge—that prove she'd been attacked."

"No. Just what she told me. And then later the kid confessed."

"Yes. Just one other question, Mr. Kirk. Do you feel certain in your own mind that when the girl mentioned the name Dexter—Robin Dexter—she was telling the truth?"

"Well—yeah—"

"I mean, you don't think it's possible that she was just—throwing you a name, any name, to cover up for somebody?"

Kirk moved in his chair and rubbed at the back of his neck. "I suppose it's possible. Anything is possible. It sounded to me like she told the truth. Why wouldn't she?"

"All right," Dick said. "Thanks for coming in and for everything. You're a good citizen."

Kirk got on his feet. "I don't know about good citizen," he said. "I just want to be in the clear."

"I understand," Dick said.

Al Levy followed his witness into the hall but stood with one foot holding the door open, so Dick knew he wanted to talk with him some more. He heard Al give Kirk instructions about where and when to show up the next day, and then Kirk walked away down the hall. Al came into the office and let the door swing shut behind him.

"Thanks for the time," Al said. "I guess we're ready to go. Gideon will try to get another continuance, but I don't think Judge Harris is in the mood for it. I think we can have a jury in the box tomorrow afternoon."

"Any chance the Dexter boy will plead guilty?"

"Not a chance, not now. Even if he wanted to—he might even get off with probation—his old man won't let him."

There was a pause. Al Levy shifted a file of papers from one arm to the other. "You have some doubts about this case?" he asked. "You asked Lonnie Kirk whether maybe the girl was using Dexter to cover up for somebody else."

Dick met his eyes. "No, no doubts," he said. "But it's always something to think about. Not only with the girl—with the Dexter boy too. Kids are funny. Say a buddy of Robin Dexter's was in a jam. If they're very close, Robin might sacrifice himself on the altar of friendship. It's been done."

"Sure. I know. But a thing like this? Could mean prison, a real rough jam."

"I know it's unlikely. I guess I just can't help poking around. Your case is all right."

"I think so. Thanks again for talking to Kirk." Al started out.

"Al—" Dick said, "one more question."

"Sure."

Al turned back into the room, facing the desk. Dick could see that he was in a fighting mood, ready to fight for his case, suspicious that Dick would make an effort to temporize, water down, crawl out from under.

"How rough is this trial going to be publicly? How blue?"

Al Levy's dark brown eyes moved in his square face. He shifted the file of papers again and put one hand in his pocket. From the bulge it made, Dick could tell that the fist was clenched.

"I don't know," Al said. "It depends on what Gideon decides to make of it. He won't pull any punches."

"How about you?"

"Me, I've got no plan to entertain the jury with a big juicy depiction of forcible sexual intercourse. If Gideon decides to go into explicit details, I'll fight back."

"Of course."

There was a pause like the earlier one, only longer, and more ominous. Dick felt what was coming and braced himself against it.

"Do you want me to go light on it?" Al asked carefully.

"No," Dick said. "I told you before and I repeat—go to it."

"Okay." Al moved quickly toward the door.

"I had lunch with Senator Morris today," Dick said. "He mentioned this case, and I told him you were trying it. The Senator said, 'Al Levy is a good lawyer.'"

Al looked back from the open door. "Thanks," he said. "Thanks for telling me." Then he went out.

Dick sat for a long moment staring at the door, then pulled the telephone across the desk and lifted the mouthpiece. Ida came on.

"Will you try to get Steve Carolla?" Dick said.

"Yes, sir."

He hung up, and glanced again at the sheet of paper on which Ida had typed the summary of the Dexter case. He pushed it aside, found the messages she had given him earlier, and looked through them. One concerned a call from the city manager. He slipped it into his desk calendar for the next day. "Once a day is enough," he muttered.

There had also been a call from Liz Dexter. He extracted it from the sheath of slips and rubbed his thumb over it as if to erase her name. His throat tightened. "Goddam it!" he said. "It's not fair!"

He reached for the phone, and his buzzer sounded.

"Yes, Ida?" he said.

"I have Mr. Carolla on the line," she said.

"Okay, thanks." There was a click as the line opened, and he said, "Hello, Steve. Returning your call."

"Yeah, Mr. Kramer," Carolla said in his low-pitched, somewhat husky voice. "I'm having a few fellas over for a drink and so forth. I'd like you to come if you can make it. Sunday."

"Sunday? Just a second." He knew he had Sunday open all right, but he let a few seconds go by.

"I can make it," he said, "I'll be glad to come. Unless some emergency—"

"Yeah, I understand. About four o'clock, okay? The Senator, he's coming if he can make it."

"All right, Steve. Thanks for calling."

"Don't mention it, Mr. Kramer. See you Sunday."

He hung up. Dick took out his handkerchief and wiped his hands. In Carolla's call there was both relief and threat. His silence on the Dexter case didn't mean much. The timing of his cocktail party and the mention of the Senator could mean that Carolla already had the word that Morris wanted Dick to run for the office and was beginning right away to set things in order—or to sabotage the plan before it could gain momentum. Dick believed the Senator's statement that he hadn't spoken to anyone else about Dick as a candidate, but, as Morris had also said, 'You can't stop people from guessing.' There was no secret about his luncheon date with Morris. Many people would know about that. And Steve Carolla certainly was as talented a guesser as anyone in the state.

Better than I am, anyway, Dick thought. I won't be able to guess a thing until Sunday. If Pete Dexter is there, it will mean something different from what it would mean otherwise. If the Senator is there, that will mean still another thing—maybe. How Carolla works! he thought with grudging admiration.

His buzzer sounded again, and he spoke to Ida.

"Mrs. Kramer is on the line, sir," Ida said.

"All right," he said.

He lifted the phone and he could hear Evelyn's voice calling to Edith, the maid. He waited till he thought she was ready.

"Hello, honey," he said.

She wasn't quite ready. "Oh, Dick! Hello—I was just telling Edith I didn't know for sure whether you'd be home on time tonight or not."

"Yes, as far as I know—"

"You're not sure."

Always it had to be a little contest. Instead of "at six-thirty," it had to be "on time." Instead of "is anything likely to come up," it had to be, "you're not sure."

"I'm as sure as I can be. Unless the President of the Mercantile Trust Company decides to murder his secretary, or the Sheriff goes berserk—"

"Oh, stop that now. You're teasing. Then you'll be home on time, you think."

"Yes."

"I'll tell Edith."

"All right. How are you feeling?"

"Better. Oh—Mother called a while ago. She said she saw you drive by today and she waved at you, but you didn't see her, I guess."

"I guess not. Sorry. I had lunch with the Senator at the Greenbriar, and it ran a little late—"

"Oh, yes, I forgot about that. How is Senator Morris?"

"Just fine. He—"

"Listen, I have to run now. I promised Donna Forester I would bring her some of that special formula rose food that Mike made up for me. Her gardener is there today, and I want to get it over there before—"

"All right. Drive carefully. I'll see you at six-thirty."

"Yes, good-bye now."

"Bye," he said.

He hung up, shaking his head slowly in wonder. Women, he thought.

He picked up the note about Liz Dexter's call, fingered it idly, then crumpled it and threw it in the wastebasket. He picked up the phone again, asked Ida for an outside line, and dialed the Dexter number.

I won't be afraid of Steve Carolla or anybody, he was thinking when Liz Dexter came on the line. Even in the one-word greeting she gave, he could hear the tension in her voice. His hand tightened on the phone. "This is Dick Kramer," he said. "You called me."

"Yes," she said. "Listen—I know I shouldn't be doing this—if Pete finds out, he'll be furious, but we've been friends a long time. I mean you and Evelyn and—"

"It's all right, Liz. Go ahead. I won't say anything to Pete."

"Thank you, Dick. It's about poor Robin—"

"Yes?"

"I'm just—well—"

Dick found himself straining to help her pull herself together.

"Naturally," she said, "it's been a horrible shock to us, and I'm not condoning what Robin did—not for a minute—but I just keep—thinking—hoping—there must be some way—Her voice trailed off. He thought he could hear her crying.

"Liz," he said, "listen to me. There isn't any way out of the trial. There just absolutely isn't—"

"But, Dick—" Her voice was on the edge of failure.

"Please listen, Liz," he said. "There's nothing I can do personally. It's all up to Robin and his attorney, Mr. Gideon."

"I don't understand," she said dully.

"The law takes a certain course," he said, and thought, Oh, Christ. "Look—and I say this not as a suggestion, just to give you information—and Gideon would be able to give you the same—the easiest way for Robin to get through it is to plead guilty."

There was a long pause, and he wondered whether she had left the phone. Then she came back.

"What would happen then?" she asked.

"There wouldn't be a jury. Just the judge and the two attorneys, and the reporter and the clerk. The judge would accept the plea and set a date for sentencing. Robin would go home on bail."

"But that's just—then what—what kind of sentence—?"

"I'm not through yet. Then a probation officer would go over the case and talk to Robin and make a recommendation for probation. The judge would take that under advisement. If the judge should decide that Robin is a good enough risk, he might very well suspend sentence and put him on probation. He would be free, then, except that he'd have to report to the probation officer regularly." He paused.

He was making it sound too good, too easy. It might not be all that easy. "Of course," he said, "he'd have it on his record."

"A criminal record," she said hoarsely. "My son—"

"Well, quite a few very eminent people have had criminal records," Dick said, "back in the past. Not that we encourage it." Not very funny, he thought. Watch it.

"Then you think he ought to plead guilty," she said.

"I didn't say that. I can't say what he ought to do. I'm just trying to explain how it might go under certain conditions."

"Guilty," she said, and her voice began once more to break down. "But his father wouldn't permit—oh, God—oh, goddam it to hell."

He could hear small, measured thuds, as if she were banging her fist on the table. He had never heard Liz Dexter use profanity before, and it was something of a shock, though he could understand it all right.

"Liz—" he said.

The pounding went on for a while, but she didn't say any more. After about half a minute the phone dropped into the cradle at the other end. Dick hung up slowly.

Ida came in with the letters and opinions he had dictated in the morning. It was a neat stack of paper about an inch and a half high. It would have to be read, some of it hurriedly, some carefully, word by word. It was after four o'clock, and he had to contend with the drowsiness induced by the gin and wine he had had for lunch.

"Thanks, Ida," he said. "No more calls unless urgent, and no more visitors unless emergency."

"Yes, sir," she said.

When she had gone, Dick left the office and went to the men's room down the hall. He took off his coat and shirt and washed with cold water. It was awkward drying himself with the paper towels, but when he had finished, he felt better and no longer drowsy. He dressed, returned to the office, and began to work his way through the stack of correspondence.

CHAPTER 5

DONNA FORESTER

She was in the kitchen when the front doorbell rang. She was drinking a strong Scotch and soda and looking out the window. Gino, stripped to the waist, was working close to the house, shaping the last of the scalloped beds in the design they had agreed on.

Not as much done as we'd planned, she thought. Huh, Gino? Slight interruption. Oh, you big, sweet, magnificent lover—

When the doorbell rang, she jumped and almost dropped the highball glass. Steady—she thought.

She had bathed and dressed after Gino had left her to go back to work, and she knew she was impeccable to the outward eye. Still she jumped and felt sudden panic.

She set the glass carefully on the kitchen shelf and started toward the front of the house. Going through the living room, she caught sight of Evelyn Kramer's blue Mercedes parked at the curb.

Oh, no, she thought. I can't bear the idea.

But she went on and opened the door. Evelyn was at the door, wearing a pair of pink stretch pants and a pink sweater, clutching a tin can of some sort in one arm. It occurred to Donna that Evelyn was too skinny to wear stretch pants. They just didn't work.

"Evelyn!" she said. "How nice to see you."

"Hello, Donna. That rose food I was telling you about that Mike made up for me, remember? I feel so guilty for having put it off so long—"

"How thoughtful of you. Come in."

"I suppose you've already got everything in and watered and all by this time."

"Not by a long way. Sit down, dear, and let me get you a drink."

"Oh, I don't think—I mean, it seems so early."

"Oh, come on. One drink won't hurt you."

She turned and walked quickly to the kitchen, leaving Evelyn no choice but to follow. The half full bottle of Scotch and her own glass were on the shelf, and she saw Evelyn's busy eyes go over them.

By the time she gets home, Donna thought, she'll have it figured out that I'm drinking myself to death.

"You like Scotch, don't you?" Donna said.

"Yes, but just a little—teensy—"

"With soda all right?"

"Fine."

Evelyn's eyes shifted to the window. Outside, Gino was raking up leaves and cuttings, piling them on a square of burlap sacking. She still had the can of rose food in her arm and she shifted it, as if uncertain whether to let go of it or not.

"Here, let me take that," Donna said. "Ooh—it's heavy."

"It's loaded with minerals," Evelyn said and giggled. She released the can in exchange for the highball glass.

"Thanks for bringing it," Donna said. "I thought we'd get some plants in today, but Gino just now finished getting the beds ready, and it's almost quitting time."

"I wish I could afford one full time," Evelyn said. "A gardener, I mean."

"Oh, Gino's not full time," Donna said. "This was a special day—" the glass in her hand slipped, and she gripped it tightly—"trying to get that bedding finished."

Bedding, she thought. That's fine. That's just great. Shut up now. Let her do the talking. She's got the tongue for it.

"Shall we sit down where it's more comfortable?" she said as she led the way out of the kitchen.

She sat in the living room, trying to listen to Evelyn with one ear and Gino with the other. But Gino's sounds were distant and elusive, and Evelyn's high-pitched, nervous voice was an incessant pelting.

"Carl's away again?" Evelyn said and submerged Donna's one-word reply in a new flow of words.

Donna finished her drink, noted that Evelyn still had some in her glass, and excused herself. In the kitchen she poured a double shot into the glass, peering out the window at the same time, so that she spilled some of the Scotch. Gino was at the far end of the yard, dumping the cuttings into his truck. She glanced at the clock and saw that he would be leaving any minute.

Don't go! she thought desperately. Stall around a little while, Gino. Please—I'll get rid of her—

Evelyn was calling to her from the living room, but she couldn't make out the words. She took a giant swallow from her glass and nearly choked on it.

Gino—

He was standing by the truck, putting on a shirt and looking toward the house. Donna started into the living room, then stopped.

"One more minute, Evelyn," she called. "I have to speak to Gino before he gets away."

Evelyn said something, and Donna returned, almost running through the kitchen. She was opening the screen door when she realized she still had the glass in her hand. She made herself go back and set it down, then walked out into the back yard. By the time she reached the truck, she had got back most of her composure.

"It looks just beautiful," she said. "Thanks, Gino."

"Well—I'm sorry—I didn't get any of the plants in—"

"Don't be sorry. Plenty of time. Do you have any time tomorrow?"

"Tomorrow—" He pushed a big hand across his face and brushed at the stiff black hair on his forehead.

"Don't change anything on account of me," she said.

"In the afternoon," he said. "Maybe about three—"

"If you have time," she said. "And Gino—"

"Yes, ma'am?"

"Never mind. Oh, I almost forgot to give you the check. Wait just a minute."

"It's all right," he said. "No hurry."

"But a whole day's work. You can surely use the money. Do you have a date or anything tonight?"

"Well—"

"Wait right here. I'll get you the check."

She ran back across the lawn to the house. She looked into the living room, where Evelyn was sitting hunched forward on the sofa, holding her empty glass between her knees.

"Just one more minute. I'm sorry," Donna said. "I have to write Gino a check."

"It's all right," Evelyn said. "Don't mind me."

Donna went to the bedroom, found the checkbook in the bedside stand, and opened her pen. "Gino"—her lips moved. "Gino what? My God, I can't think of his last name! Gino, Gino—" She wrote the date and the amount and signed the check.... I can't ask him what his name is, for God's sake! she thought. If I leave it to be filled in, does he know enough to just fill it in? Oh, goddam it!

She went by the rear hall to the kitchen, carrying the check, and out to where Gino waited by the truck. When she handed it to him, she was close enough to smell the sweat under his shirt.

"Here, Gino. I was hurrying so fast—I just signed it and wrote in the amount. You can fill it in—"

He nodded, his face impassive. His eyes, beside the high Roman bridge of his nose, were very dark, with highlights flecking the eyeballs in the late sun. He didn't glance at the check but just pushed it into his damp shirt pocket.

"Gino," she said in a small voice. She managed to refrain from touching him. She had a feeling that Evelyn Kramer was looking out the kitchen window. "Do I have your telephone number?" she asked. "In case something should come up about tomorrow?"

"I don't know. I gave it to you—"

"Tell me again, now, in case I lost it."

He told her the number slowly, distinctly. She repeated it with her lips silently.

"And you have mine," she said.

"Yes," he said. "Yeah. I've got yours."

My number—you've got—she thought. "Good-bye Gino," she said. "Thanks again."

She didn't wait to watch him climb into the truck but turned quickly and went back with that running stride to the house. She looked out as she closed the door, and he was backing the truck carefully down the drive.

Evelyn wasn't in the kitchen, and she took time to breathe deeply half a dozen times to settle herself and make her hands stop shaking. Then she picked up her glass and went into the living room.

"Sorry to dash in and out that way," she said. "I guess I'm not organized today. Let me get you another drink."

Evelyn squealed and held the glass up out of reach. "Oh I wouldn't dare," she said. "One is all I can take before dinner."

Donna sat down with her drink. "How is Dick?" she said. "Busy, I guess, as usual."

"Yes, busy. This case of Robin Dexter has him upset. I'm sure he'd rather not have a trial at all, but you know how the law is."

Donna was shocked in spite of herself. No way to talk, Evelyn, she thought. I know what the law is, and your husband is the biggest lawman around here, and it doesn't make any difference whether he wants to try Robin Dexter or not. He has to do what has to be done and—oh, the hell with it.

"He had lunch with Senator Morris today," Evelyn said casually.

"That's nice," Donna said. "I suppose they have to keep in close touch." She slid that in pretty smoothly, Donna thought. Lunch with the Senator—look at me.

There didn't seem to be much else to say. Evelyn stirred restlessly.

"Sure you won't have another quick one," Donna said.

"Oh, no, I couldn't." She got up uncertainly. "I'd better get back. Dick will be home for dinner tonight, and I've got to help Edith."

Edith, my full-time maid, Donna thought. And then she thought, Come on, Donna, knock it off. It's only that she doesn't have anything else to talk about. She got up and opened the door.

Evelyn started out and turned back. "Oh, the rose food," she said. "There's enough, I think, for all your first planting. You just put three tablespoonfuls in a gallon of water and—you know how to do it. It works wonders for me."

"I appreciate it," Donna said. "Come over in a couple of days, and we'll see how it's working."

"All right—'bye now."

"Good-bye," Donna said. She waited till Evelyn was safely off in her Mercedes, then closed the door, sat down on the nearest chair, and finished her drink. She sat looking into the empty glass for a few minutes. Her hands weren't shaking any more, but she could feel her heart beating extra hard, as if she had climbed a steep hill.

Suppose she had taken a notion to come over around lunchtime, she thought, and suppose instead of going to the front door she had gone around to the back, having the rose food and all, and me in the kitchen with Gino unbuttoned—my God, I wonder whether anyone else was watching!

She got up, went to the kitchen, and poured Scotch into her glass. She didn't bother with ice or soda. She carried it into the bathroom and looked at herself in the mirror under the bright lights. Her face looked all right. It looked pretty damn good, in fact. As it should, she thought.

She paused in the bedroom and caught sight of the photo graph of Carl in the easel on her dressing table. Fury twisted deep in her. "You son of a bitch," she said through her teeth. "How do you like it now?"

She felt sick to her stomach and sat down on the edge of the bed to finish the Scotch. When the glass was empty, she set it on the nightstand and lay back on the bed, blinking at the ceiling, her arms flung outward.

Gino, she thought, my Gino, baby.

She raised herself on her elbow and smoothed the bedspread with her other hand. Gino, she thought, when you get home among your Italian friends, you won't—will you? You won't go bragging about laying the woman up in the country club district, will you? Please, Gino, you won't brag about it—What if he can't help it? Seventeen, eighteen—maybe it's a big thing in his life. Who wouldn't brag about it? But, Gino, please—

She pushed herself off the bed and went to the kitchen to get another drink. The bottle was nearly empty and she searched the cupboard under the sink till she found another. She made a long one this time, with ice and soda, and went to the living room. She sat, drinking it slowly, thinking about Gino.

Not till three o'clock tomorrow, she kept thinking. "Twenty hours," she said aloud.

He's in the shower now, she thought, washing the sweat off and whatever remains of me on him. Getting ready to go out with his Italian girlfriend—what's her name? Lewkie. For God's sake, Gino, don't tell Lewkie. Don't try to be a big man around Lewkie.

What do they do, I wonder? Go to a show, go look at television somewhere? Sit in the car and neck? Gino—

She had another drink and then another. It grew dark in the living room. At eight-thirty she decided to drive to the club for dinner. She fixed her face, smoothed her dress with her hands, and left the house. She was slightly unsteady on her feet. When she backed the car out of the garage, she scraped the left rear fender against the neighbor's fence.

AL LEVY

Al Levy's wife, Doris, looked into his study at eleven-thirty, yawned, stretched her arms, and leaned against the doorjamb, waiting for him to take notice of her. Al was in his shirtsleeves at his big desk, which was stacked on all sides with books and papers, so that she couldn't see his face or head but only the hunch of his thick shoulders and part of the back of his neck. Like some kind of frog crouching among the books, she thought.

After a while he leaned back, shrugging as if to ease the tension between his shoulder blades. His head turned, and he caught sight of her. He leaned back all the way, took off his glasses, and dropped them on the desk. She was standing with one shoulder against the jamb, one hip jutting at a sharp angle, and the full curve of her flanks thrusting under the housecoat she was wearing. Al's eyes moved in his head slowly, looking at her, and she got that tingling sensation in the thighs that she always had when he ogled her. You'd think a person would get over that, she thought, after a few years. Thank God she hadn't.

"Is that any way for a nice Jewish boy to think?" she said, shifting her position.

"Come here," Al said.

"Come here, yourself."

"Who's the man of the house?"

She pushed languidly from the door and walked to where he was sitting. "You got me," she said. "You're a fast boy with the questions."

"Got to be." He put one big arm around her buttocks and began with his free hand to unbutton the housecoat. Doris glanced at the pile of papers on the desk, pages of typewritten notes heavily laced with penciled revisions.

"What kind of kid is this Dexter?" she asked.

Al opened the housecoat with his fingers and kissed her navel, making a loud smacking noise. "Just a kid," he said. "The headshrinker said he was normal, responsive, and guilty as hell."

"If he's normal, how can he be so guilty?"

"Come on, you went to law school the same as me."

"Not quite the same. I quit, remember?"

Al hugged and released her. "Look," he said, "am I normal?"

Doris shrugged. "Aside from a few quirks—I guess so."

"All right. If I get sore and give you a belt in the nose, am I guilty?"

"Of what?"

"Of belting you! Wife-beating, it's called."

She frowned thoughtfully. "Well—it would depend on whether you had a right to belt me—the motivation."

"Don't be sly with me," he said, slapping her behind. "The next word you're coming up with is provocation."

She put the palm of her hand on his face and rubbed his nose roughly. "Okay, provocation," she said.

Al pulled her hand away from his face, kissed her palm, and switched off the desk lamp.

"Provocation is inherent in all degrees of sexual shenanigans," he intoned. "The law allows for it. But the law holds there is a place to stop. This girl is sixteen years old. She wanted to stop."

"Stop what?"

Al got up from the chair, turned her to face the door, and gave her another swat. "You know damn well stop what," he said.

"But if she let him fool around—"

"Come on, bedtime."

Going up the stairs, he put his hands on her buttocks, urging her upward.

"I thought you had a trial on in the morning," she said. "That's in the morning. Right now I got something else on."

She made a guttural sound in her throat.

"Do you want me to take a shower first?" he said.

"Let's not be vulgar."

In the bedroom they raced each other, undressing. She won and scrambled into bed, then pulled the blanket over her head. Al pushed his way under it and found her.

"So fool around a little," she said.

"You know I will."

"What if I say stop?"

"The law doesn't recognize marital rape."

"Oh-ho! Some law."

"Come here."

"Yeah—"

Pretty soon he said, "You going to say stop?"

"Yeah. Start stopping."

"You can talk plainer than that."

"Yeah, yeah, yeah. Come on, big baby. Give—me—it."

* * * *

Al was half asleep when he felt Doris get into bed and roll hard against his back.

She put an arm around his waist. "Is it going to be one of those juicy trials?" she asked.

"Hmm—how do you mean, juicy?"

"Like you go into all the details. 'What did he do then? Did he take out his penis?' Answer: 'Yes, he did.' 'And did he put it in you?' Answer:—and so on, hour after hour?"

"I don't know. Maybe. Depends."

"That will be rough on the kid—the girl, I mean."

Al moved heavily in the bed. "Maybe. I guess so."

After a while she said, "Might be kind of hard on Mr. Kramer, too, if it gets a big play. If he plans to run for Senator."

"We talked about it today," Al said. "He doesn't like the case, and I don't blame him. But there's no way out of it now, and he knows it and he'll be all right."

Doris began to snore softly. Al disengaged her arm gently, turned onto his back, and folded his hands under his head.

"It's rough, though," he said aloud to the dark. "Rough all around."

RICHARD KRAMER

Dick Kramer lay in bed, wishing Evelyn would turn off the light. She was sitting at the dressing table, putting some cream on her face. Now and then she would pause, lean close to the mirror, pull at her narrow face, and inspect it carefully. Dick turned over in bed.

"I'm worried about Donna Forester," Evelyn said.

"Oh?" he said.

"She's drinking so much."

"Well, I guess she always drank pretty regularly."

"But all by herself. When I went over there this afternoon, she had a glass in her hand all the time. She kept running out to the kitchen to get some more."

Dick didn't say anything.

"You know what I think?" Evelyn said. "I think it's because of Carl. I think he's cheating on her."

"Is that what everybody is saying?" Dick said.

There was a pause.

"What do you mean by that remark?" she said. "That's not very nice."

"I'm sorry. I didn't mean anything."

"It's just something I figured out by myself."

"All right. I really don't know whether Carl is cheating on her or not."

Evelyn turned off the light, and Dick heard her get into the other bed. After a moment she reached up and switched off the pink shaded lamp on the stand between the beds.

"Would you ever cheat on me?" she asked.

"Of course not," he said.

"Did you ever think of it?"

"Never."

Some time went by. Then Evelyn said, "Aren't you going to kiss me goodnight?"

Dick threw back the cotton blanket, got out of bed, leaned over the other bed, and kissed her mouth quickly. "Good night," he said.

"Good night."

After he had got back in his own bed, he lay on his back, unable to sleep. Evelyn always fell asleep instantly. He had lain awake many nights envying her. Clear conscience, he thought, and his mouth twisted wryly. Clear conscience, hell, he thought. Metabolism.

I wonder how she would look if she got fat? he wondered. Like that one in Chicago I couldn't make it with that night I was—when? Seventeen? No, I was nineteen. My God, it's forever. I was never nineteen years old. But I was that night, and she scared me to death—"Don't take your pants off, honey, somebody might come in."

There were girls, though. Elegant, bright girls. At nineteen, twenty, twenty-one—but I never had a dime to take anybody out. Those few times with Karen—but it was so late in the semester. We only just got acquainted when she had to go home to Chicago. I wonder what happened to her? She was tall and very slender, like Evelyn. I wonder if that means anything? I don't think so. My mother wasn't like that—kind of blocky and short, with that bleached hair. Karen didn't have any money either, I remember. I guess that's why we got along all right those few times. The simple pleasures—movie, walk through the park, have a late snack, and walk to the dorm. It was good then.

What if Evelyn had been poor like Karen? he thought. No—I loved her, really. It wasn't the money. The money helped though, didn't it? Not Evelyn's, but her mother's. Those tight times—setting up the office—campaign expenses. Generous. Always generous. Mother Stevens is quite a woman. Aside from the money—gutsy. I wonder what happened about Evelyn?

He couldn't make himself visualize Evelyn as fat like the whore in Chicago, or as resembling her mother in any way except around the eyes sometimes. Nor as Karen—quiet, slim, with that suppressed eagerness and joy to live. He couldn't let himself think about the money.

But it's all paid back, he thought self-righteously. Every nickel. Out of salary. A good salary and good management. Of course, without those contributions there wouldn't have been that salary, nor before it that fairly rich practice. All that I am or hope to be, he thought.

He turned on his side suddenly, thrusting, as if to push the thoughts away. After quite a long time he drifted into an uneasy sleep.

LONNIE KIRK

There were four customers at the bar at the *Highwayman's Inn* at one-thirty in the morning. Lonnie Kirk was putting things in order for the night, polishing glasses and stacking them on the backbar. The customers were two couples together, well known to one another and to Lonnie.

"One more belt for the road, Lonnie?" one of the men asked.

Lonnie made four bourbon highballs with water and cleared off the used glasses, dunking them in the detergent basin as he lifted them down.

"We're going over to Ralphie's," one of the girls said. "Why don't you come along, Lonnie? We'll wait for you to close up."

"Not me," Lonnie said. "Not tonight."

"Lonnie's got to go to court," one of the men said. "How about that, Lonnie? You got everything ready, all rehearsed?"

"No rehearsals," Lonnie said soberly.

"You mean the D.A. didn't tell you what to say?"

"No," Lonnie said. "He asked me a few questions."

"The whole thing is silly," the other girl said. "No guy can rape a girl if she really doesn't want him to."

"I wouldn't know," Lonnie said.

"They pay your expenses?" one of the men asked. "You have to go in there, have lunch—"

"No expenses. It's my duty as a citizen. The D.A. told me."

"Well, maybe you'll have a ball," the man said.

Lonnie finished polishing the glasses and set the last one on the backbar. I wish they'd hurry up and get the hell out of here so I can go home and get some sleep, he thought. "I don't know," he said. "I never was in court before."

CHAPTER 6

Judge Harris's court came to order at twelve minutes after ten on Friday morning. The courtroom was one of three still in use as such in the old courthouse, and it was inadequate for its time. The air sometimes was quite bad, and in winter the old steam pipes used for heating got pretty noisy. Because Judge Harris was the senior judge of the circuit and presided over the majority of criminal trials in the county and because of its hallowed location, Department Two in the courthouse was maintained for his use. The judge had been heard to remark that "Trying a serious criminal case in that annex on the Mall—like trying to shoot an X-ray with a flashlight." Nobody had ever been able to figure out exactly what that meant, but Judge Harris's preference was plain, and he had the full support of the District Attorney. This was no combination to fight.

Though the newspapers and the radio had played it down, the sensationalism promised by the Robin Dexter case had drawn a crowd. Two sheriff's deputies had to be posted outside in the main corridor to assure enough seating for the jury panel, which consisted of sixty persons. They occupied two-thirds of the available seats, and the last row was roped off and reserved for witnesses and interested officials, such as the District Attorney and members of the Sheriff's Department. That left about twenty seats for casual onlookers, and these were filled long before ten o'clock.

Al Levy was sitting in the back row with Dick Kramer when the bailiff rapped for order. He had to hurry down to the counsel table in front of the bench and just barely made it. As he left his seat he had asked over his shoulder, "Any last minute suggestions, boss?"

And Kramer had said, "Nope. It's all yours."

It was both comforting and alarming. Al thought about it as he rushed down the aisle. If Kramer had reservations about the case, he might withhold help if Al should need it. But no, Al thought, standing at the table for the judge's entrance. Kramer wouldn't do that.

The bailiff opened the session, and Judge Harris gathered his robe and sat down in the squeaky swivel chair with the high back while the clerk read the formal charge in the case of the state versus Robin Dexter.

At the long mahogany table on the judge's right, facing the bench, Al Levy sat alone with his brief bag. Opposite, on the judge's left, Harry Gideon and his partner, Sam Crowell, flanked Robin Dexter, who slouched low in his chair, looking down at the table top. While the clerk was reading, Harry Gideon leaned close to his client and whispered, "Remember—don't talk while the judge is talking."

Robin nodded curtly, and Gideon started riffling through a thick file of papers.

When the clerk had finished, Judge Harris looked at the two counsel tables, then out over the room. "The courtroom," he said, "is a public place and open to all interested persons to the extent to which they can be accommodated. The nature of some of the testimony in this case may sometimes provoke strong reactions. I assume we're all civilized people here, and the court expects civilized people to behave in a certain way. In the event of any disturbance, I will ask the bailiff to clear the room."

The room was silent.

"A few words to the jury panel," Judge Harris said. "Ladies and gentlemen, the court appreciates the fact that many of you have suffered some inconvenience, possibly even some loss of income, in making yourselves available for jury duty. This is a trial of a serious crime—the crime of rape. Some of the facts in the case may be unpleasant, even re-volting. The court has no wish to subject anyone to experiences that may be excessively painful to their sensibilities. Any of you, therefore, who feel that attendance at this trial may prove emotionally distressing are excused. Those of you who leave will report to Department One—that is, just across the hall."

The judge waited two or three minutes. Nobody got up to leave.

He always does that, Al Levy was thinking. I wonder if it's because he figures that after his little speech nobody would dare leave. That way, we're sure of enough jurors to get the thing going.

"Is the prosecution ready?" Judge Harris asked.

Al Levy dipped his head. "Ready, your honor."

"Is the defense ready?"

Harry Gideon nodded. "Defense is ready, your honor."

"The clerk will call the jury," the judge said.

He settled a pair of glasses on his nose and began looking through some papers. The clerk, picking the names from a box, called out in a clear voice. Jurors got up one by one and made their way down the aisle and into the jury box against the wall on the judge's right hand.

* * * *

Dick Kramer sat through Judge Harris's opening remarks, then left the courtroom and went to his office. He wasn't sure why he had sat in on even that much of the trial. Customarily he stayed out of the courtroom unless he was prosecuting the case personally. He had had some vague idea that his presence would indicate that he was solidly behind the case and not equivocating. And he had thought that it might be encouraging to Al Levy, though he wasn't at all sure of this. It might have the opposite effect.

When he reached the office, Ida was out for her coffee break, and there was a message on his desk that he couldn't quite get the drift of. He made a routine call to the office of the Supervisors, and when it was completed, Ida had come back.

"What's this about the grand jury?" he asked.

"Well," Ida said, "they got into a kind of a fuss and asked me some questions, which I said I couldn't answer, and you would be in any minute. So they said they were going to take a recess, and maybe around eleven o'clock—if you had time,—you could drop in there and straighten them out."

"Did they say what item they were hung up on?"

"No, but I have a hunch it's the Sanderson thing."

"Oh. All right. Unless they change their minds before then, I'll go down at eleven."

"And I told Mr. O'Brien you'd maybe be able to see him around this time."

"Sure. Will you ask him to come up?"

A red light flashed on his intercom, and Dick picked up his phone and opened the line to the Sheriff's office.

"Kramer," he said. "What is it?"

"We've got three kids here—I don't know what to do with them." The voice belonged to Ed Sherry, administrative assistant to Sheriff Donahue.

"What are you being asked to do with them?"

"Put 'em in juvenile detention."

"What's the problem?"

"Well, they were booked in the city jurisdiction, and a detective brought 'em in here and said he had orders to turn them into the county facility instead of the city—"

"Who gave him the orders?"

"I don't know. Somebody at city headquarters."

"Have you got room for them?"

"I guess we got room, yes, but we don't have a qualified attendant in there right now."

"How old are the kids?"

"Twelve, fourteen."

"What did they do?"

"Stealing. Some store over in Crudsville."

"Oh, come on—twelve years old?"

"The way I get it, they were doing pretty good. Before daylight—they had a couple of big wheelbarrows, working from the alley—this was a hardware store and they had pretty well cleaned out the power tools and a bunch of other stuff, when they got caught."

"Did the haul get put back in the store?"

"I don't know. I suppose so."

Blake O'Brien came in, and Dick motioned him into a chair.

"What is it about the qualified attendant?"

"Well, the juvenile law says we got to have a duly qualified probation officer, plus a standby female officer—a matron—for all offenders under the age of fifteen. I can get one or the other but not both. We're all chopped up by vacations."

"There's a complaint on the kids, right? How firm is it?"

"Looks pretty firm. The city police put them through the whole routine."

"All right. Turn 'em over either to a probation officer or a matron—a matron would be better—and put 'em up temporarily. I'll take the responsibility. Check back in a couple of hours."

"Okay, Mr. Kramer. Thanks." Dick hung up. "Excuse me, Blake, couple of quick calls."

"Sure," Blake said. "Better if I come back later?"

"No, it won't take long. Ida, get me the city manager." Dick searched through a file on his desk and looked to O'Brien for help. "You know who's in line on the volunteer defender list?"

"Not for sure," Blake said. "Manny Silverman had a case a few days ago, but—"

"Manny's had enough. Ida—"

His buzzer sounded, and Dick picked up the phone, covering the mouthpiece with his hand.

"Yes, Mr. Kramer?" Ida said.

"Will you find out who follows Manny Silverman on the defender list and try to get him on the phone?"

"Yes, sir."

"Hello," Dick said into the phone, "Richard Kramer speaking. I'd like to talk to Mr. Bazzard."

"One moment, sir," a secretary said.

Bazzard came on the line.

"Listen," Dick said, "about these juvenile offenders—"

The city manager was prepared for the call. "Yes," he said, "three youngsters about twelve years old were sent to the county facility."

"On your orders?"

"At my suggestion."

"Aren't you pushing things kind of hard?" Dick said.

"We talked about this yesterday—"

"I know we did."

"I've taken the necessary steps to negotiate this business of juvenile facilities with the supervisors. Meanwhile the city facility is inadequate for offenders of this age. When the acting police chief called me, I said I had talked with you about it, and my suggestion was that they be sent to the county."

"You did the first thing that popped into your head, is that it?"

"I did the humane thing," Bazzard said. "Among other defects, the city juvenile detention hall is a firetrap, and this is the season."

Dick's mouth tightened, then relaxed. "All right," he said. "We've put them up temporarily. I'm not against humanity, but the next time something like this comes up, it would be smart of you to clear it first."

"With you?" Bazzard said.

"With me—or with the Sheriff or the acting Sheriff. I'll alert them."

"Very good," Bazzard said. "Is that all?"

"That's all."

Dick hung up, shaking his head at Blake O'Brien. "He's the coolest guy in the world," he said. "I've got a little tangle with him about five times a week."

Blake nodded. Ida called from her office, "I have Mr. Orcutt on the line."

Dick's forehead creased. "Bill Orcutt?" he said to Blake. "I thought he'd retired."

"He likes to keep his hand in," Blake said drily.

"How old is he?"

"About eighty-five now, I think."

"These are just kids."

Blake shrugged. "He might resent being bypassed if he's next on the list."

"Yeah," Dick said. He opened the line and said hello to Orcutt. "Listen, Bill," he said, "I wouldn't bother you with a thing like this, but it came up all of a sudden—feel free to turn me down—"

"Go ahead, Dick," Bill Orcutt said. "I'm just sitting here looking at my navel."

"Well, over in juvenile hall there are three young kids from Cruds-ville. I don't think they have a lawyer. You might be able to spring them."

"Too hot to handle?" Orcutt said.

"I just want 'em out of juvenile hall."

"What are they in for?"

"Burglary."

"Oh, my!"

"The loot was returned—they got caught in the act. If you find out who signed the complaint, you could probably do the whole thing on the phone."

"All right. May I use your name?"

"I'm glad to see you haven't lost your sense of humor," Dick said. "Thanks, Bill."

"Not at all. Thanks for calling."

Dick leaned back in his chair and rubbed his forehead with both hands.

"Sorry, Blake, for the delay. My time is yours."

O'Brien uncrossed his ankles, sat up in the chair, and consulted some notes. "This woman Berryman—Nadine Berryman," he said. "I've been working on the case about a week—prostitution and a drug rap."

"Yeah?"

"She's in county hospital. I think she's got a story to tell, and this might be the day for it. If you could be there, too—"

"How'd she get in the hospital?"

"She threw a wingding. Started the other day. She was quiet enough for a couple of days; then she started yelling around and throwing up, and they had her in the infirmary. But she gave the nurse a bad time, so they moved her to county. She's evidently been on the stuff for quite a while—mainliner—and she's in fairly pathetic shape."

"How's she getting along in the hospital?"

"Not too good. They had to put her in a private room, and she gave everybody a bad time, including a couple of interns. They give her a certain amount of sedation—not too much—and she's quiet a couple of hours at a time."

"What is it about telling a story?"

O'Brien hesitated. "Well—on account of the narcotics thing, tied in with prostitution, some eager-beaver reporter from the *Courier* is work-ing overtime. He talked to me a couple of times, and I put him off. But he also, I guess, got to her some way and put a bug in her ear."

Dick felt a cold wind at the back of his neck.

"His angle is," Blake went on, "that the stuff is coming on the river, unloading somewhere in Crudsville. He can make it sound like they unload it in bushel baskets right under the cops' noses. Donahue and the city people are both working on it, trying not to make too much noise, but they've got nothing yet. I don't know how much the reporter really has got, if anything except hunches. But we know that the Berryman woman has been getting it and we're pretty sure she doesn't go out of town for it."

"You said the reporter put a bug in her ear."

"Yeah. I think he persuaded her that she could make a deal with us. Anyway, the last couple of days she's been saying, 'Let me talk to Dick Kramer. You get the D.A. over here, and I'll tell him plenty.'"

Dick rubbed his nose and scowled. "We drag that goddam river," he said, "about once a month looking for stuff. If there's traffic, I don't think it's coming in here."

"That's what I like to think," O'Brien said. "But if it should be, it looks pretty bad on the statistics."

"Yeah."

"And whether it is or not, this reporter can put on quite a show unless we get on top of it."

"Has the Berryman woman had any kind of hearing?"

"No. She was picked up ten days ago and booked. She hasn't been well enough for a hearing."

"You've talked to her?"

"Several times."

"Is she rational?"

"Off and on. I can't tell whether she's faking any of it."

Dick looked at his watch. "Unless there's a change," he said, "I have to see the grand jury at eleven. Might take an hour. Could you make it to the hospital around twelve-thirty?"

"Sure."

"All right. We'll go talk to her. You might call them so they won't let her fall asleep while we're there."

O'Brien nodded, got up, and went out. Dick called to Ida, asking for the Sanderson file. She brought it to him, and for ten minutes he read in it rapidly but carefully, his finger following the lines of the typescript.

CHAPTER 7

Riding in Blake O'Brien's compact car, with Blake at the wheel, Dick put his head back and tried to ease the tension in his neck. It had been growing since his conversation with the city manager, and he knew it wouldn't let up till he could get to bed that night. But that night, he remembered suddenly, he had to play bridge at the club. Oh, no, he thought. Not tonight.

"The grand jury is nervous about bringing in an indictment against Sanderson," he said. It was some relief to be able to talk to someone about his problems, someone who understood them and knew how to keep his mouth shut, like Blake O'Brien.

"Yeah?" Blake said. "I don't wonder."

"Some of 'em have this big image of Happy Jack, and they can't shake it. Funny thing."

"Mmm."

"I went through the bill for them and made a few points they said they were confused about. I tried to explicate some contract law. I don't know how well it went down. The line between simple default and larceny is kind of fuzzy."

"It's fuzzy to me," O'Brien said.

"Bound to be. But I think the county's case against Sanderson is sound."

"Sure. But everybody thinks he's a great guy."

"He is a great guy. But he tried to pad out his bank account with the taxpayers' money, and that's stealing."

"What did they say to that?"

Dick laughed a little, letting his head loll against the seat. "They've picked up a little terminology. 'Exemplary,' they kept saying. It's just 'exemplary.'"

"Yeah. Just holding Happy Jack up as an example so somebody else won't try the same thing. So why all this fuss about such a great guy?"

"Uh-huh. I had to get a little serious. 'Look at the pictures,' I said. 'That's part of the road Sanderson contracted to build for the county. He bid on the job. There were specifications. It was specified that over this stretch where the soft spot is, down in the bottoms, the concrete mixture had to meet a certain standard, and it had to be reinforced. All that was in the bid and the contract. But Sanderson cheated on the reinforcing and he cheated on the mixture. And the road didn't hold.'

"So one of the diehards said that the inspector on the job let him get away with it, and I had to explain no he didn't, Happy Jack was too fast for him. The inspector checked the steel, which Sanderson had on the site. It was all right. He checked the concrete on a surprise visit, and Sanderson had it loaded with sand. He waited while it was dumped and a new mix started coming on the job. That night Sanderson exchanged the steel for a smaller gauge, had it right on hand for first thing in the morning, along with some more loads of the substandard concrete. He worked pretty fast, starting at seven in the morning, and he must have had somebody tailing the inspector. Because when the inspector got out there on his routine call, he had the steel covered with the cheap cement, and he was pouring a thin layer of the specified mix over the top. The inspector did everything that was expected of him. He checked the mix, and it was all right. He ran a probe down to make sure there was steel under it. He'd already seen the load and okayed it. You can't pinpoint the gauge of the steel with that probe, and you can't feel the consistency of the concrete, and Sanderson knows it as well as anybody. So it wasn't the inspector's fault. It was Sanderson's, all by himself."

O'Brien didn't say anything.

"Sorry to go on like that," Dick said.

"Oh, hell," Blake said.

"How's Al's trial going?"

"As usual, I guess. He came in around noon. They haven't got a jury yet. Gideon is stalling. Al said the only questions he's asking the jurors are 'Have you or any of your children ever been subjected to forcible rape or sexual molestation?' and 'Do you believe there is any fundamental biological or sexual difference between people of different nationalities?' Gideon's asking quite a few questions. I think by now Al hopes he'll take the rest of the day for it, so Al won't have to make his opening pitch with that long weekend for it to cool off in."

"Yeah."

"And I guess here we are."

Blake drove into a parking slot to one side of the hospital ambulance entrance. It was marked "Sheriff's Office—Official Cars Only."

"Is that reporter likely to be hanging around the hospital?" Dick asked.

"Yeah, he's likely."

"What's his name?"

"Lambert. Peter Lambert."

"I think I know him by sight. But give me a nudge if you spot him, all right?"

"Sure."

They went in by the ambulance entrance and took an elevator to the fourth floor. They had to check in at the nurse's station and wait while a nurse went to the Berryman woman's room to see whether she could talk to them now. Dick asked Blake whether he had seen any sign of the reporter on the way up, and Blake said he hadn't.

The nurse came back and said Mrs. Berryman wasn't feeling well, but she would talk to the District Attorney for a few minutes.

"Is there a nurse with her?" Dick asked.

"No, she's been quiet this morning."

"I'd like a nurse in the room with us, if you can manage it," he said.

"I'll see." She went into an anteroom and came back after about a minute. "I can go with you for about fifteen minutes," she said.

"And Mr. O'Brien?"

She looked doubtful. "I don't know. She's a little—difficult. She said, 'The D.A. I'll talk to the D.A. Nobody else.'"

Blake O'Brien shrugged. "I'll wait here," he said. "If you want me, just look out and wiggle your finger."

"Okay."

Dick and the nurse started down the hall. "I hope she's in a good mood," the nurse said.

"She hard to handle?"

"Brother! The language she uses!"

Dick clucked in sympathy. They reached the door, and the nurse opened and held it for him. The lights were dimmed, but he could see that there were two beds in the room and only one was occupied. A woman raised her head to look at them. Her reddish hair was a wild tangle.

"Mr. Kramer?" she said. "Richard Kramer?"

"Yes," he said. "I'm Richard Kramer."

Her head sank back onto the pillow. "Welcome to my boudoir," she said.

Her head lifted again, and she stared at the nurse.

"What's she doing here?"

"I asked her to come," Dick said.

The woman snorted. "To protect me?"

"No, to protect me," he said.

She laughed hoarsely. "That's pretty good," she said.

He moved nearer the bed, and the nurse stayed behind near the door. Nadine Berryman had subsided again and was lying on her back with her eyes closed. She made a large mound under the hospital sheet. He could see by the dim lamplight from the bedside table that her face was pockmarked, though not disfigured.

"Mrs. Berryman," he said from some distance, "I understand you have something to tell me."

"Kramer?" she said, "Dick Kramer?"

She's faking, he thought. "Yes," he said. "I have a few minutes—"

A tremor went through her, and he saw sweat break out on her forehead. Pain, he thought. Maybe it's real.

"Listen—" she said.

He went to the bed and leaned over her. She raised herself on one elbow, and her eyes opened, looking for him. "Listen—can you do anything for me?"

He thought he could see now that she really was in serious pain. "I don't know," he said.

"If I do something for you?"

"You're under arrest," he said, "and the charge is pretty serious. I can't make a deal with you, if that's what you have in mind. I'd like to hear what you have to say. I can't promise you anything."

She lay down again. She was breathing heavily with her mouth open, and there was a sour smell to her breath. "I need some kind of relief," she said. "They won't give me enough—see—I've been on the stuff for about a year and I need it. I'm going to kick it as soon as I get out of here, but I can't do it all of a sudden like this."

"I understand," Dick said. "What did you want to tell me?"

"If you would tell the doctor it's all right, you know. You're the boss. He'd listen."

"I'll speak to the doctor," he said. "I can't promise anything."

She raised one hand languidly, beckoning. "Listen Dick—Mr. Kramer—is that nurse still here?"

"Yes," he said. "I asked her to stay."

"Can she hear me?"

"No. She's way over by the door."

"Have they got the room bugged or anything?"

"No. Go ahead. Don't worry."

She went through another of those convulsive shudders, more protracted this time. She drew her knees up and put her left fist in her mouth till it passed.

"I'm sorry," he said. "Can you tell me now?"

She was short of breath, and the words came out in spurts, so low that he had to lean close to hear them.

"I've been getting the stuff from a guy named Ben. I don't know his last name. He gets it out of the river."

"Out of the river?"

"They throw it in the river, and he fishes it out. I watched him once. Down by the docks in Crudsville."

"You mean they throw it off a barge or something?"

"I don't know what kind of goddam boat. Down by the docks."

"Which docks? North or south?"

"I don't know—south I think—way down past the big coalyard, you know."

"Can you remember the exact location?"

"No—there were a lot of trees. The ground was wet, swampy."

"Is it a one-man operation? Just Ben, all by himself?"

"I don't know. He's the only one I know. He does all right. There's quite a few around town hooked."

He didn't respond. He was thinking about the riverbank on the Crudsville side.

"I guess you wouldn't know about that," she said.

"About what?"

"Being hooked—how many there are."

"I don't usually know unless they get in trouble."

"Yeah."

"Can you tell me where this Ben person lives?"

Her head moved from side to side on the pillow. "No, I don't know," she said.

"All right. I'll leave you alone now. Thanks."

She reached out and found his hand by chance. He let her hold it for a moment. Her hand was clammy and cold. "Listen—you'll talk to the doctor, like you said?"

"Yes, I'll talk to him. Try to get some sleep."

"Sleep—hah," she said.

"I'll speak to him right now," Dick said, pulling his hand free of hers.

"Okay," she said. "Thanks for coming."

He had taken three steps toward the door when she said, "You don't remember me, huh?"

He turned to look back at the bed. "Remember—? I'm afraid—"

"Nadine," she said. "Nadine Gorman. Walnut Street High School. Nineteen thirty-six. I remember you, Dick Kramer. You were on the debating team. You wouldn't remember, but I remember you."

"Nadine Gorman," he repeated.

"That's right. Berryman was the name of the man I married."

"Well, what do you know," he said. "It's a small world." What do you say now? he was thinking, because we went to high school together thirty years ago.

"Yeah," she said. "Nadine Gorman. That was me."

"Try and sleep now," he said. "I'll speak to the doctor."

She mumbled something, but he couldn't make it out. He nodded to the nurse, and they went out to the hall.

"Anybody special taking care of her?" he asked.

The nurse shrugged. "Whoever's around. Interns."

"Does the chief resident know anything about her case?"

"I guess so. He follows all the cases. I think he saw her once or twice."

"Would he be in now?"

"Somewhere, I think."

"I'd like to talk to him."

"All right. Down at the desk."

They walked down to the desk, and Blake O'Brien got to his feet as they approached. The nurse picked up a telephone and started asking for Doctor Prettyman.

"Get anything?" O'Brien asked.

"Maybe," Dick said. "She told me the story. She's pretty sick. I don't know whether she made it up or not."

"Dr. Prettyman is in his office," the nurse said. "Do you want to speak to him on the phone?"

"Please," Dick said, taking the phone from her. "Doctor Prettyman?"

"Yes."

"This is Richard Kramer, the District Attorney. You have a patient from county jail—"

"Yes, I know we have."

"You're familiar with her case?"

"I've looked into it."

"What kind of shape is she in?"

"I don't understand the question. She's alive."

"What does she need in the way of treatment?"

"She needs a fix! She's a junkie! A user!"

"I know. This is what I'm trying to say—the way things are developing, she is probably the most crucial witness I've got, and I need her and I want her to be able to testify when the time comes."

"Well, what do you want from me?"

"I just want her taken care of as best you can."

"She needs a fix. Is it all right for me to give it to her?"

"I'm not in charge of the hospital, and I don't know anything about medicine."

"Okay. The best thing I can do for her right now is to give her a fix."

"You're the doctor," Dick said and hung up. "Let's go," he said to Blake. He remembered to look back and say thank you to the nurse, who bobbed her head and went about her business.

"By God, I hope I never get sick and have to go to a hospital," Dick said.

"I'm with you," Blake said. "How did it go?"

They had the elevator to themselves. "She said there's a guy named Ben," Dick said, "who supplies her. He gets it out of the river, down at the south end of the docks on the Crudsville side. They throw it off a boat of some kind, and he picks it up."

"That's it?"

"That's about it. She told me we went to high school together—she and I. And she asked me to speak to the doctor about getting her some relief."

"Will he do it?"

"I think so. He wanted me to take the responsibility for it. I should prescribe medicine."

"There's no law against a doctor using a fix as treatment when necessary."

"I know it, but it's risky medicine and it's very risky public relations-wise, if you know what I mean."

"I see."

They left the elevator and started out by the ambulance entrance. Blake caught at Dick's sleeve. "Our boy is here," he said.

"Who?"

"The reporter."

"Oh, great."

"Brush him?"

"No, I guess not."

They walked out to the car, and a young man in horn-rimmed glasses approached on an angle from the ambulance loading platform.

"Hi, Mr. O'Brien," he said. "Mr. Kramer."

Seeing him, Dick remembered his face. "Hello, Lambert," he said. "How are you?"

"Fine. Could I hitch a ride back to the courthouse? My car's busted."

Dick was hungry. He had planned to stop somewhere on the way back and have lunch with Blake and try to work something out to follow up Nadine Berryman's story. But he couldn't face the prospect of sitting through lunch with the reporter.

"Sure, climb in," Dick said.

It would have been courteous to have shown Lambert into the back seat and to have sat with him, letting Blake drive like a chauffeur. But

Dick wasn't in a mood to be courteous. He motioned to the back seat and climbed in beside Blake in the front, putting the reporter at some disadvantage.

Not that Lambert was easily discouraged. They had barely got out of the hospital parking area when, leaning forward from the back, he asked: "Mr. Kramer, is it true that your department is about to crack down on the narcotics traffic on the river?"

Dick cringed inwardly at the hard thrust of the question but managed to stay cool on the outside. "Can I break that up a little?" he said. "In the first place, I don't know whether there is any narcotics traffic on the river. In the second place, if it should turn out that there is such a traffic going on, my department certainly will crack down on it."

"Well," Lambert went on, "you're holding a woman named Berryman on a prostitution charge. Is it possible that she is a key to the narcotics trade in the county?"

Dick shrugged heavily. "As you know, I can't discuss individual cases like this until after the court disposes of them. Whether Mrs. Berryman knows anything about any source of drugs locally, I don't know. If she should, then, of course, she would be an important witness."

The reporter let some breathing time pass, but he wasn't finished yet. Blake O'Brien had made the last turn and was heading for the ramp that led down to the Sheriffs parking area when Lambert asked, "Is it true, Mr. Kramer, that if Senator Morris should announce his retirement from politics as of the end of his term, you plan to run for the United States Senate?"

This time Dick was prepared, and the shock was lighter. He was even able to laugh with a genuine sound.

"You're having a busy day, aren't you?" he said. "Let's wait and see whether Senator Morris does retire and take up that question later. Right now, no comment whatever. Okay?"

"Okay," Lambert said.

The three of them got out of the car and started up the ramp toward the courthouse.

Things were fairly peaceful, Dick was thinking. Now all of a sudden I've got to get on top of the public relations, along with everything else.

"Listen," he said to Lambert, by way of dismissal at the side door of the courthouse, "you're enterprising and I admire you for it. The *Courier* is a good newspaper. But don't crowd me too hard. I won't withhold anything that I can tell you legally, and I won't force anything on you that you don't want. You give me the same break, all right?"

Lambert hesitated. "Well, we're not in quite the same position," he said.

"I know," Dick said, "but within reason. How's that?" Lambert looked at Blake O'Brien, then at Dick again. "Okay," he said, "within reason."

"Thanks," Dick said, holding out his hand. "Just don't leave me alone altogether."

"Never fear," Lambert said and shook hands with him.

Dick and Blake O'Brien got into the elevator and started up to the third floor.

"You have time to do a little investigating?" Dick asked. "When do I start?"

"Right away. Let's get a rundown first on every guy named Ben or Benjamin known to the police. And get a list of every known user in the area, whether in or out of jail. Then we'll get hold of the cops who are on the beat in that section of Crudsville and get set for a stake-out."

They left the elevator and walked to Dick's office.

"How much do you have on your desk that needs clearing?" Dick asked.

"Not much. A few loose ends—"

"Can one of the clerks help?"

"Sure."

"All right. Find one who's not busy, and I'll unhook him from the judge. I'll try to get Donahue and Parsons, the city chief, to huddle with us this afternoon. Give me a ring anytime."

"Yeah," Blake said and went out on the balls of his feet. O'Brien had been gone only half a minute when Dick picked up his phone and called him. A secretary answered, and Dick said Mr. O'Brien was on his way to the office, and would she have him call Mr. Kramer the minute he got in—before calling anyone else.

Ida hadn't gone to lunch yet. "If you've got a girl to handle the phone," Dick said, "you'd better go. Will you have somebody send me a sandwich and some coffee?"

"What kind of sandwich?"

"Any kind—cheeseburger."

"Cheeseburger?"

"Yeah." He looked up at her in the doorway. "Anything wrong with that?" he said.

"You don't eat right," she said.

"I know it," he said, "but let's try to keep it out of the papers, huh?"

"All right. Mr. Orcutt called and said he got the three boys out of jail, but it wasn't easy."

"Did you tell him to send the county a bill?"

"Yes, I did, but he said to forget it."

The telephone rang, and Dick picked it up without waiting for Ida to get to her desk.

"Blake O'Brien," the voice said.

"Yeah, listen—instead of getting a list of men named Ben, better get a list of anybody beginning with 'B.' I'd like to keep this thing wrapped up tight as long as possible. I don't want Ben, whoever he is, to get any wind up."

"I've got it."

"And that's going to make a lot more work out of it, so the sooner we get started, the better."

"Right, chief."

Ida was on her way out. "Cheeseburger, for sure?" she said. "With everything?"

"Yeah—no, hold the onion."

"All right," she said. "But an onion is a vegetable and—" Dick waved to her, and she went out. Sitting at his desk, he let his head drop forward. The stiffness in the back of his neck had grown into a steady ache that extended to the top of his head. He would have to remember to do something nice for Ida, he thought. Ida was forty-two and homely and loyal, and had worked for him for over ten years, with only minor complaints, and he owed her a great deal. But what? What could I do for her? he wondered.

The girl Ida had got to cover the switchboard during her lunch break looked into his office. "Are you in to anyone who calls, Mr. Kramer?"

"No," he said. "Mr. Levy and Mr. O'Brien I'm in to—and if the red light flashes, of course—and Senator Morris. That's all."

"Mr. Steve Carolla?" she asked.

"Oh, yes, I guess so. Mr. Carolla."

"All right, Mr. Kramer."

"And my wife," he called as she turned away. "I'm in if my wife should call."

"All right."

He rubbed the back of his neck vigorously, but it didn't do any good. He got up, left the room, and went to the men's room, where he stripped to the waist and went through the cold water ritual. When he got back to the office, the lunch he had ordered was on his desk. He opened the sack, got the coffee and the cheeseburger out, and began to eat methodically. When he finished, he still had the headache, but he felt stronger. He began making telephone calls to the Sheriff and the city police chief and when he had them lined up for a meeting at four that afternoon, he felt better still. He felt strong enough to tell Evelyn when she called him at two-thirty that he couldn't make it for the bridge date that evening. She emitted sounds of rage and, a little later, pain, and he rode it out patiently.

"What do you have to do?" she asked finally.

"Some very urgent things. I can't talk about it on the phone."

"Business or pleasure?" she asked.

"Business, naturally."

"Dick, I just don't know—the last minute—what can I tell them?"

"Well, can you find someone to go with you? No reason you shouldn't go and enjoy yourself."

"Some man, you mean?"

"I didn't have anything particular in mind. Surely they can find a person to play bridge."

"I don't want to go without you," she said. "Besides, how would it look?"

"Oh, for God's sake. What do you mean how would it look? You're going to play bridge, not strip poker or something."

"Dick!"

"I'm awfully busy, darling. If you just call—"

"I can't. What excuse can I give?"

"Give the simple, honest excuse that I can't make it."

"You never can make it."

He tightened his grip on the phone and took a long, deep breath.

"What time will you be home?" she asked.

"I have no idea."

"I guess I'll go over to mother's for dinner," she said.

"That sounds like a good idea."

"But I don't want to drive home alone late at night."

"Well, maybe it would be wise to spend the night there."

A pause.

"Would that make you happy?" she asked.

"I don't understand the question."

"Oh, all right, good-bye!" she snapped and hung up.

The wrangling conversation had angered and depressed him, and he sat for some time drumming with his fingers on the desk, unable to concentrate on the pile of papers in front of him. Then Blake O'Brien came in with the R and I lists, and as soon as he got into them, working with Blake, name by name, his depression lifted.

At ten minutes after three Ida came in. "I just had a report from Department Two," she announced with some self-importance.

Both men looked up, waiting for the news. Ida took her time over it.

"They got a jury about ten minutes ago," she said. "Judge Harris asked Mr. Levy if he was ready to proceed. Mr. Levy said yes he was ready, but he asked the court's permission to offer a stipulation."

She paused and looked at her manicure. Dick, leaning across the desk, shook his hand at her. "Ida, come on with it!"

"Mr. Levy then said he was prepared to stipulate, with the concurrence of defense counsel, that the testimony of the plaintiff regarding the events of the night in question, transcribed from a preliminary hearing, was correct and germane. This would make it unnecessary for the plaintiff to take the stand. As the plaintiff was a young, sensitive girl, this seemed to Mr. Levy a reasonable stipulation."

She paused again. Dick ran his hands through his hair.

"Judge Harris asked counsel to approach the bench, which they did. Mr. Gideon was upset—red in the face, I think, was the phrase I heard. Mr. Levy was unperturbed. Judge Harris dismissed the jury for a recess and asked counsel to join him in chambers. Which is where they are now."

"Thank you, Ida," Dick said.

"You're welcome," she said and went away.

Blake O'Brien was chuckling. "Oh, that Levy," he said.

"Yeah," Dick said. "Now, by the time they get it hashed out in chambers—and Gideon can never agree to the stipulation—it will be time for the weekend recess. So on Monday morning Mr. Levy can start swinging with continuity and keep it going."

They bent over the lists once more and resumed their tedious, essential check-out.

CHAPTER 8

Evelyn Kramer had called her husband from the club, where she had had lunch with Donna Forester, and Peg Farrell, and some other friends. After the call, being upset, she had gone into the women's lounge and tidied up, and at a little after three she had decided to call Donna Forester and see what she was doing for the evening, if anything. She couldn't be doing much, with Carl out of town on one of his trips.

As she left the lounge she ran into Peg Farrell, who said she had just tried to call Donna and hadn't got any answer.

"That's funny," Evelyn said, "she was in such a snit to get home by three that she kept looking at her watch—"

"Maybe she had to stop off somewhere and get the watch fixed," Peg said.

Evelyn stared at her.

"Never mind," Peg said. "Are you coming to the bridge tonight?"

"No." Evelyn sighed. "Dick can't make it."

"Oh, that's a shame. Well, you can come anyway, can't you? There's always a loose bridge partner around the place."

"Oh, no. Dick doesn't like me to be out alone that way—at night," Evelyn said.

"I see," Peg said, moving away. "See you soon."

Evelyn stood looking after her, then went slowly into the main lounge and looked for someone to talk to. There wasn't anyone she knew, and pretty soon she went to the telephone and dialed Donna Forester's number. There was no answer. She hung up, thought about it for a while, then picked it up again and dialed her mother's number. Her mother answered.

"Are you busy tonight?" Evelyn asked.

"No, nothing special. Why?"

"Well, I thought—Dick has to work late tonight, and I thought I might come over and take potluck with you if you're not going out."

"Of course. Any time. Do you want to spend the night in case Dick is late? You might bring a nightie and toothbrush."

"Oh, I don't know yet. I'll see."

"Well, come when you're ready. Just walk in. I'll be around somewhere."

"All right. Thanks."

She left the club, found her car, and started to drive home. On Park Drive she overlooked the stop sign at Hartford Street, and a car crossing in front of her swerved wildly and blasted its horn. She pulled up at the curb and sat there, waiting for her hands to stop shaking.

"Had to stop and get her watch fixed—" Her mouth formed the words Peg Farrell had spoken earlier. That's some kind of inside joke, Evelyn thought, that they won't let me in on. Probably something dirty. Donna Forester.

She started forward again, forcing herself to drive carefully, her heart pounding. Donna and Dick get along pretty well, come to think of it, she was thinking. At that Christmas party last year they had a wonderful time together. In fact, I didn't see much of Dick at all that night. And with Carl away so much—it would be the most natural—I mean, it would be so easy—.

By the time she got home, she could feel an angry pulse beat in her temple, and her hands were moist with sweat She ran from the garage into the house. Edith was in the kitchen reading the papers. Evelyn ran up the backstairs and into the bedroom, picked up the telephone between the beds and dialed Donna Forester's number. She got no answer, even though she let it ring twelve times. She hung up, folded both arms across her belly, and rocked back and forth on the bed. She was crying. "No— no," she moaned, "you can't do this to me!"

After a while there were steps on the stairs. Edith looked in at her. Evelyn was aware of it, but didn't look up.

"Anything wrong, Mrs. Kramer?" Edith asked.

Evelyn pulled herself together with obvious effort and lifted her chin. "No, Edith. I'm all right. Thank you."

Edith lingered a few moments, then turned away and went downstairs. Evelyn reached for the phone and drew her hand back as if she had burned it. "No, I won't give you that satis—" Half a dozen times she reached toward the instrument and stopped herself. The seventh time she picked it up and dialed Dick's office. Ida answered.

"This is Mrs. Kramer," Evelyn said. "May I speak to my husband, please?"

"Well, he's in conference, Mrs. Kramer, and he asked me not to—"

"Conference?"

"Yes, Mrs. Kramer. He has the Sheriff and the Chief of Police with him, and Mr. O'Brien, and he gave strict orders they weren't to be disturbed."

"Oh! Well, would you give him a message for me—if he's there—"

There was a pause.

"Oh, he's there all right, and if it's urgent, I'll take a chance—"

"No, don't do that. Just tell him, please, that I decided to go to mother's for dinner tonight?"

"I'll tell him."

"Thank you, Ida."

She hung up and lay back on the bed, holding herself with both hands. I don't think Ida would lie about it, she thought. Anyway, he's too smart to let anybody else in on it right in his own office. So maybe he really is in conference. But it can't go on forever. What about tonight—that he can't talk about on the phone and all that. Ooh—it hurts!

She cried some more and then she got up and washed her face. That made her feel better. Then she called down to Edith to make her a cup of tea. The idea of the tea made her feel better, too. She tried not to think about Donna Forester and her drinking all that Scotch the day before.

Donna was nervous about something, Evelyn thought. About me. She was nervous at lunch today, too. She didn't know I was going to be there.

Donna Forester…Donna Forester…"

DONNA FORESTER

She drove the car carefully, but not wasting any time, along the South River Highway, going south out of town. Gino sat on the far side of the seat, big and stiffly uncomfortable, speaking only when she spoke to him. His big brown hands moved over his thighs, not quite ever coming to rest. Should I ask him to drive? she thought. I wish I knew what he was thinking.

She had decided just before he arrived a little after three that it was too risky to have him right in the house, what with neighbors and unexpected visitors. So she had said when he came to the kitchen door, "It's too nice a day to grub around a garden. How would you like to take a ride out in the country?"

"Well—sure—"

"Do you have to be anywhere special today, later?"

"No."

"All right, then. It's not as if we were goofing off altogether. I want to show you something—a real natural outdoor garden—south. Have you been out South River Highway?"

"Not lately."

"You'll appreciate it, I think. You appreciate things, Gino."

"Some things, I guess."

"Then let's take my car and just go. Why don't you run your truck into the garage while I back mine out? Your tools and things won't be a temptation if they're out of sight."

"Whatever you say."

She was glad she hadn't tried to invent some elaborate excuse, such as, "There are some wildflowers in this place, and I want to see what you think about transplanting them."—or some nonsense like that. There were enough complications without piling up subterfuges.

"It's not far now," she said. "You know where the Highwayman's Inn is?"

"I guess not."

"It's a good place to eat. Maybe we could have dinner there if you'd like. Anyway, the place I want to show you is just past the Highwayman's Inn about three miles."

He didn't say anything.

"Are you feeling all right, Gino?" she said. "Would you feel better if you were driving?"

"Oh, no," he said. "I feel fine."

"I'm glad."

I wish I could think of him as just a kind of servicing agent or something, she was thinking. But I like him, goddam it! It would be better, though—for him, too—just have a ball and sooner or later say good-bye. Only I like him and he's all I've got and it's going to kill me to say good-bye.

The road curved, and the afternoon sun struck at her eyes. She adjusted the visor and suddenly she was sleepy, trying to blink herself awake. The car swerved, not dangerously. Gino looked at her, then looked away.

I wish I hadn't had that extra drink before lunch, she thought. Why do I get so racked up? Because, she answered herself, I wasn't sure whether he would come or not.

They passed the Highwayman's Inn, a low, rambling structure set among the trees on the river side of the highway. Beyond it they were in the country. Thickly wooded patches alternated with open fields, summer brown now. The fields were fenced from the highway, but the woods were open. Now and then narrow, unpaved lanes led into them.

"Who owns all this?" Gino asked, waving vaguely.

"A man named Dexter owns most of it," she said. "Old family in town."

"Dexter—there's a rich kid named Dexter being tried now," he said, "for ra—for what he did to a girl."

"Yes, I know," Donna said. Let's get off that subject, she thought. Let's not dwell on that. Damn it, he's so good! she thought. He didn't want to say "rape" to me.

She put her hand on his thigh and felt him respond to the touch, his muscles drawing slightly, then swelling. "Thanks, Gino," she said, "for going along with an old woman."

"You're not old," he said.

Easy, she warned herself, don't make a liar out of him.

She caressed his thigh, and he leaned toward her suddenly and kissed her cheek. She shivered. "That was sweet," she said.

He put his arm on the back of the seat, over her shoulders, and kissed her again and stroked her thighs with his free hand. "I could go for you, I think," he said.

"I'm glad." It was the first time she had ever heard him try to make any kind of a joke, and it warmed her.

"Is it all right to fool around with you while you're driving?" he asked.

"You know it is," she said. "But take it easy. I have a tendency to close my eyes."

"That's all right, I'll watch the road."

"I'd rather you'd watch me."

Pretty soon she squeezed her legs tight together suddenly. "Ooops," she said. "Better wait till we get there, Gino. It's more dangerous than I thought."

"Okay," he said and took his hand away.

"But don't forget where you were."

"I won't lose my place," he said.

"You doll," she said. "You sweet, loving doll."

"You're the doll," he said. "I'm a guy."

"Excuse me. Yes, you're a guy."

She concentrated on the driving then, pushing the car around the curves on the river bluff. The wooded areas were more frequent now and wilder, and after a couple of miles she slowed, looking for the turnoff.

"It's along in here somewhere," she said.

"What kind of a place is it?"

"Well, it's just kind of a nice woodsy place—you'll see in a minute."

She missed the turnoff, an obscure dirt lane hidden in foliage, and had to stop and back up in order to turn into it. There was a dip, and the car lurched, then leveled off, and they were in the woods, winding among high trees, leaving the river behind.

"Peaceful in here," Gino said.

She looked quickly to see whether he was making a pun and decided he wasn't. His face was relaxed and serious.

"Yes it is," she said. "So peaceful. I haven't been here for a long time. I used to come every once in a while to get away from things."

"With somebody?" he asked.

"With—You mean with some guy? No, never," she said. It was true, and she had said it honestly, but she couldn't let herself hope he believed it.

"Just me, huh?" he said.

All right, Gino, she thought. Just you. "That's right," she said.

The deeply rutted road had washed out in spots, and she had some brief panic when a rear wheel got hung up on a hidden rock. But there hadn't been any rain for about ten days, so it came off all right. The woods thinned after a while. They crossed a shallow meadow, and she pulled up in a clearing at its far edge. There was the sound of running water.

"Well, this is it," she said. "How do you like it?"

"Nice," Gino said, opening the car door.

He didn't come around the car to her side, and she let herself out and joined him. He was looking around at the meadow, a brownish turf peppered with small flowers—yellow, orange, and blue.

"I hear water," Gino said.

"There's a creek in the woods," she said. "I've got everything here— swimming hole and all."

He put his arm around her, hugging, and she felt her rib cage buckle.

"You've got everything all right," he said.

She pushed against him to loosen the embrace, pulled his head down with both hands, and kissed his mouth.

"Come on," she said, "let's go into the trees and lie down in the river—or however it goes. Listen, there's a thermos full of lemonade in the trunk. And something to sit on."

"Lemonade?" he said.

She had a sudden sagging feeling that she had let him down. "Yes— you don't drink, do you? I mean, being a football player and all."

"No," he said. "Once in a while a glass of beer."

"I'm sorry. I could have brought some beer."

"It's all right," he said.

She handed him the key to the trunk, and he gave her a slap on the behind as he moved away.

But it's not all right, she thought. I made a point of his age. He didn't like it.

He took the folded blanket and a quart thermos bottle from the trunk, handed her the blanket, and closed the cover. They walked away from the car toward the sound the creek made back in the trees. Except for the water and the rising and falling buzz of cicadas, it was still. In the shade, the thick grass underfoot was springy and greener than out on the meadow. They walked hand in hand to the sloping bank of the stream. There were willow trees along the water's edge, with grassy clearings between them and the woods.

She dropped the blanket to the ground, and Gino reached for her, pulling her close. "Come on, let's do it," he said, nuzzling at her neck.

She felt a momentary revulsion, stiffened, and was on the point of pushing him away. Then she gave in. "Don't you want to get rid of that jug?" she said.

He dropped it and began pulling her dress up with both hands. She pushed him away then.

"I'll do it," she said, panting a little. "I have to wear this dress to dinner, remember?"

"Okay," he said, pulling off his shirt.

He was ready before she finished spreading the blanket, and he pushed against her, tumbling her into the grass. She turned under him.

"All right, Gino, yes, all right—but easy, easy, baby—"

"Don't call me baby," he said.

"No—all right—I won't—"

It wasn't the way she had planned it, with the long, sweet buildup. He was urgent and rough with her. She wrestled under him, trying to put him off just a little to give herself time.

"Wait, Gino—" She gripped his penis firmly and pushed against him.

He looked down at her quizzically. "Change your mind?" he said.

"No," she said. "But take it easy. All right? Don't worry—I see you haven't lost your place."

He smiled then, and she drew him down and into her, and the fury had gone out of him.

"That's better," she said. "That's so good, Gino. All right now. Is it safe to close my eyes?"

He didn't answer. She blinked and through her eyelashes saw the soft storm cross his face as he filled her.

RICHARD KRAMER

At five-ten Blake O'Brien left Dick's office to pick up an early dinner. After the Sheriff and the city police chief had left, they had had a rather sharp argument about the planned stake-out. Dick's idea from the start had been that he would join it personally. Blake O'Brien had argued against this—gently at first, then more sharply.

"You are the boss," he had said finally, "and it's not for me to tell you what to do. But I don't think it would be smart or useful for you to go down there by the river and sit in a car—or maybe up a goddam tree or something—till dawn's early light."

"It's that I want to get on top of this, if there is anything, right away," Dick said. "I'm not trying to be a hero. I'm not on television—"

"Right. I know it. So if anything should turn up, I'm sure you'll be the first to know and you'll have dibs on the first interrogation. And I'll be there to see that it works that way."

"Oh—*you're* going to be there."

"Yeah. Because somebody ought to be there from this department, but not you. It's like—look, Mr. Kramer, say it was some big man, with the fate of the whole county in his hands and enough power so that it would take a little negotiation to cool him and cut him down to size. Then, I would say, you ought to be there, right on the spot for the take-over. But this is a nothing. This is a jerk, a pusher, a little independent snot. Let's not send an elephant to step on a flea."

Dick gave him a look. "You're very persuasive when you get into the colorful language," he said. "All right. I yield to your sense of proportion. But don't think I'm going to relax."

"Okay. You do what you have to. I'll go get some dinner and make a contact with the men on that duty. You'll be available?"

"Oh, yes, I'll be available. Good luck."

He was embarrassed when Blake had gone. He couldn't imagine why he had been so set on joining the stake-out. Blake had been quite right about the elephant and the flea, and he wished he hadn't pushed it so hard. It must have made him appear overanxious—*infra dig*, as the phrase went. He decided it was because of the pressures that had been building around him all day—the reporter from the *Courier,* the wrangle with Evelyn, the uneasiness with the prostitute Nadine, with whom he had gone to high school. Some simple, direct activity would be a relief, a kind of vindication of his own existence.

Ida came in with the message that his wife had called to say she would be having dinner with her mother. He picked up the phone and dialed his home number. Edith came on and said that Mrs. Kramer had left to go to her mother's.

"All right, Edith," he said. "Thank you. If you'd like the evening off—"

"Oh, I don't have anything to do, Mr. Kramer," she said.

"Well, as you wish."

"Will you be home? Shall I fix you some dinner?" she asked.

"No, thanks. I've got to work late tonight."

"All right," she said.

He hung up and he was thinking, what is it about me that Edith hates so much? What did I ever do to her?

His buzzer sounded. "Mr. Carolla," Ida said.

He picked it up. "Hello, Steve," he said.

"Hello, Mr. Kramer. Fella just called me a while ago, fella from across the river. Said he got robbed this morning. Fella's got a hardware store—three kids—punks, he called 'em. So he went to all the trouble to make out a complaint and all, and the next thing he knows, the kids got a lawyer and they're running around the streets."

"I'm familiar with the case," Dick said. "I understand they got caught in the act, and the merchandise was returned."

"Yeah, I guess so. It don't matter to me. But this fella was kind of mixed up. 'Where'd they get a lawyer all of a sudden?' he was wondering."

"Anybody can get a lawyer," Dick said. "That's the nice thing about the U. S. A."

"Yeah. I guess—you got some accommodations trouble, huh, Mr. Kramer?"

"I wouldn't call it trouble."

"Whatever you say. Don't worry about the kids. I was just reporting what the fella said."

"I appreciate your calling," Dick said.

"You won't forget my party on Sunday, huh?"

"No. Would you rather I wouldn't come?"

Carolla chuckled deeply. "Listen, Mr. Kramer, without you it wouldn't be a party," Carolla said and hung up.

Dick felt a shooting pain in the back of his neck where before there had been the steady ache. He's out to get me, he thought. I'm for the kill as fast as he can make it.

Ida came in with a thin sheaf of onionskin, the transcript of the day's session in Department Two. He started to read it, but stopped halfway down the first page. He flipped to the last page and saw that nothing had happened that he didn't know about from Ida's earlier report. He put the transcript in his incoming basket and began straightening up his desk.

"Do you want me to get a bite and come back?" Ida asked from the doorway.

He was startled. He looked at his watch and realized that his shirt collar was unbuttoned and his coat draped over the back of his chair. "No," he said. "What time is it? Past quitting time."

"Well," Ida said, "I thought maybe if you were going to be working late, you'd like some help."

He was both touched and suspicious. But when he looked at her face, it was open and clear. She hadn't been pushing anything. Why would I think she was pushing anything? he thought.

"I'll be all right," he said, "but thanks very much. Just so the phone is plugged in to ring in here. I'll keep the Sheriffs switchboard informed if I go out."

"Okay," Ida said, "then I guess I'll go." She started away, then turned back.

"You ought to go get yourself a good dinner," she said "with—"

He laughed and held up his hand, palm out. "With vegetables," he said. "Thanks, Ida. I'll do it."

"I hope so," she said and went away.

It took her a few minutes to clear her desk and get ready to leave the office. When she had gone, he felt an oppressive quietness. He had worked late many times in this office and he couldn't remember having had the feeling before, the feeling of isolation, of having been deserted. He knew it was an irrational feeling even while he was experiencing it, but he couldn't shake it off.

He looked at the phone and thought about calling Evelyn at her mother's, just to check in with her. Then he shrugged the impulse off. He didn't feel up to another wrangle.

He looked at his watch and it was five-forty-five. Besides the ache in his neck he now had a stomachache. I need dinner, he thought. A good dinner, with vegetables. A cocktail—just one—in a cool, quiet place and a good dinner might knock the tension out, he decided. Then I can come back and put in a good night's work.

He flipped a switch and spoke to a woman on the Sheriffs switchboard. "Richard Kramer," he said, "just reporting in. I'm expecting some telephone calls in the course of the evening. I'm leaving the office now for dinner. Until about seven-thirty I'll be at the Greenbriar Hotel. Then I'll be back in the office."

"All right, sir," she said. "Thanks for calling."

He picked up his coat and went out, then stopped in the men's room to freshen up and adjust his tie. Then he went downstairs and into the ramp that led to the parking area. He had nearly reached his car when it occurred to him that he couldn't go to the Greenbriar Hotel without driving past Mother Stevens' house, and if she and Evelyn happened to be watching at the moment—.

There was a phone booth in the parking lot, and he walked over there, but it was in use. He got in the elevator and rode up to the third floor. He walked down a long corridor to a door marked: Communications—sheriff's dept, personnel only. He went in, and there was a desk in a reception area just inside the door. Beyond the desk was a barricade and beyond it the main communications system of the department; a long, U-shaped table, with a switchboard at the far, closed end and individual phones along both outer sides of the table. Deputies were manning about half the phones. Two women sat with their backs to the room at the main switchboard. There was a steady buzzing undertone, punctuated by crackling sounds. Lights flashed on and off the switchboard. Dick felt a squirming spasm of distaste. Have to be a goddam computer to answer the phone, he thought.

He got the attention of the young woman at the front desk. "I'm Richard Kramer, the District Attorney," he said. "I just called in about my whereabouts, and want to report a change."

"Yes, Mr. Kramer—"

"I told the operator I'd be at the Greenbriar Hotel. That has been changed. I will be at—

After a moment she said, "Yes, Mr. Kramer?"

She was alert, with pencil poised.

"I'll be at the Andrew Jackson, downtown," he said, naming the first place that came into his head. He hadn't been in the Andrew Jackson for five years. He wasn't sure they had a dining room, but surely they had something.

"All right, Mr. Kramer," she said. "I'll call this in."

"Thank you," he said and left quickly.

That is really something, he thought. They're all in that room together. All she'd have to do would be to raise her voice a little and call out, "Hey, Nancy, the D.A. will be at the Andrew Jackson instead of the Greenbriar." But no, she's got to go through the routine, put in a call.

Going down to the parking lot in the elevator, he realized he was lashing out at the system for no reason except his own embarrassment. The D.A. can't make up his mind, they would be saying. He found the car keys in his pants pocket. And a D.A. that can't make up his mind, he thought, is going to have one hell of a time running for the U. S. Senate—if they let him.

Carolla, he thought as he got into the car and got it started. Steve Carolla. What have you got cooking in that fine Italian head?

But the feeling of his own cowardice nudged Carolla out of his mind. It was merely craven of him to change his dinner plans because he didn't want to drive past his mother-in-law's house. How could he be afraid of his mother-in-law?

She had been nothing but good to him. That was the trouble maybe. She had been too good. Without wanting to, she had put him in the position of being obligated the rest of his life.

Horseshit, he thought. She doesn't feel that I'm obligated. Only I feel that way. What she really did, she bought herself a son-in-law, a husband for her daughter.

The only thing about that is, I accepted the deal. And the trouble with that is, I did it because I truly wanted Evelyn. At the time.

And not now? What about now?

CHAPTER 9

Although Sunday had been a more relaxed day than Saturday around the house, Dick felt more relief than anything else when it was time to go to Steve Carolla's stag cocktail party. Saturday had been miserable. Late Friday night he had called Evelyn at her mother's house to ask whether she wanted him to drive her home. She had said it didn't matter, she could spend the night there if that would be more convenient for him. So then he couldn't leave it at that and drove out there to get her. Mother Stevens had been wryly hospitable and had offered him a nightcap, which he had declined. Evelyn had gone along with him all right, but in almost total silence, and he hadn't tried to force a conversation. He hadn't been in a talking mood himself, for that matter. The last report he had had on the stake-out had been negative, and he had felt himself at a standstill, blocked, cut off from the current of activity that, if it had sustained itself, would have given him some outlet for his frustrations. He had been unable to understand Evelyn's hostility and silence and after a while he had given up trying.

On Saturday Evelyn had spent nearly the whole day in her room, and Dick hadn't felt up to invading her privacy. He had gone to the office for a few hours on Saturday afternoon and worked his way through a stack of dull but essential reports on county administrative matters. It had been in the office, when he had finished the work and was trying to develop a positive attitude about going home, that he had put together a few recent remarks by Evelyn and decided, with amusement at first and then with annoyance, that he understood part of what was going through her mind. He hadn't spoken of it until Sunday after a late, leisurely breakfast, when he had relieved Edith of Evelyn's morning tray, carried it up to her himself, and sat on the other bed while she picked lackadaisically at the food.

"How're you feeling?" he asked, making it sound as hearty as he could without shouting.

"Oh, pretty good," she said.

"Breakfast all right?"

She looked at him for a minute. "It's my regular breakfast," she said. "I'm used to it."

He fought down resentment and pushed on with it. "Other night," he said, "you asked me whether I ever cheated on you."

She wouldn't look at him.

"I don't know what made you think of it," he said, "but I told you I never would and I just thought I'd repeat that to make it clear."

There was a pause.

"All right," she said. "You made it clear."

Talk about a hostile witness, he thought. "And when I explain that I have to work late at the office," he said "that is really what I'm doing, and that's what I was doing Friday night." Enough, he thought then. Don't go on and on about it.

He waited about a minute, and when she didn't respond, he got up, patted her shoulder under the sheer bed jacket and started out. She let him get to the door before she said, without looking up, "I never said anything about you cheating on me."

He had an odd feeling inside his head, as if someone had reached in and tilted his brain. "Oh," he said. "Then I guess I was mistaken. I thought it was your phrase."

"I mean I never accused you of cheating on me," she said, "if you're going to quibble."

He gave up, shrugging. "Never mind," he said. "Let's not quibble."

He went down to his study and tried to read, but his attention was fickle and went on and off like a blinker signal. He reread the story Lambert had turned in for the Saturday morning *Courier*. It had been fair enough reporting, and he had had the good grace not to mention the political thing. The narcotics problem had been worked over lightly, and Dick's department had been given the credit for its control in the past. The Berryman woman hadn't been mentioned by name. Dick was relieved by the tone and reserve of the piece and by the fact that in the Sunday *Courier*, in the weekly resume of county business, the editorial writers hadn't taken any potshots at him. But he knew it was an uneasy peace. Senator Morris might not announce his retirement publicly for some time to come, but the insiders knew his job was up for grabs. Dick had the inside track so far, but it was early, and he could be jostled out of the running by almost anyone with a reasonable claim. His department was clean; nobody could build a major scandal like a funeral pyre around him. But it wouldn't have to be major. A slipup in the Sheriff's office, one corrupt officer, narcotics traffic on the river—these could be made into a chain of fuses that might set off an explosion at exactly the wrong moment. That was why he had been so driving about the stake-out for the man named Ben after getting the tip from Nadine Berryman.

Too intensive, he thought with some embarrassment. Too eager beaver. If Blake O'Brien hadn't cooled me off Friday afternoon, I might have fixed everything good! And if anything should happen to Nadine Berryman—

On an impulse, he picked up the phone on his desk and dialed the county hospital. After some waiting he got connected with the resident.

"How's the Berryman woman?" Dick asked.

"What do you mean how is she?"

The doctor's chip-on-the-shoulder attitude irked him, and he forced himself to clamp down, cool it. "I assume she's still alive," he said. "Is she more cooperative than she was the other day?"

"Let's see—she hasn't made any big scene, I guess."

"Is she in condition to be discharged?"

"Is that a yes-or-no type question?"

"Not necessarily."

"Let me put it this way, Mr. Kramer. She's better off here than in jail. On the other hand, we're not surrounded by empty beds. We could use the room. If she were a private patient, I'd want her to stay a while. But she's a county patient, charged with a crime, and it's not really up to me."

"I understand. All right. I'll check in again."

"Okay, Mr. Kramer."

Lot of personal attention from the D.A., Dick thought, on a case of prostitution and using. The doctor will be thinking about that. Likewise Mr. Lambert of the *Courier*. If things go wrong enough, it could be made to look as if the county were pampering drug addicts because Richard Kramer had gone soft on a whore he went to high school with—probably an old girlfriend—

He got up suddenly, as if to escape the plague of anxieties, and banged his knee against the underside of the desk. "Goddam!"

There was a knock at the study door.

"Yes?" he said.

Edith looked in. "Mrs. Kramer wondered whether you'd like an early dinner today?" she said.

"Oh, no, I don't think so," he said, "unless she does. I've got that cocktail party this afternoon—Mr. Carolla—"

"I see," she said. "I'll tell her." She closed the door quietly.

What the hell now—we communicate through Edith? he thought. Edith is our message center?

He looked at his golf clubs in the corner. I could get over there and do nine holes, take a shower, and maybe feel better at Carolla's, he thought.

But then he decided it was not a time to go off by himself and give Evelyn more reason to complain.

Stick, he thought. Stick and sweat. The one thing about time—it passes.

It passed very slowly. At twelve-thirty he took advantage of Edith's temporary absence from the kitchen to fix himself a peanut butter sandwich. Evelyn hadn't come down yet. He started up the stairs to look in on her, then changed his mind and went down again.

At about one-fifteen he tried to do some more reading but couldn't keep his mind on it. He took his putter and a few balls from the golf bag, went out in the back yard and practiced putting. After ten minutes he began to relax and found himself concentrating on the putts and not worrying about the phantom worries that had beset him earlier.

Who wants to be Senator, anyway? he thought. It's nice right here. I like it here.

Edith called from the service porch, "Mr. Kramer, you're wanted on the phone."

He took the putter and balls with him and went inside. She had the phone off the hook in the kitchen, and he said he'd take it in the study. He sat down at the desk and spoke to Blake O'Brien.

"Sorry to disturb your Sunday," Blake said.

"I'm glad somebody's disturbing it. Go ahead."

"A thing has come up on that drug thing—"

Dick's hand squeezed on the phone. "You found Ben?" he said.

"No—no luck like that. In fact, maybe no luck at all, even the reverse."

"All right, let me have it."

"A couple of city cops picked up a suspect on the street—suspicion of pushing. Routine. They didn't find anything on him, but they brought him in on suspicion of drunk driving. He was hopped up and they figured—anyway, they brought him in. Very small-time character."

"Yeah. Go ahead."

"So on account of the alert and the stake-out they called me, and I went in and spent some time with him, and the cops were there, too. Well, he didn't have anything useful to say and he wasn't in bad enough shape that they could really book him and hope to make it stick—obviously he wasn't drunk. I was about to call it off and let him go, having run out of questions. And then one of the cops, just trying to be helpful, asked him, 'Do you know a guy named Ben?'"

"Oh, great," Dick said.

"And naturally the fella said he never heard of such a guy."

"Uh-huh."

"So—to get it over with—if we let him walk out of here, and if he does know a guy named Ben, there goes our stake-out and everything for the time being."

"You're still holding him?"

"Yes. We don't have anything to hold him on, and he's too hot to let go."

"How long can we hold him without getting in trouble?"

"From now? He was picked up about eleven o'clock. We might keep him hanging around till after dinner. I think we could get in trouble if we hold him over night."

Dick lifted his hand as if to drum with his fingers on the desk top, then balled his fist. The decision was for right now and it was all his.

"We'll have to let him go. Maybe we can salvage something. Put a tail on him and stick close—if he does know this Ben, and if he got the message, he might lead us to him. At least that way we'd find out who the guy is. That's all we could hope for now that I can think of."

"Not much of a hope."

"I know, but we can't hold him. We'll have to let the stakeout go and get at it some other way."

"All right, if you say so."

"I'll listen to suggestions."

There was a pause.

"I haven't got any," Blake said.

"Okay. Thanks for getting down there and for being on top of it. Call again if you want to talk. I'll be at Carolla's for a couple of hours between four-thirty, six-thirty. It's all right to call me there. Otherwise, see you in the morning."

"Sure, boss. Have a good day."

"I'll certainly try."

It was a little after two-thirty, and he had an hour before he'd have to dress for Carolla's party, so he stretched out on the couch in the study. After a while he felt himself beginning to doze off. He got up, set the alarm on his desk clock for three forty-five, stretched out again, and let himself fall asleep.

* * * *

He could hear Evelyn stirring around upstairs and he decided to shower and shave in the downstairs bathroom in order to be out of her way. When he went up to dress, wearing his bathrobe, Evelyn was at her dressing table, working carefully at her face. There was the fragrance of powder and toilet water in the room, and she had laid out one of her most engaging cocktail dresses on her bed.

"Well—" Dick said. "Very stunning around here!"

"I thought I'd try to be ready on time for once," she said.

"That's very cooperative," he said. "Got a big date?" He was heading into the wardrobe, loosening the belt of his robe.

"Haven't I?" she said. "Edith said there was a cocktail party—at Steve Carolla's?"

He felt as if someone had plunged a cold fist into his belly. I explained to her. I'm sure I did.

He looked out from the wardrobe. She was applying rouge skillfully. Her narrow shoulders were hunched in concentration.

"I thought I explained," he said. "This is a kind of business thing—men only."

She looked up at him with her rouge-pat poised. She had that wounded deer look in her eyes that had wrung him so when they'd been younger. It was wringing him now.

"Men only?" she said.

"Yes. Some of the county committee, maybe the Senator—people like that—cracker-barrel stuff. I won't stay long, but I have to show up."

"Oh," she said. She lowered her arm slowly to let it rest on the dressing table, the rouge pat dangling between her slim fingers. "I didn't understand," she said quietly.

I told her yesterday, goddam it! he thought. I know I did. "Didn't I tell you yesterday?" he said.

She looked up again. "Did you?"

"I'm sure I did."

"Well, maybe I didn't hear you," she said.

He hovered there, looking at her helplessly, unable either to approach her or turn away.

"It's all right," she said. "I'll find something to do."

She got up, turning away from him, which released him, at any rate, so that he could go on with his dressing.

When he came back to the bedroom, she was standing at the bed, fingering the hem of her cocktail dress. One more try, he thought.

'Tell you what," he said. "I'm not going to stay at this thing long. You go ahead and get dressed, and as soon as I can get away, we'll go some nice place for dinner. How about that?"

She was slow to answer. "I don't think so," she said. "It's depressing on Sunday, everything half empty—"

"We could go to the club. The steaks are always good."

She shook her head, sat down on the bed, her face lowered. "No," she said. "I don't want to. The Dexters might be there."

So there was no way, he thought. No way at all. "Well," he said, "if you change your mind, anything you decide will be fine with me. I'll try to get back by five-thirty."

"Don't hurry," she said listlessly.

He went out of the bedroom and down the backstairs. I know damn well I told her explicitly the exact thing about the cocktail party, he thought. I remember where we were—just before dinner, having a drink in the living room, and I told her, so help me God, and how could she forget overnight?

CHAPTER 10

From the terrace of Steve Carolla's Mediterranean style home you could look out over the city toward the river and over the rolling green hills and valleys of the West Hills Golf Course and Country Club. It was the same club Dick Kramer belonged to, along with the Foresters and the Farrells and the Dexters and all the old-line families in town (Richard Kramer had married into it), and Steve Carolla had made it the hard way. Born in Crudsville to an alcoholic foundry worker and his deaf-mute wife, Steve had climbed to the country club eminence on steel cleats, using his fingernails when necessary, and at times on his hands and knees. He had made it by physical strength and stubbornness, by a certain amount of luck, and by a shrewdness in picking the sure winners among uncertain losers. He had been with the organized unions when they were winning and had left them when they began to lose, and he had managed to land on his feet with the Italians and most other downstate minorities in his pocket. He had been able to keep them there by using the steel cleats when called for and by gentler means, including the distribution of largesse, and the stronger his political power grew, the more securely he could claim the allegiance of the underprivileged. He could do a lot for them, but he would never be able to do as much for them as they had done for him. But they would never know this. He was myth to them, myth and legend, and at the same time he was an actual, living man. To the members of the West Hills Country Club and their associates in business and politics he was nearly all myth—and thus fearful. He had been made a member of the club because most members either were obligated to him in some substantial way or were afraid to vote against him. Those who had voted him in were fond of saying, "But he never has abused the privilege, you have to admit that."

He had a kind of native sense of taste—or a canniness in imitating the tastes of those among whom he chose to live—and the house, though large and prominent on the high knoll above the country club, was well designed and carefully furnished and in no way ornate. The broad terrace was nearly bare of furnishings, contained no statuary, and was therefore a comfortable and relaxing place to entertain men. As far as anyone knew, Carolla never entertained mixed parties. His wife, Rose, a plump Italian girl from Chicago, was never in evidence during one of Steve's frequent cocktail gatherings. Few of the men present this Sunday afternoon had ever set eyes on her.

Half a dozen were gathered on the terrace when Dick Kramer arrived a little after four-thirty. Senator Morris was not among them, and this was a disappointment. The Senator was the only one of the "courthouse gang" he felt secure about at the moment. He saw that Pete Dexter was there and braced himself as he crossed to the group. He was prepared for almost anything except Pete's quick smile and hearty handshake. Must be that pseudo-military mystique, Dick thought. Good soldiers never cry.

He shook hands with Ernie Smart, slender and silver-haired, one-time state attorney general and nominal chairman of the county committee. Ernie had status without effective power; nobody paid much attention to him, but he looked good in the papers.

Also present were Al Crandall, state assemblyman from the district; Ivo Morelli, a lawyer and Steve Carolla's chief aide around the wards; the county tax assessor, Chuck Connors; and the decrepit but bright-eyed and still acid-tongued Otto Mannheim, retired U. S. district judge. Before attaining the judgeship, Mannheim had filled out the unexpired term of Senator Morris's predecessor in the Senate and was probably on closer terms with Morris than anyone else in the state. Dick was glad to see him.

"Have to mind my manners now," Mannheim said as they shook hands, "with the enforcer on the scene."

"You bet," Dick said. "I'm after you."

"You sure are—at least forty years."

Dick laughed. "You don't look a day over thirty-eight," he said.

Steve Carolla came from inside the house and shook hands with Dick. "Kramer," he said. "Nice to see you. Come on over and get a drink."

Mannheim, leaning heavily on a gnarled walnut cane, held out an empty glass. "Bring me some more of that dago red, Steve," he said.

"Sure, Judge," Carolla said, taking the glass. "I made that myself. You like it all right, huh?"

Mannheim made a face. "House wine," he said. "I'll drink anything."

Carolla laughed deep in his throat. "Okay, Judge. I'll send you a case in the morning."

Dick went with Carolla to a bar that had been set up in a corner of the terrace. While Steve filled the judge's wine glass Dick made himself a whiskey and water highball.

"The Senator said he'd try to make it by five," Carolla said.

"Good," Dick said, "I'll be glad to see him."

"How's Mrs. Kramer?"

"She's fine, thanks. And your wife?"

"Okay. Rosie's strong as a horse."

"But prettier."

Carolla shrugged. They rejoined the group, and Carolla handed the judge his wine. Ivo Morelli and Ernie Smart were arguing the merits of a couple of race horses that had run in the money the day before in California. It was common knowledge that Morelli ran a book in the next county, down and across the river.

"…not in my book," Ernie was saying. "That horse will never go out at seven to two again."

"You haven't got a book," Morelli said, "I hope."

"Mr. Kramer," Chuck Connors said, "when are you going to let Ivo move his book across the river, closer to home?"

Dick shrugged. "Any Saturday night," he said. "I won't close it till Monday."

Morelli laughed happily. It was an old joke.

"Cleanest county in the state," Mannheim grumbled. "It's got so you have to take off your shoes to walk in the courthouse."

"That's right," Dick said, "and we're installing footbaths next week."

"Well," Ernie Smart said, "Dick's got to get it clean in a hurry so he can move on to higher things."

There was a silence. It hadn't been a graceful remark, but it had been thrown out, and it was Dick's job to field it.

"Better believe it," he said. "I had an offer just the other Jay from the Civil Liberties Union. Doesn't pay much, but lots of prestige."

"You'd fit in there good," Pete Dexter said. "How's your Russian?"

Not much of a remark, Dick thought, but maybe the best Pete can do under the circumstances.

The session was beginning to wear on him already and he excused himself to walk back to the bar, where he added ice to his drink, but no whiskey. That strained feeling in the back of his neck was getting worse. He had expected to be the punching bag in this preliminary workout. He knew he was being tested, and not for good fellowship, but he didn't know what directions the blows would come from nor what the gloves would be loaded with. He wished Senator Morris would show up to divert some of the attention. He also wished he knew what Carolla was specifically pushing. Because there had to be something. Steve Carolla didn't spend time and liquor on casual Sunday afternoon parties.

When he rejoined the group, they were talking about Happy Jack Sanderson, and it broke off as Dick arrived. The pause was awkward.

"Go ahead," he said. "All right to talk about Jack Sanderson. I've got no axe to grind."

Morelli smirked. "It's all up to the grand jury, right?"

"Sure," Dick said.

"I just happened to remember," Chuck Connors said, "two years ago Jack Sanderson practically gave the county committee a blank check to help out in the Congressional fiasco."

"He could afford to," Dick said. "It was the county's money."

Judge Mannheim introduced some oil into the sticky silence. "A good crook is an asset to every community," he said. "Trouble with bad crooks—they hang onto all of it, Greedy."

"Too many crooks spoil the broth, huh?" Morelli said with excessive delight.

Nobody could think of a reply to that one, so the conversation got away from Sanderson.

I wonder if that's it with Carolla? Dick thought. Sanderson. I didn't think they were buddies. It couldn't just be over campaign money.

There was a ring at the front door, and Carolla left the group.

Good, the Senator, Dick was thinking.

But Steve came back with Floyd Cantrell, one of the county supervisors, beefy, loud-voiced, concealing a basic friendliness under a gruff manner.

"Hi, everybody—fine bunch of bums gathered together—get me a drink, Steve. I need the hell out of it! I been—let me tell you where I've been."

He shook hands all around, plunged toward the bar, met Carolla returning, and relieved him of a tall drink.

"City manager," he said after a long pull at the glass. "Bazzard—buzzard. Got me cornered. That son of a bitch has got to go!"

"How could he corner you on Sunday?" Ernie Smart asked.

"On the goddam golf course! I got around in good season, time for a couple of beers. My own foursome there—Tom Kelly, Joe Dykes, and a fella from upstate—and here comes Mister Bazzard just a steamin'! Nothing to do but introduce him around, and he's got to talk to me—big deal—urgent business—"

"Come on," Pete Dexter said, "get to the business."

Floyd glared at him and took another swig from the glass. "I'm coming to it. He's got a hair up his ass about juvenile hall—'facilities,' he calls 'em. City facilities no good, got to use county facilities and all that shit. Said the District Attorney—"

He broke off and looked around with mock concern, shading his eyes with one hand. "Is there a district attorney in the house? Oh, yeah—you," he said to Dick. "Well, anyway, said the D.A. told him he'd have to get together with the supervisors on it. So he goes into this goddam sob story about three little dago punks—excuse me Mr. Carolla, Mr. Mo-relli—three poor little tykes that got picked up by the cops and no place to take care of 'em. So I asked him, 'What did they do?' 'Robbed a store,' he said. 'Then, Christ, throw 'em in the jug!' I said. 'They're only twelve years old,' he says, and I said, 'Old enough to steal, ain't they?' Well, we didn't get very far that way. And then I says, 'Looks like the D.A. is passing the buck to the supervisors,' and he says, 'I have the greatest respect for Mr. Kramer.'"

Cantrell ran his tongue over his lips and repeated, "I have the great-est respect for Mr. Kramer. That's nice. So then I says, 'I expect to be seeing Mr. Kramer this afternoon, and I will sure as hell talk to him about these lousy broken-down facilities.' And that is how come I am late to the party."

"So you got here," Carolla said. "Have another drink."

"Yeah, Mr. Carolla I will," Cantrell said. They went off toward the bar as the doorbell sounded again.

"Maybe Mr. Sanderson would be willing to contract to build a new juvenile facility for Mr. Bazzard," Morelli said.

It was a better joke than his previous try and drew some laughter. Floyd Cantrell came back with a fresh drink, and a minute later Carolla returned with Senator Morris.

"There he is—man of the hour." Otto Mannheim said.

The Senator's face was set and grim. He nodded to Mannheim, shook hands with him, then with Morelli and Pete, and nodded at Dick and the others.

"Gentlemen, I only have a minute," he said. "I've had a call from Washington—Mrs. Morris suffered a stroke at noon today and is in the hospital. I've arranged for a special plane and I just stopped in to say hello on my way to the airport. I was at the club when the call came."

Through the muttered expressions of sympathy Dick could almost hear his mind calculating. The realization was shocking, but he couldn't make himself stop. The Senator's tragic personal position gave Dick a double opportunity—to make a legitimate escape from the party and to do the Senator a service.

Morris had already begun to detach himself from the group as the idea came to Dick, and he watched the timing of his own move carefully.

Carolla went with the Senator as he moved to leave the terrace, and the others stayed behind. Dick was certain then that his plan would work. Carolla wouldn't leave his guests for long. He excused himself and joined Carolla and Morris as they walked through the broad living room toward the front door. Outside on the curving drive a taxicab waited, its motor running.

"Let me drive you to the airport, Senator," Dick said. "I brought the big car and I can use the siren if necessary."

Morris seemed to hesitate, then accepted, as Dick had expected him to. "Thanks, Dick," he said. "It would be a help." He turned to Carolla. "You'll excuse me if I take him from your party?" he said. "I'll send him back."

Carolla's dark, full face didn't change. "Sure," he said. "Don't apologize, Senator."

Morris shook hands with Carolla. "Thanks, Steve. Keep in touch, all right?"

"All right, Senator. I'm sorry about the bad news."

Morris nodded. Dick opened the front door for him, and as he went out he held out his hand to Carolla.

"Many thanks, Steve," Dick said, "for including me. Give me a ring when it's convenient, okay?"

"Sure, Mr. Kramer," Carolla said. "Nice to see you." Outside, the Senator dismissed his cab while Dick opened his own car and got it started. Morris climbed in and sat with him in the front seat, and they rolled down the drive to the street.

"I appreciate this, Dick," Morris said. "But I apologize for pulling you away from the affair."

"Don't give it a thought," Dick said. "I wish some magic voice would bring you word that Mary is all right."

"Well, I guess magic went out with the middle ages," Morris said.

It was a twenty minute drive to the airport, and they rode the first fifteen minutes without any conversation to speak of. Traffic wasn't heavy, and Dick didn't have to use the siren. With a U. S. Senator as passenger, he'd have felt perfectly justified if it had been necessary.

They were on the broad boulevard that ended at the airport, four or five minutes ahead, when Morris suddenly asked, "What's this narcotics thing I hear about? Traffic on the river?"

"I don't know anything for sure," Dick said. "May I ask how it came to your attention?"

"I can't say right now. It's in the wind. I know you're on top of it, but—how hot is it?"

"That's what I don't know. We are on top of it all right. Slight hitch this afternoon—a zealous city policeman tipped a witness by accident."

"Yeah, well, that's how it goes."

They slowed and had to wait in line as traffic funneled into the airport entrance. It would have been ostentatious and not really effective to have used the siren at this point.

"You've thought about our talk the other day?" Morris asked.

"Yes. Unless you change your mind, I'm available."

"Good." Then he said, "It's not my mind exclusively, of course."

"I understand that."

They got through the gate and headed for the distant terminals. The Senator seemed to be trying to reach a decision. He said nothing more till they had completed the circuit of the landing strips and pulled up at the loading ramp of the charter terminal where he would hoard his plane.

"Listen," he said, "I can pretty well make my views stick with the committee and up around the statehouse. But Carolla is powerful and he's independent. Right now he's thick with Pete Dexter, and Pete, unfortunately, is not the best friend you've got in the world. He doesn't mean much politically, of course, by himself, but with Carolla he's a threat. A lot depends on the outcome of this case against the Dexter boy. If you win it, Carolla will shy away from Pete because he won't stick with a loser. And if that happens, there won't be much of any way for Pete to hurt you."

"All right—"

"But there's something else. I'm not sure what it is because Carolla hasn't let me in on it, but he's got something else up his sleeve. Last few years he's begun to feel his power, and it feels good. I think he's got a man in mind—somebody he can manage all the way."

Morris looked at his watch and opened the car door. "I've got to go," he said. "I know all this I'm saying is pretty vague. Just wanted to put you onto whatever there is. Watch Carolla and watch Pete Dexter. They'll try to dump you if they can before you can even get started. You're all right so far, but win that case, Dick, and stay on top of the narcotics thing. Good-bye now. Thanks for the ride. Give my best to Evelyn."

"Yes, and I'll hold the thought for Mary."

"Okay. So long."

Dick watched him walk away and disappear in the terminal. Then he put the big car in gear and pulled away.

* * * *

He realized, somewhere downtown, that he was running late and had promised Evelyn he'd be home promptly. He made a turn, drove into the parking at the Sheriff's office, and went into the phone booth. He didn't have change, and there was nobody in sight to make change for him, so he walked up the ramp to the courthouse and went to his office.

He called his home. Edith answered, and he had to wait a while for Evelyn to come on. He explained about the Senator and the trip to the airport and asked whether he could pick anything up for her on the way home. She said no.

"I'm sorry about Mary Morris," she said.

"Yes. I'll be right along. Want to make a couple of other calls while I'm here."

"All right," she said and hung up.

He sat for a while in the white, specific light of his desk lamp, then dialed Al Levy's home. Al came on, and he could hear voices and music in the background.

"I won't keep you—" he said.

"It's all right, chief," Al said. "What's on your mind?"

"Just wanted to congratulate you on that ploy in court Friday. You got it the way you wanted it."

"Yeah, that worked out. Gideon was hot as a griddle, but Harris took it all right. Now I'll get a little better continuity with the presentation and all."

"It was very good work. How do you feel about it all in all?"

"The case? Good. I feel fine. We could lose, but not without a fight."

"All right. Nice going. Let me know if I can help."

"Sure, chief. Thanks for calling."

Dick hung up, switched off his lamp, and went back to the car.

By the time he reached his own neighborhood, it was growing dark. The Senator's words were still running through his mind. He wished they had been more specific so he'd have some idea of what he might be up against. But it had been good of Morris to say as much as he had.

He was passing Carl Forester's house when Donna suddenly backed into the street in front of him apparently without looking. He managed to swing the big car to the left toward the Forester drive to avoid hitting her. He heard Donna give a yip as her car swerved, its back wheels hitting the far curb and going up over it. There she stopped. Dick got out and crossed the street to look in at her.

"My God," she said. "That's pretty embarrassing—almost smash into the D.A. himself."

"Hello, Donna. You all right?"

"I guess so. Thanks, Dick. I'm sorry—"

"No damage," he said.

She found a handkerchief and fanned herself vigorously. She was panting a little. There were two bright red spots high on her cheeks and her mouth was vivid. She was fragrant and dressed up, as if to go out for the evening.

Good-looking woman, he thought. There was also the smell of whiskey on her breath. "Sure you're all right?" he asked.

"Oh, sure—except I seem to be sliding downhill—frontwards."

"Well, for one thing, your back wheels are up on the curb."

"Oh," she said.

"If you want to ease them down into the street, I'll take a look and see if you've knocked anything out of line."

"All right."

She let the back end bump down into the street, and he took a look. The car looked all right. I wonder how many she's had, he thought. Ought not to be driving. Maybe I ought not to let her. I could arrest her for drunk driving—The thought was ridiculous and he pushed it out of his mind.

He went back to the window. "The car's all right," he said. "But you seem a little shaky. Going anywhere I could take you?"

"Oh, no! No, thanks. I'm all right—just scared for a minute. It was so clumsy. But I'll be all right."

Reluctantly Dick backed away from the car. "Drive carefully," he said.

"Yes, sir," she said. "You bet your life."

"Good night." He waved as she pulled away and drove off slowly down the street.

Hitting the bottle, he thought. Evelyn mentioned it. Something about Carl cheating on her. Seems a shame. Who would cheat on a good-looking woman like Donna?

CHAPTER 11

DONNA FORESTER

She drove slowly and carefully through the country club district, making herself settle down. Lucky it was Dick Kramer, she thought. It might have been some jerk—he would have yelled at me and I'd have yelled back and that would have been a mess.

On the South River Highway she drove back toward town and turned onto the Fifth Street Bridge, crossing toward Crudsville. She hadn't been in the slum part of town for years and she had an almost lightheaded anticipation as she looked over and down toward the bright, uneven lights along the river bank.

Where Gino lives, she thought. I ought not to do this though. I should have called first. But if his mother answered, or his father or somebody—I can hear it now: "Hey, Gino, who's the fancy lady calling you up alia time?"

But I should have called, anyway. Because what if he isn't there? I can't go knock on the door and ask for him. I'll just have to hang around and hope he'll show up. Cross that bridge when I come to it.

She giggled and the car swerved slightly. Cross what bridge? she thought. One bridge at a time.

She paid attention to her driving and got safely across the bridge. There seemed to be only one main street, the one along the riverbank, and she drove very slowly, bumping over the humps and the interlacing railroad tracks. There was a strong smell of oil and the rank river smell. She found it stimulating.

Guts, she thought. Takes guts to live over here—like Gino's guts. Oh, my sweet, hot Gino!

She hadn't seen him since that Friday afternoon up by the creek in the woods. Sunday morning she had slept late and then she had worked outside in the yard—weeding, trimming in the hot sun, trying to dissipate the longing for him with her muscles. But then after lunch she had done all the outside work there was to be done, and there was no place to go, nothing to do. It was warm in the house, and after she showered, she sprawled on the bed, naked, and wondered whether if she concentrated on him, Gino would pick up the wave somehow and come around to see her.

It was easy enough to concentrate on him, but it was also disturbing. Like trying to catch your breath while falling, she thought. Oh, Gino—please! But Gino hadn't come, nor telephoned.

Carl telephoned around two-thirty to say he'd be another couple of days the way things were going. She said she was all right, thanks for calling.

"Tuesday night, I think," he said.

"Okay, Tuesday night." She hung up. "And fuck you," she said aloud. No, she thought—Gino, Gino—

It had taken her from then until six o'clock to make up her mind to go look for him. She had made herself a drink at three-fifteen and another at ten minutes to four. Then she had drunk three more between four-thirty and six, and at six she had decided to go.

She got into the business section of Crudsville and had to stop and find Gino's address on a slip of paper in the glove compartment. The name of the street meant nothing to her. There were some youngsters hanging around on the corner in front of a variety store. She rolled the window down and called to them, asking, "How do I get to Columbus Street?"

A boy stabbed with his thumb over his shoulder. "Three blocks up, turn right," he said.

"Thank you." She heard them giggling as she pulled away and turned the corner, going away from the river.

There were rows of four-family brick apartments and occasional duplexes. The streets were badly lighted. Some of the buildings had front yards with grass in them. There were no trees. But after three blocks, when she found Columbus Street, there were some old poplars along the curb on one side. The houses on Columbus Street were farther apart than those near the river, and some of them were single-family frame houses, generally well kept. Nice, she thought. The street where he lives is a nice street.

She checked his house number again and crawled along the street till she found the place. It was a frame house with a porch that ran across the front and curved around one side. There were some trees in the yard and along the curb, and she stopped under one and looked at the house. There were lights on, so someone surely was home.

But Gino might have gone out somewhere—Please God don't let him have gone somewhere yet!

She sat there for about ten minutes, and nobody came out or went in. She wished she had thought to bring the bottle of Scotch with her. Then she was relieved that she hadn't But her throat was dry, and there was a hot feeling around her ears and down the back of her neck.

I'll go knock on the door, she thought. I'll say I'm one of Gino's customers and my telephone was out of order and I wanted to tell him to be sure to bring some rose food—She got all the way out of the car, turned around once and got back in. Oh, no! she thought. Don't do that.

A screen door opened on the porch, and Gino came out. In the light from one of the windows, she saw he was wearing a sport shirt and slacks. He leaned back into the house for a moment and then came down the steps toward the sidewalk. Her heart was pounding, and her ears burned.

What if he doesn't like it? What if he's cross with me? I couldn't stand it—

She watched him stride down the walk with that lazy-looking athlete's swagger. He paused, glanced both ways along the street, looked for a moment at her car, then started on past her. She rolled the window down quickly, leaning across the seat.

"Gino."

He stopped, peered in at her, and came to the car. "Hey, what are you doing over here?" he said.

"Well, I was driving around and I just said to myself—I'll go see if Gino's home. And—here I am."

"Well—how are you?"

"Just fine."

He moved uncomfortably, looked away, and hunched his shoulder toward the house. "That's where I live," he said. "With my folks."

"I know. It's a nice house."

"It's just a house."

She released the door lock and flipped the handle. "Want to get in?" she said.

He looked away again, then opened the car door. "I guess—for a minute." He slid in beside her, and closed the door, and sat slouched in the seat with his head back.

"Got a date?" she asked.

"Well, I told Lewkie I'd take her to the show. James Bond show."

"Oh," she said.

Pretty soon he said, "I didn't expect to see you over here," he said. "You should have called me or something."

"I know. It was just spur of the moment."

"Uh-huh." He sat there with his head back, and after a while he looked at his wristwatch.

"I mustn't keep you," she said.

"It's all right. The show doesn't start till eight o'clock."

She laughed a little in her throat. "I thought maybe you might call me," she said.

"Well, I—"

"It's all right. I had quite a time. After I took my shower—it was so warm in the house—I was lying on the bed without anything on and I thought if I think hard about Gino, maybe he'll come see me."

He turned to her, laid his arm on the back of the seat, and put his hand on her thigh.

"If I'd known you were lying there without anything on," he said, "I'd have got over there, instead of watching the ball game on TV."

"That's very flattering," she said.

"It was a lousy ball game."

He tightened his arm on her shoulders, twisted her to him, and kissed her mouth, long and hard. She was panting when they finished and she put one hand on his face.

"Gino—"

He put his hand under her dress, forced her legs apart and touched her, not roughly. "How about it right now?" he said, kissing her ear.

"No," she said. "No, Gino, not in the street in the car—"

He brought their mouths together again, and she gave in to it for a moment, then tensed and pulled his hand out from under her dress.

"Not here like this," she said. "Besides, you've got a date."

"I can be late."

Oh, Christ, she thought. "No. You go ahead with Lewkie. Don't keep Lewkie waiting."

"Don't be mad at Lewkie," he said.

Why not? she thought. Why the hell not?

"Hey, you want a drink?" he said. "We've got some wine my father made himself. It's good wine." He was half out of the car.

"No, Gino, please," she said. "I have to go now. Have a good time at the show." She turned the key in the slot and pushed the starter button.

He lingered on the edge of the seat. "Look, maybe later—after the show—"

"No," she said. "It will be too late. You have to go to work early. I'll see you pretty soon."

He got out of the car, closed the door, and leaned in. "Come again," he said.

"We'll see. Good night, Gino."

"Good night, Donna."

She saw he was clear of the car before she pulled away, spinning the tires in the dry leaves in the gutter. She was crying. She brushed the back of her hand across her eyes furiously. You fool. You goddam fool, she thought.

She drove aimlessly up one street and down another till she found her way to the business section. There was a cocktail lounge on the corner with a red and blue light over the door. She found a place to park and got out. In the doorway of the bar there was a strong odor of urine and stale beer. Her stomach lurched. She could hear loud voices and louder music from a jukebox inside. She turned and went back to the car.

By the time she got back across the bridge and on South River, she felt cooler. Her stomach was churning badly, and she knew she ought to get something to eat, but she couldn't bear the thought of going home.

The club—she thought. Then, No not the stinking club.

She turned south on the river road and drove fast, both windows open, the breeze pelting her ears and tossing her hair. She drove several miles and turned in at the Highwayman's Inn. There was only one other car parked in the guest lot.

Inside, two couples were finishing a dinner in the small, somberly decorated supper room that adjoined the bar. She sat down in a booth and ordered a Scotch and soda and a steak sandwich with French fries. She got through two drinks before the food was served. The two couples had left, and she had the place to herself.

She ate slowly, forcing herself to cut and pick up and chew, chew, chew the tasteless steak. Then she had another Scotch and soda. Halfway through it she left the booth, went into the bar, and sat on a stool. The bartender was a youngish, somewhat dapper man, with carefully groomed hair and a sleek, tapering figure.

"Is it all right for me to sit here by myself?"

He looked at her long enough to be slightly insolent. Then he said, "For a high-class woman like you, yes," he said. "Some types, I'd say no."

"Thank you," she said. She finished her drink and ordered another. "Is it always like this on Sundays?" she said.

"Most of the time," he said.

Pretty soon she said, "My name's Donna. What's yours?"

"Lonnie," he said. "Lonnie Kirk."

"All right," she said. She drank slowly, holding the moist, cold glass against her palm, watching Lonnie Kirk at work behind the bar.

Her stomach was burning so fiercely she couldn't lie still. She had gone upstairs at nine-thirty, thinking that if she could just manage to get to sleep early and sleep through, she would be able to get through the next day. Another reason she had gone up early was to get away from Pete, who had had too much to drink at Mr. Carolla's cocktail party and had been ill-tempered through dinner, impossible to talk to about anything but especially about Robin and the trial. Robin had gone out for the evening, and she had wanted to talk to Pete in his absence, but every time she had opened her mouth, Pete had snapped at her, and she hadn't been able to say any of the things she thought might help.

After half an hour of tossing and turning she knew she wouldn't be able to sleep without taking something. She got up and took two of the stomach pills, and then decided to take a Seconal, too. One Seconal usually didn't do it for her, especially when her stomach was hurting, but she didn't want to take a chance on sleeping too late. She knew Pete and Robin would leave without her in the morning if she weren't ready to go. At least, she thought for the hundredth time, poor Robin doesn't have to be in jail all this time.

She had been afraid to tell Pete about her conversation with Dick Kramer. She had broached the idea, somewhat timidly, that it might be better for Robin to plead guilty, but Pete had cut her off, shaking his square-jawed face at her in fury. "Unthinkable—ridiculous!" he had said.

But she couldn't give up the thought. Dick Kramer had practically promised her that it would be the best way. The publicity would end, and Robin wouldn't have to go to prison—she wouldn't be able to stand it if he had to go to prison. She'd kill herself.

After a few minutes the pills had had some effect on her pain, and the Seconal had quieted her enough, so that she could expect to go to sleep soon. She set the little traveler alarm clock on her bedside stand for seven in the morning, just in case. She was drowsing off when she heard Pete come upstairs. She waited with a kind of hopeless expectancy for him to look in on her, but he passed and went on down the hall to his own room.

She lay there for a few minutes, listening to his movements as he got ready for bed. When he was quiet, she got up, put on a robe and slippers, and went down to his room. His door was open, and she went in a few steps and saw him lying there, bulky and tense in the dark. It occurred to her that he looked impatient even in sleep, as if the fact of unconsciousness were a plot against him.

"Pete," she said, "may I say something?"

"Certainly," he said.

"I haven't told you this," she said, "but the other day—I had a talk with Dick Kramer." She waited, holding her breath.

"Well," he said after a minute, "what for?"

"It was about Robin. I felt so desperately helpless—I—asked him what would be best to do."

He rose on his elbow in the bed, looking at her. "You asked Dick Kramer what would be best to do?"

"Yes, I did. And he said—"

"Oh, my God," he said. "Listen, try to get it through your head—Dick Kramer is the prosecutor. It's like U. S. Grant asking Robert E. Lee what would be best to do about Bull Run!"

"I understand that," she said, "but he's also an old friend."

"There's no friendship in court!"

"All right—please listen."

He sighed heavily and lay back on the pillow. "All right, go ahead."

"He said the most sensible thing for Robin to do would be to plead guilty. There wouldn't be any publicity. It would be quiet and simple, and there would be a probation officer, and Robin wouldn't have to go to prison or anything, and—it just seems to me it makes sense. Will you consider it? Talk it over with Robin and Mr. Gideon—?"

"No," he said firmly. "I will not consider it."

"Pete—"

He got up on the elbow again and spoke in that mockingly patient voice, as if she were in, kindergarten and he were explaining some elementary fact of life. "In the first place," he said, "Robin didn't commit any crime. He went out with a little Italian cunt, and she teased him and led him on, and then when she tried to chicken out, he wouldn't let her. He just did a perfectly natural, healthy thing—"

"I don't see that it was so perfectly natural—"

"Will you let me finish! In the second place, it would suit Dick Kramer just fine if Robin would plead guilty. It would take Dick Kramer off a hot spot. He thinks he's going to run for the United States Senate. Certain other people around town aren't so sure he'll make it, including me. He won't make it if this case blows up in his face. That will make it pretty clear that he tried to build himself up with a big, juicy, sensational trial, full of sex and class prejudice, and people won't like that. He might get a few Jewish votes, a few do-gooders, but he won't get any other votes. And he won't even get the Italian vote because Steve Carolla will take care of that."

She wanted to double over with the renewed pain in her stomach, but she managed to stay upright. Her temples were pounding. "You—"

she said. "You're using Robin—as a pawn—in a political quarrel. You're just using your own son—!"

"I am not!" he said. "It's a matter of honor, and I know whose side I'm on, and that's all there is to it."

"Honor?" she said. "Honor?"

She moved away from him into the hall. "Whose honor?" she shouted. "Yours? Robin's? Mine?"

"Go back to bed," he said calmly. "You're hysterical."

She turned suddenly and ran back to her own room. Inside she tripped and fell on her hands and knees. She crawled to the bed and got on top of it and waited a long time till the room stopped reeling. Then she took two more of the stomach pills and another Seconal and lay there with her eyes open, waiting for morning.

LEWKIE

Gino and Lewkie came out of the theatre a little before eleven and walked slowly toward home. After a few steps Lewkie moved close to him and slipped her hand into his. He held it lightly.

"Ooh—" she said, "that place where the scorpion was crawling on him—I almost threw up!"

"Pretty good scene," Gino said.

"What if it happened to you?" she said. "Would you be cool like that—just wait till you could kill it?"

"Not me," Gino said. "I hate spiders and all that stuff. I'd probably jump out the window."

"I think you'd be cool, Gino," she said.

"Okay."

After a couple of minutes she said, "Guess who I saw this afternoon."

"Who?"

"Guess."

"With the people living around here, I have to guess?"

"Betty Petrucelli," she said.

"Oh? How is she?"

"She's all right, I guess, but she sure is snotty lately. 'How is it at the trial?' I asked her. 'I don't really know,' she said. 'It just started.' So then I asked her some perfectly proper question about it—about that night, when it happened, you know—and her nose goes about a mile in the air, and she says, 'I'm not permitted to discuss it outside the courtroom. Mr. Levy told me not to.'"

"Well, she sure discussed it plenty before the trial started."

Lewkie let a moment pass. "She did?" she said casually. "What did she say?"

"I couldn't repeat it to a nice girl like you."

Pretty soon she said, "Well—listen, do you think he really did it—forced her like that, the way they claim—"

"Really raped her? Yeah, I think so, the way she told it."

"She told you?"

"Sure she told me."

"Just the two of you?"

"No, there was a whole bunch of us hanging around."

"A whole bunch of guys—and she told you those things—?"

"She didn't use any bad words, if that's what you mean."

"I bet she did."

"No, she didn't. She just said what happened."

"How could she tell you what happened without—?"

Gino put his arm around her and pulled her hard against his side. "Come on, knock it off, huh?" he said. "I'm telling you the truth."

She struggled till he loosened his hug.

"What if she has to get up in court and tell all those things in front of a bunch of people? I'd die, Gino, I'd just die!"

"Well, that would end the trial, I guess."

"Oh, you!"

She separated herself from him and swung off quickly down the walk ahead of him. He caught up with her at her front door.

"You can't come in," she said. "It's too late."

"All right."

"But you can walk me to the door."

"Gee, thanks."

In the dark doorway of the apartment building where Lewkie lived he put his arms around her, and she tilted her face so he could kiss her.

"You're thinking about that Betty Petrucelli," she said.

"I am not."

"Well, you're thinking about something. About the last three nights you haven't kissed me the same."

"The same as what?"

"You know what I mean."

He pulled her close and kissed her again, long and deep, till she pushed away from him and leaned dazedly against the wall.

"That's—more like it," she said.

"You take a little walk with me down to the park," he said, "and I'll do better than that."

"Now cut it out, Gino. Just kiss me once more nice and say good night."

He kissed her sweetly. Her mouth was warm and open. She put her fingertips on the back of his neck, clinging lightly, and he wasn't thinking about anyone but Lewkie.

CHAPTER 12

It began quietly in Monday morning's *Courier,* on the editorial page. Dick Kramer almost missed it as he read through the paper at breakfast. It was the last item in the main editorial column and it was brief.

Political ambition has led many honest public officials astray in the past. This heartland area has been well served both in the national and state Capitols for many years. The *Courier* hopes this tradition of honest public service will continue as new leaders accept the torch from whose who, perforce, must retire.

> A criminal trial getting underway in Superior Court today unhappily throws harsh light on an ugly and all-too-human incident. It happened in our community, which is accustomed to facing up to its sins as well as its virtues. It is to be hoped, however, that restraint will prevail on both sides as the courtroom battle proceeds. This paper, serving the families of Gilesport and the surrounding area, believes that the District Attorney's department understands as well as anyone else that a display of lurid legal fireworks does not provide the best illumination on the road to political advancement.

Dick's first reaction was of amusement, but that wore off quickly. Under the stiff, euphemistic phrasing lay the blunt warning: "All right, Richard Kramer, go ahead and prosecute Robin Dexter—but don't forget who your real friends are." It was highly improper and completely unactionable.

So all right, you put me on notice, he thought. We'll see how it goes.

He went upstairs and looked into the bedroom. Evelyn was still asleep, and he left the house quietly without waking her.

When he reached his desk a little after nine, there was a message from Al Levy. He asked Ida to call Al and invite him to come up if it was convenient. Levy came in a minute and a half later.

"You read the morning editorials?" Al asked.

"Yeah," Dick said.

"What do you think?"

Dick waved his hand as if to brush away the very question. "Important thing is, what do you think and how do you feel about the case?"

"I think there's going to be a lot of pressure from so-called right-thinking people. But about the case I feel all right."

"Then there's no problem, as far as I'm concerned."

"Good. I'll be glad to let you read my notes for this morning—"

"I don't have to read them."

"Okay, chief. Thanks for the vote of confidence."

"Give it hell, Al," Dick said, and Levy went out.

His buzzer sounded, and he picked up the phone. It was Blake O'Brien. "New development," Blake said. "Hang on."

"Go ahead."

"Nadine Berryman—"

"She's talking?"

"She's dead."

The phone slipped in Dick's hand. He shifted it to the other ear. "When?" he asked.

"I just got the call about three minutes ago. Nurse found her dead. Maybe an hour ago."

"What did she die of?"

"They haven't started the autopsy yet, but it looks like—hang on again—an overdose. The big fix."

"Goddam it."

"Uh-huh."

"Have you talked to that resident doctor?"

"No. He's not available right now. No doubt he feels himself to be in an awkward position."

"He's not alone. Have we got any cops over there yet?"

"Yes. In fact, I had deputies posted in that corridor the last two days—took that liberty."

"Good going. I'm afraid we're up to our nostrils. How are you fixed for water wings?"

"I thought I'd get over there myself and try to keep things moving along."

"Thanks. Keep in touch."

"You know I will."

Dick called to Ida and asked for the narcotics files.

"Whole thing?"

"That's right. Old and new. And see if you can find a clerk or somebody with some free time to start through it."

She was bringing him the files, two thick stacks of manila envelopes in various stages of deterioration, when the telephone rang. He picked it up without waiting for Ida to catch it. It was the resident at the county hospital. His voice was even-paced and quiet.

"I wish to talk to you on the level," he said.

"Go ahead," Dick said.

"Pursuant to our conversations of the last few days," the doctor said, "I have been treating the patient Nadine Berryman, an admitted user of drugs, with gradually diminished doses of opium derivatives. That is to say, I have been attempting to put her through the early withdrawal stages the easy way—for her. I have, without exception, administered these drugs myself, personally. The last time I treated her was at about nine-thirty last night. She was quiet, and her heart and blood pressure were satisfactory. Sometime early this morning the patient Berryman died. An autopsy is in progress, but it appears likely, from the signs, that she died of an overdose of some opium derivative. The dose I gave her at nine-thirty last night could not possibly have caused her death." He stopped abruptly, catching Dick unawares.

"You have that written down, it sounds like," Dick said.

"I have."

"All right, hang onto it. Mr. O'Brien from my office is on his way to the hospital. Anything you can do to help him will be appreciated. If you're questioned by anyone else, police or anyone, just say you've talked to me and have nothing more to say at this time. They won't insist."

"Thank you, Mr. Kramer." He hung up.

Pretty good man, Dick thought. If I get anything wrong with me, I hope I can get him to take care of me.

"All the clerks are busy," Ida said, "but I could get someone to sit on the phone—"

"Good idea. It's a tedious job. I want a complete list of names from the arrest records for narcotics offenses as far back as we've got 'em. I want the list alphabetized. Not only the offenders, but the arresting officers, witnesses, and attorneys, if and when."

"Okay, Mr. Kramer." She carried the files back into her own office. A moment later she looked around the edge of the door. "The grand jury would like to see you," she said.

He made a face.

"Sanderson again?"

"Looks as if."

"Oh—"

Ida disappeared, and he suppressed the word that was on his lips.

* * * *

In the grand jury room he listened with apparent patience to a summary of the difficulties the jury was having over the Sanderson case. He answered a few questions as they came up. The questions were easy enough, but it was obvious when the summary ended that the jury's hang-up was based on personal, emotional reluctance to bring in an indictment against a popular citizen, a good family man—against genial Happy Jack Sanderson.

With an effort he pushed his mind clear of the narcotics preoccupation and the easy legalisms he had perpetrated in answering their questions.

"May I say a few words about this case?" he said. "I have nothing personally against Jack Sanderson. I'm not out to get him. Jack Sanderson got himself in this fix. It's hard to believe, I know, that a man with so much going for him would go to such risky lengths to squeeze out a few extra dollars on a routine public works contract. But the evidence is pretty clear that Jack Sanderson did.

"We're dealing with the concept of responsibility. But I'm not going to get into a lot of abstract thought. Just look at what actually happened because Jack Sanderson cheated the county on that public road he built. That road gets a lot of use. Farmers use it every day. Produce goes over it.

"A farmer named Warden hit that road down in the bottoms in a loaded pickup truck. The road went out. Warden broke an axle, blew out two tires, and if he'd been going a little faster, he might have rolled over. If someone had hit it in the middle of the night, say a light car full of youngsters, at sixty-five or seventy miles an hour, some of them could have been killed. Luckily, it was Warden who hit it—in broad daylight—and he reported it so it could be closed.

"It couldn't be patched. It had to be dug up and rebuilt. That took time, and all that time the road was closed. All the traffic—good, solid, useful traffic—had to detour around by the old road through the Walnut Park district. A lot of time and money were lost. Because Jack Sanderson tried to pull a fast one."

He had spoken quietly, as a neighbor speaks, and the room was quiet when he finished.

"It's not for me to tell you to bring in the indictment," he said. "Legally the case is sound, in my opinion. I've just tried to give you the ethical basis of it. The decision is up to you. Thanks for listening."

He went out, unhurried, and there were some murmurs of appreciation. He thought he could sense respect in them. But you never know, he thought. You never can be sure.

Back in the office there were some routine calls, and he disposed of them and looked in to see how Ida was making out with the lists.

"Maybe late this afternoon," she said. "I didn't realize what I was getting into."

"Maybe you could lead-pipe someone into helping," he said.

"I'll see how it goes."

The young woman who was filling in on the switchboard looked around. "Mr. O'Brien is on the line, Mr. Kramer."

He went to his desk to take the call.

"The autopsy report confirms the resident's opinion," Blake said. "Overdose."

"The resident is positive he didn't give it to her."

"Yeah. I talked to him. He let me read the statement he read to you on the phone."

"Could he have made a mistake—if he was pooped, which he probably usually is—"

"I don't think so. I have some things—could we get together for an early lunch?"

"Sure. The Downtown Club?"

"Fine. Little after twelve?"

"I'll meet you there."

He hung up and asked the girl on the switchboard to place a call to Senator Morris in Washington. (…if he's easily reached," Dick said. "I don't want it to go through as urgent."

"All right."

It took about five minutes.

"Senator Morris will be on the line in a minute," she said.

Dick picked up the phone. After a while Morris spoke.

"I wondered how Mary is," Dick said.

"Well, she's alive, and she's got a good chance."

"That's great news."

"Yes—yes it is. I'm hanging around Walter Reed Hospital most of the time. Just happened to come into the office for a couple of minutes."

"Well, I won't keep you. I wanted to know how she was."

"I appreciate it. How are things back home?"

"All right, I guess. Nothing to disturb you about."

"Something on your mind, Dick, go ahead."

"The only thing—you mentioned yesterday the narcotics business—"

"Yes?"

"It may be bigger and uglier than I thought. Got some new information."

"I don't like the sound of that. Anything I can do from here?"

"No, we're on it pretty good, but I'm glad to have a chance to alert you. I'll keep you up on it."

"Please. And stay on it, Dick. This is the kind of stuff can kill you."

"I know. Thanks for the time, Senator."

"Don't mention it. Thanks for calling."

Dick hung up, asked the girl to call a taxi for him, and went down to the men's room to wash up.

At the Downtown Club, a men's restaurant in the Port Hotel, he found an isolated table in a back corner. Blake O'Brien hadn't arrived and Dick ordered a glass of tomato juice in lieu of a cocktail. He drank it slowly and was on the last swallow when Blake came in.

"Sorry I'm late," Blake said. "I had to spend some time cooling out that Lambert guy from the *Courier.*"

"How far in did he get?"

"I'm not positive, but it looks like all the way. When I got to the resident's office, Lambert was coming out. He'd dropped in on a routine call—part of his beat, he said. He knew the Berryman woman was dead. He nailed me to the wall for about three minutes, and I mumbled this and that and got away. In the office that statement the resident made was all neatly typed up in plain sight on his desk. Lambert may have read it."

"Great."

"A good reporter with his nose out can read anything that's legible while standing on his head looking in a mirror."

"Well—have a drink?"

"No, thanks. Anyway, the indications are that Mrs. Berryman was murdered—first degree. No accident."

"What kind of indications?"

"She had a visitor—it was a real fluke. Her lawyer visited her."

"What lawyer?"

"That's part of the fluke. Nobody caught his name."

Dick looked at the backs of his hands. "Explain this fluke. It smells."

"It sure does, but we're stuck with it for now. The officers I assigned to watch her were in plain clothes. She wasn't in the prison ward. No need to flash a lot of uniform. These officers were scheduled for relief this morning—seven o'clock. By coincidence this is the time of the nurses' shift change. So there's that period around seven when everything changes. That's when her lawyer visited her."

"Anybody challenge him at all?"

"Yes, naturally, one of the deputies asked him for an I. D., and he had a Bar Association card. The officer didn't write down the name—why should he? He wasn't guarding a killer or the President of the United States—just a sad whore. Naturally, she's under arrest; she could have a lawyer. None of the nurses paid any attention. Most of them didn't know what was going on."

A grizzled waiter in a red vest took their order and went away. Dick picked up his knife and doodled with it on the folded linen napkin beside his plate.

"So the theory is that this guy, this quote lawyer unquote, went in with a needle and gave her the dose."

"That's how it looks from here at this time."

"No leads to the lawyer at all?"

Blake shook his head. "The officer's description was so vague it was pitiful. Nobody else saw him."

"How are they doing with the investigation?"

"Okay. Jack Kearney from the Sheriff's office is on it He's a good detective. You want me to stay with it?"

"No, Kearney will probably do better if he's on his own without a prod. Besides, I'd like you back around the office."

"Whatever you say."

"Let's eat lunch and do something in the brains," Dick said. "I'm all of a sudden hungry."

"I know what you mean. Nervous stomach."

Dick grunted and bent over his plate.

* * * *

When Dick got back from lunch, four reporters were waiting in his outer office. Lambert was there for the *Courier,* and there were two local radio newsmen and a wire service man whose beat brought him through town every couple of days. It was no time to play hide and seek with them, so Dick invited them in. Lambert appeared to be the unofficial spokesman for the group, and most of it came from him. One of the radio men had a recorder, but Dick managed to beg off from a verbatim session extempore.

He gave them the bare facts on the death of Nadine Berryman, absolving the hospital of responsibility. Then he gave them some fill-in in response to questions. Lambert didn't bear down on the narcotics thing till after they had got through the homicide. Then he got into it.

"Doesn't this mean, Mr. Kramer," Lambert said, "this murder of a crucial witness, that the stakes are pretty high? Doesn't it mean that the narcotics traffic in the area is bigger time than you suspected?"

"It may well mean something like that," Dick said. "But when we talk about narcotics, we're dealing in relative terms when it comes to bigness. Any narcotics traffic is big because it's dangerous and potentially explosive. Statistically narcotics is not among the leading classifications of crime—certainly not in this state, even less in this county."

"Well, statistics are one thing," Lambert said, "and the drug traffic is something else."

"Exactly what I said," Dick said.

The other reporters laughed appreciatively, but Lambert wasn't ruffled. "What are you doing about it?" he asked. "I mean by way of investigation?"

"For one thing, we're looking for whoever it was who gave Nadine Berryman an overdose of drugs. For another thing, we are reexamining the history of the narcotics problem in this area in order to estimate its possible extent, and we are actively investigating every specific lead we can develop to whatever drug traffic there may be as of today."

"Have you developed any leads yet?"

"None that I can mention at this time."

"Then you do have some leads."

"I can't answer that now," Dick said. "You understand the nature of police work well enough to know why I can't." One of the radio men moved in and eased Dick somewhat off the hot spot Lambert had put him on.

"In your opinion, Mr. Kramer," he asked, "does a substantial traffic in drugs necessarily mean that one specific person is in charge of it—some Mister Big?"

"Well, Dick said, "there is organization. The stuff is hard to come by, and there are a lot of risks involved and considerable money, and usually, I would say, in any area there is a Mister Big, yes."

"You have any ideas about a Mister Big in this area?" the reporter asked.

"I have ideas. I don't have any names in mind, if that's what you mean. I assume that if drugs are coming in here in any quantity at all, somebody is dragging down the profit."

"But no idea who might be in this area?"

"None at all."

Lambert shifted the ground suddenly. "Can you comment on the trial of Robin Dexter?" he asked.

"No," Dick said. "It would be improper at this time."

"Do you think it was improper of the *Courier?*" Lambert asked, "to editorialize on the trial in this morning's edition?" Dick swung slowly in his chair and looked out the window toward the Sheriff's office. After a minute he swung back.

"I think it was mighty close to being improper," he said. "Mighty close."

"But was it improper in a legal sense? Are you thinking of taking any action?"

"No, of course not," Dick said. Then he laughed quietly. "Part of a newspaper's job is to ride herd on public officials. I wouldn't want to frighten the *Courier* into neglecting its duty."

The radio men laughed, and Lambert retreated momentarily. The wire service man asked, "Are you in touch with Senator Morris on this narcotics problem?"

"Not exactly. I've talked with Senator Morris in the last few days several times. But it's not the Senator's beat really, and he can't be expected to give his valuable time to it. It's the responsibility of this department, and we're "staying on top of it."

"Do you expect to enter the race for the Senate when Morris retires?" Lambert asked.

"Oh, come on," Dick said. "We talked about that the other day. Remember? This is no time to comment."

"If you should enter that race"—Lambert persisted—"what effect would this narcotics problem have on your chances?"

Dick came forward in his chair, put both feet on the floor and both hands flat on the desk. "That's enough now," he said. "If you'll excuse me—lots to do—"

"Thanks, Mr. Kramer," one of them muttered, and they left the office, Lambert bringing up the rear. He paused, looking back from the door as if to say something, but after a glance at Dick's face he went out in silence.

The girl on the switchboard came in with some telephone messages and a copy of the transcript of the morning session in Judge Harris's court. Dick returned all the calls but one and read through the transcript hastily. Al Levy's opening argument was clear, precise, and not inflammatory. He promised facts and established a rationale for the justice of bringing the case to trial without resorting to sentimentality. Gideon, naturally enough, had been more emotional and had taken the only course available to him in the light of the evidence—he would prove that his client had been led on by the plaintiff till nature's demands had to be met and that it was not rape in the moral or legal sense of the word.

Gideon had gone on at some length, and in the morning session there had remained only enough time for Levy to begin to question his first witness, a police officer in a Crudsville precinct who had taken down the information Lonnie Kirk had given him after he had driven the Petrucelli girl home. There had been frequent objections by Gideon on the elements of the officer's testimony that were hearsay, and it had been a protracted questioning. Court had recessed at ten minutes past twelve and would resume at one-thirty.

There was nothing for him to do about the trial, and he turned his attention to Ida and her lists and to the problem of the man named Ben, and the mysterious visitor who, quite possibly, had murdered Nadine Berryman early that morning.

CHAPTER 13

By Wednesday morning no leads had been developed in the hospital murder case, and a long and painstaking search of the lists Ida had compiled had yielded nothing usable about any possible big-time drug czar. It had thrown some light on the extent of the drug traffic around Gilesport over the past fifteen years, however, and Richard Kramer found this light harsh and unwelcome.

"Why is it shocking to me?" he asked Blake O'Brien. "I've been around long enough. I ought to have known about it."

O'Brien shrugged.

"Assuming our records are correct," Dick said, "—and I figured this out just for the hell of it—there's been over a million dollars' worth of traffic just in this area since the beginning of the Korean war. It dropped way off during the war and for about a year after. Then it climbed pretty fast for about five years and dropped off again when Peterson was D.A. Now it's up again."

"It's disconcerting," O'Brien said, "but not necessarily disastrous."

"Any words of comfort you can come up with will be acceptable," Dick said.

"I made a curve too," O'Brien said. "You can see that while there's a lot of activity while the traffic is up, there aren't too many convictions. Lot of interrogations, arrests, some indictments, but not much resolution of the cases."

"So," Dick said.

"You look at those lists Ida made and you see a lot of offenders, but you also see a lot of lawyers. Your ordinary scrabbling hophead isn't usually in a position to get a lawyer, and a lot of these lawyers have been very sharp and effective."

Dick held up his hand for quiet and looked down the lists. "Let me try to get with you," he said. "The big legal activity could mean that there's enough money involved—enough money in the hands of legal-minded operators—to set up protection. By protection I mean devices to protect the pushers—maybe even some users—against police action in order to keep the traffic in operation."

"Which means good organization."

"A solid, legal-minded organization," Dick said. "Let's think about that."

"The *Courier*, tomorrow or the next day," Blake said, "is going to start asking us to come up with 'Mister Big.'"

"All right. We'll come up with Mister Big."

O'Brien gave him a look. "Whoever he may be," he said. Dick nodded soberly. "Whoever he may be, by God," he said.

O'Brien picked up his papers and left the room. He had hardly disappeared when Al Levy looked in from Ida's office. Dick looked at his watch and saw that it was ten-fifteen. He blinked. "Come in, Al."

"Recess." Al said.

"How are we doing?"

"Well, we may be dead," Levy said. "I'm yelling for help."

"What is it?"

"My chief witness is chickening out."

"You mean that bartender—Kirk?"

"No, he did all right for me. Gideon couldn't shake him. I mean the Petrucelli girl. I'm going to have to put her on the stand—probably this afternoon."

"Well?"

"She's not sure she wants to—in front of all those people. She's afraid of Gideon mostly, I think. He's rough, and she's had a chance to see him in action."

"What do you want me to do?"

"I thought if you could talk to her—we could get her between us—she might stiffen up."

"Sure. In your office?"

"I think it would be better psychologically if I bring her in here."

"All right. Oh—is there anyone with her—her mother, anybody adult?"

"Yeah, her mother. She's all right. Just sits there. No interference."

"Good. Be sure to bring her, too."

"Right now?"

"Yeah, now."

Al started out, then came back to the desk. "I'd better sketch it for you—her deposition—to the magistrate over in Crudsville about three months ago—that's in the record. Naturally Gideon wouldn't stipulate that we'd rest our case on it without calling the girl. I just won a little time on that—

"I understand."

"So now the girl's shaky about it. She's not one to come out strong—she kind of wiggles around things. Instead of saying she won't take the stand, she's beginning to forget things, you know? I was going over that preliminary testimony with her, trying to freshen her memory, and she started giving me this, 'Maybe it wasn't like that,' 'Maybe he didn't—I forget.' Like that. So she got a little upset, and it finally came out—she doesn't want to take the stand. I explained to her that if Gideon called her, she'd have to take the stand and that I'd protect her to the best of my ability. But—she's still a kid—maybe you could give her the fatherly confidence—"

"Bring her up. How much time have we got?"

"Well, I told the judge I might be a few minutes late, and he said, 'I hope you use your time to good advantage,' whatever that means."

"That means you can have maybe an extra ten minutes."

"Yeah. I'll go get the girl."

While he waited Dick asked Ida for the preliminary testimony of the Petrucelli girl, and he was leafing through the transcript when Al Levy ushered in the girl and her mother. Dick stood up.

"Mrs. Petrucelli? I'm Richard Kramer. Won't you sit down?"

"Yah," she said and sat down. She was large-bodied and very dark-skinned, with competent-looking hands and a stolid expression.

"This is Elizabeth Petrucelli, Mr. Kramer," Al said.

The girl nodded shyly. She was stolid, like her mother, but with large, restless eyes that made her sometimes more attractive than she really was. Her figure was good, but her face was too block-like to be pretty.

"Please sit down," Dick said. "What do they call you?"

"Betty," she said, "mostly."

"All right, Betty. Mr. Levy tells me he expects you to take the stand today to testify. I thought we might talk it over for a few minutes."

"Okay," she said.

"Some people feel a little nervous about taking the stand," he said. "It's like stage fright. You don't know what it's going to be like, and there's the microphone and all, and people listening. But it's not any-thing to be frightened about, really. Not when you're in the right."

"Well—I—" she said. She looked at her mother and rubbed at her mouth with the back of her hand. Her mother wasn't any help. "I guess I'm nervous," she said. "After all—it's kind of personal."

"Sure it is," Dick said. "It's the most personal thing in the world and maybe, therefore, the most important. It's because it's so important that we have to ask you to take the stand. The accusation against the defen-dant is very serious, and he has a right under the law to face his accusers. But you are in the right, remember. You don't have anything to be afraid of. You're telling the truth."

"Sure, I know, but—sometimes I forget things."

Dick shrugged. "Everybody forgets details after that length of time. The main thing is, according to your testimony at the preliminary hearing this boy forced you to submit to sexual advances against your will. That's about it, isn't it?"

"Well—yes. That's about it."

"And you put up a fight, didn't you?"

"I sure did."

"You really didn't want him to do it, did you? You weren't just teasing him?"

"I wasn't teasing. I didn't want him to do it."

"That's the most important thing," Dick said. "That you didn't want him to do it and you put up a fight. That's all Mr. Levy wants you to say. He'll ask you the questions in a way that will make it easy for you to say it. It doesn't have to take long."

She gave Al Levy a sidelong glance, then looked into space. "It's not Mr. Levy I'm worried about," she said. "How about that other one—Mr. Gideon?"

"Mr. Gideon will ask you questions—maybe quite a few questions. He will try to confuse you, perhaps. That's where we get back to the basic, important thing. He will try to make you say that you were teasing and that you really did want Robin Dexter to do it and that you didn't put up a fight. That would not be true, would it?"

"Well—no. I told the truth."

"So that's all there is to it. You tell the truth and you won't have any reason to be nervous or ashamed of anything."

She looked at him for a few seconds with those large, mobile eyes, then lowered them. "All right, Mr. Kramer," she said.

"You'll be all right," he said. "It takes courage to testify on the witness stand. I think you've got it."

She shrugged and looked at Al Levy, who got to his feet. "Time to get back," he said. "See you later, Mr. Kramer."

Dick nodded.

Al held the door for Betty and her mother. Behind their backs he looked at Dick and raised his thumb quickly. Dick responded with a smile. When the door closed, the smile wore off.

The law, he was thinking, is ridiculous. But it's all we've got.

When he saw the transcript of the morning session, sometime after lunch, he saw that Betty Petrucelli hadn't yet taken the stand. Gideon had called Lonnie Kirk back for more cross-questioning and hadn't got anywhere with it. Among other exchanges, one in particular demonstrated the strength of Al Levy's witness.

Question: How long a time did you spend with Miss Petrucelli, Mr. Kirk?

Answer: Just long enough to drive her home—across the Fifth Street Bridge and around Crudsville a little.

Question: And did you make advances to her?

Answer: Did I what?

Al Levy rose to object, then changed his mind and said he'd let the witness answer.

Question: Answer the question, Mr. Kirk.

Answer: Do you mean did I fool around with her? Certainly not. What do you take me for—stupid?

Question: You mean you didn't find her attractive enough to fool around with?

Answer: Attractive—I don't know—got nothing to with it.

Question: Attractive girls don't appeal to you, Mr. Kirk?

Answer: Not when they've got blood on their legs that some other guy put there—

Question: That's enough. No more questions.

Answer: Besides which, I certainly wouldn't do it and then go turn myself in—

Question: That's all, Mr. Kirk.

"The most honest of honest men," Al Levy had said, "because he will testify in his own exclusive interest." Dick smiled and pushed the transcript aside.

His buzzer sounded. He picked up the phone, and it was Evelyn.

"Dick, I'm half out of my mind. I don't know—something has got to be done—"

"Whoa," he said. "Straighten it out for me."

"What do you mean? I'm sick. I can't go on like this—"

"Go on what like this?" he interrupted, with calculated brutality. As a matter of practical psychology, hysteria sometimes gave way only to harsh treatment.

"There's no place I can go anymore," she said. "I went to the club for lunch—nobody would speak to me!"

"I don't understand—"

"Because of this horrible thing with the Dexters. And the horrible things in the paper this morning."

"Look, Evelyn, sweetheart," he said, "you're very upset Will you please do something for me?"

"What?"

"Lie down wherever you are—on your back. Close your eyes, take ten deep breaths, then start from the beginning."

There was a pause, not long enough for ten deep breaths, but when she came back, her voice was quieter. "It's just that I have this horrible feeling all the time that I can't go anywhere, that somebody is always watching me. I feel—dirty."

"No reason in the world for you to feel dirty," Dick said. "So there's a trial going on—trial for rape. You're not on trial, and I'm not on trial." (Hmm, he thought.) "It's just something that has to be done. The same thing with the drug traffic. With murder. These things are my business and my responsibility, but I'm not guilty of them. I just work here."

"I wish you worked somewhere else."

"Well, I've got my eyes on something else, but it will take a little time."

"You mean Senator? That would be even worse."

"Oh, I don't think—"

"Politics is dirty!"

He counted to five and took one deep breath. "Somebody been talking to you?"

"No!" she said. "Nobody talks to me. That's the trouble. I feel dirty!"

He tried firmness again. "I don't know what to suggest" he said. "I'm sorry you have these feelings. There isn't really any cause for them except what you make of them inside yourself. Try to think about something else. Maybe if you went shopping—"

"I don't want to go shopping. I don't want to go anywhere. I'm embarrassed to be seen in public. I want to go to bed and pull the covers over my head."

"Then try that," he said. "But try being easier on yourself."

Her voice went dull and remote. "All right," she said. "Maybe I can do what Donna Forester does—drink."

"I wish you wouldn't, but one good stiff belt right now might help," he said. "Give it a try."

She hung up.

What is wrong? Dick thought. How do I fail her? Why can't she grow up?

He dialed a number, and after a few rings Mother Stevens answered. "Listen," he said, "Evelyn is having a bad time. I don't know what to do for her."

"You mean she's sick?"

"Well, not really sick—I mean, no disease. She's upset about things. About the stuff in the papers and this rape trial—I was wondering, could you give her a ring, talk things over with her?"

"I could give her a ring. She never was easy to talk to, but I'll do my best."

"Thanks."

"Dick—how are things, by the way, really?"

"With Evelyn and me—?"

"No, the job things—this narcotics business and all?"

"Nothing to worry about," he said. "They get sticky, but we're working on it Don't believe everything you read in the papers."

"That's for sure. All right, I'll talk to Evelyn."

"I appreciate it."

"Drive out and see me some time."

"I will."

When he hung up, he felt a little guilty about passing the buck to his mother-in-law, but at the same time, as a practical matter, it seemed a good move to have made. Evelyn had been fighting him for feminine reasons of her own, and he couldn't hope to understand them. But he could hope for a truce, and a mediator like Mother Stevens might be able to bring it about.

* * * *

It appeared that she had brought it about that evening. He had made a particular effort to get home on time, and Evelyn had been cheerful and chatty. They had cocktails in the back yard and he took a tour of her flower garden and found it enjoyable.

"You've got a real green thumb," he said.

"Right now it's more of a black thumb," she said. "I really worked this afternoon."

"It shows. You feel better, huh?"

"I feel all right. Mother called, and we must have talked about an hour."

"Good for her—and you."

She didn't ask him anything about the "dirty business," they had a leisurely dinner, and he even felt relaxed enough to watch television with her until nine o'clock. Then he was yawning, ready to go to bed. He had homework in the study but decided it wasn't urgent enough to be worth the risk of putting Evelyn off again. It had been the most comfortable evening he'd spent at home for a long time, and he didn't want to lose his hold on it.

"Bedtime?" he said when the program ended.

"Uh-huh," Evelyn said, yawning deeply.

He helped her up from the chair and headed her toward the stairs. "You go ahead," he said. "I'll lock up." He gave her a gentle swat, and she swayed in from it and yipped.

"Don't be long," she said.

Edith had gone to her own room at the back of the house downstairs, and he checked the lock on the service porch and the kitchen door, then went to the front door. Looking out, he saw the evening edition of the *Courier,* folded, lying on the grass in the front yard.

I guess she didn't have the heart to pick it up one more time, he thought. He had a feeling of tenderness for her, as if he ought to protect her from the reality of daily life as impressed on newsprint in all its fictitious splendor.

He went outside to the yard and picked up the paper, soggy with dew, carried it into the house, and locked the front door. He was about to pitch the paper into the wastebasket in his study but then he paused. He couldn't resist taking a look at it. Just glance over the front page, he thought. Only take a minute—

He opened it, spread it out on his desk, and looked at the front page. There was a rerun of the article under Lambert's by-line from the morning edition, the one beginning a series on the traffic in narcotics in the area. It had been hard-hitting but not insidious, and Dick hadn't felt strongly about it earlier in the day and had no drive to read it again. He was lifting the page to turn it when a headline caught his eye in the lower right corner.

DIVIDED RANKS REPORTED IN DISTRICT ATTORNEY'S OFFICE

Unconfirmed reports indicate that the trial of Robin Dexter for rape was nearly quashed because of reluctance on the part of District Attorney Kramer to push for a conviction. Al Levy, Deputy District Attorney, prosecuting the case, said late this afternoon that as far as he knew, he had the full support of his chief. Rumors persisted, however, that the case went to trial only after a bitter fight within the department....

There was a little more, but he didn't bother with it. He folded the paper slowly, tightly, punching it into a hard square with his fist, and dropped it in the basket. He had that feeling of intense cold, as if someone were pressing the sharp end of an icicle against the back of his neck. He switched off the light, stood in the dark for a few minutes, then climbed the stairs to the bedroom. Evelyn was stretched out in her bed and the light was still on. He went into the wardrobe, undressed, put on his pajamas, and got a drink of water. He sat down on the edge of the bed, and Evelyn asked, "What's the matter? Something wrong?"

"No—" he said. "Nothing. Don't worry about it."

"Well," she said, "I'm your wife. If you worry about it, I guess I can. What's the matter?"

He shrugged. He didn't want to talk about it, and he didn't want to get her started again on the dirty business, but he couldn't tell whether her mood would tolerate his putting her off.

"Just something I saw in the paper before I came up," he said.

"Oh, what?"

"Little story in there about me being reluctant to push Robin Dexter case."

"In the paper?" she said. "How could it get in the—?" After a moment she said, "Well, it's true, isn't it?"

"That I'm reluctant? No, it isn't true," he said. "If I were reluctant, if it weren't a solid case, it wouldn't be in court now."

"But I thought you said a long time ago once that you didn't want to prosecute Robin Dexter."

"I might have said I wished he hadn't done it. I never said I didn't want to prosecute. Why would I say a thing like that?"

"Oh—I guess I was wrong."

"Well, let's go to sleep."

He switched off the bedside lamp and swung his legs up onto the bed. After a moment he sat up again, looking toward her in the dark. His throat squeezed tight, then opened painfully. "Evelyn—" he said, "you had lunch at the club today?"

"What—? Yes," she said. "Why?"

"You were upset afterward, said nobody would speak to you. Did you speak to anyone?"

"I didn't mean nobody would actually speak to me—"

"Was there any conversation at the club about the Dexter case?"

"Well, I guess so—yes."

"Did you take part in it?"

"I couldn't just sit there and say nothing."

"What did you say?"

There was a pause.

"You sound like a lawyer in a trial," she said. "Cross examination—"

"Please, Evelyn," he said, "I have to know. What did you say about the case? About me?"

"I just said—you were sorry about the whole thing, and if it were up to you there wouldn't be any trial."

"In other words, you gave the impression that I was reluctant to prosecute Robin Dexter."

"I didn't say reluctant—"

"What was on your mind, for God's sake? Why would you do that to me?"

"Please—" she said plaintively, "don't be cross with me. I didn't know it would get in the paper."

"It always gets in the paper!"

Cornered and guilty now, she began to fight back. "What do you want me to do?" she said. "These are my friends. They look at me as if I did something horrible. Am I just supposed to ignore it?"

He forced himself to be quiet with her, quiet and reasonable. "Listen, Evelyn, try to understand my point of view. It's the same as if, say, you were chairman of a committee at the Assistance League, and the League was pushing a big, worthwhile project that would take everybody's co-operation to put over. And then I'm having a drink at the club, say, and I start talking about the project, and telling people that you don't really ap-prove of the project, but the rest of the committee put up an argument—"

"I don't see that it's the same at all."

"The only difference is that this means my career, my reputation, my integrity, the integrity of the Department. It has an effect on everything that happens—"

"Please—stop it!" she said. She was on the edge of hysteria now.

He got up abruptly, put on a robe, and went downstairs. He sat down in the study, switched on his desk lamp, switched it off, then on again. He pulled the phone to him and dialed Al Levy's number. The phone rang a long time before Al answered. Al's voice was flat and cold.

"That item in the evening paper," Dick said, "I just saw it a few minutes ago."

"Yeah," Al said.

"You know it isn't true." Dick's hand began to sweat as the silence lengthened.

"I know we didn't have any big fight over the case going to court," Al said.

"You think I'm reluctant?"

More silence.

"I'll be honest—I don't know what to think," Al said. "You've been cooperative—you were very good with the Petrucelli girl today. But I don't know how you really feel."

Dick felt himself tightening, rising to the hard crest of the challenge. "We're talking around it," he said. "Let's skip all that about how I feel and how you feel and all that crap. What's important is what the others think—the jury, the witnesses."

"You're not telling me anything."

"All right, then we're together."

"I hope so. I really do."

"I'll be in court with you in the morning."

"That might help."

"Not to interfere."

"Okay."

"So hang in, Al."

"Sure."

Dick hung up and sat in the dark till the swelling in his throat diminished. He was not at all certain about Al's reaction to his call. He tried to imagine himself in Al's position and couldn't. He had been in internecine departmental struggles before, but he had never had to take it the way Al had taken it today.

When he went upstairs finally, Evelyn appeared to be asleep. He got into bed without speaking and lay there a long time with his eyes open, the back of his neck no longer cold now but on fire.

Too hard on her, he thought. She was feeling good. We had a chance to get in balance, back on the old terms. I threw it away. I didn't have to press her that way. But goddam it—!

But I made a deal, he told himself. She needs taking care of, more than most women maybe. I made a deal with the grand jury that I'd tell them the truth. A deal with Al Levy to support him. A deal is a deal.

AL LEVY

After Al hung up the phone, he went to the kitchen, padding in his slippers, and drank a glass of milk. It helped a little. He stood there leaning against the kitchen shelf, drinking the milk and trying to decide whether he was glad or not that the chief had called him, and whether it would be good or bad for the chief to be in court in the morning. I guess it's about all he can do now, he decided.

As he was leaving the kitchen he hit the light switch hard with the heel of his hand, and the wall trembled slightly. I hope he gets to be Senator, he thought, if that's what he really wants—if he knows what he really wants.

Upstairs in the bedroom Doris was sitting up in bed, reading a book about European politics.

"I thought I left you asleep," Al said.

"I woke up."

"Listen, you keep reading that stuff about Europe, you'll lose your equanimity," he said.

"On the contrary," she said, "it takes my mind off problems. It's escape reading."

He grunted and rolled into bed.

"Who called?" she asked.

"Mr. Richard Kramer, District Attorney."

"Oh."

She put the book down, turned out the light, and lay flat beside him. He put his hand on her belly and stroked it absentmindedly.

"Is he with you or against you?" she asked.

"He says he's with me."

"You don't believe him?"

"I don't know—should I?"

After a while she said, "Yes, I think you should."

"Okay," he said and turned over in the bed.

"Because I know how much you want to win this case," she said. "And I wish you didn't."

"What was that?"

"I wish you didn't have to win it so much."

"What are you trying to tell me?"

"I don't know exactly. It's kind of complex. I know one thing—you've got a big, hot drive to win it because you don't like this kid, this Dexter boy."

He raised himself in the bed and stared at the wall in the dark. "You're crazy," he said.

"No, I'm not. You're trying to hang this kid."

"I am not."

"I think so."

"Whose side are you on?"

"Your side."

"Then let's not have any more of this crap."

"All right," she said. "I don't want you to quit the case or anything like that. Don't even think about what I said. Only remember it—sometime."

"Women," he said.

"Uh-huh," she said. "Good night, honey."

He grunted and blinked in the dark and fell asleep almost at once.

CHAPTER 14

Whether purposely or not he couldn't be sure, but Richard Kramer walked at a leisurely pace from the back of the courtroom and reached the counsel table where Al was sitting just as the bailiff called the session to order. Al got up for the ceremony and stood until after Judge Harris had seated himself. Then he and Kramer sat down together. "Morning," Al said.

"Good morning."

Judge Harris glanced at the prosecution table, performed a discreet double take, glanced at the defense table, and nodded. "If counsel are ready," he said, "we'll proceed." Harry Gideon asked permission to approach the bench. The judge granted it, nodding toward prosecution counsel.

"Both of us?" Al said under his breath.

"No, just you," Dick said. "He's justifiably curious. Give him a little room—it's all yours."

At the bench Judge Harris leaned forward, and they conversed in whispers out of hearing of the jury and witnesses.

"I want to know whether the presence of the District Attorney," Gideon said, "is for the purpose of influencing the jury and the general public. I think it's improper—"

"If I may say a word," Al Levy cut in, "I have never heard of a case in which it was improper for the head of a prosecuting department to join his staff at the counsel table."

"In view of a story in yesterday's *Courier,* I think it is improper under these circumstances for the District Attorney—"

"All right hold it," Judge Harris said. "What's this about a newspaper story?"

"In yesterday evening's *Courier,*" Gideon said, "it was reported that the prosecution was divided about this case before it started. Now all of a sudden the District Attorney makes a big show of turning out—"

"The District Attorney is here," Al Levy said, "to assist me and advise me. That's not improper, as I understand the term."

"Then I think the court ought to take cognizance of the influence of the newspaper story on the jury, if any, to counteract the influence of this power play by the District Attorney—"

"What's your position, Mr. Gideon?" Harris asked.

"My position is that the presence of the District Attorney is prejudicial to my client's interests, and if he remains, I will move for a mistrial."

"I'll deny the motion," Harris said. "It seems to me that this influence business will work itself out about equally. The court has no intention of asking the District Attorney to leave the room. That would be a mistrial, Mr. Gideon."

On the way back to the counsel table Gideon said, "Defense moves for a mistrial, if the court please—"

"Motion denied," Judge Harris said. "Mr. Levy, you may proceed."

Sitting apparently relaxed at the long table, his hands idle, Dick was acutely aware of the movements around him and of the presence of others behind him. He knew Pete Dexter and his wife, Liz, were sitting almost directly behind their son in the first row, just over Dick's right shoulder. He was aware that Betty Petrucelli and her mother sat behind him in the first row. He knew himself to be, for those opening moments, the chief focus of attention in the courtroom, and he could feel the prickling of that attention in the individual hairs on the back of his head. But he also knew that this attention would shift as the trial got under way, so he sat it out patiently, remembering to keep his hands still and his eyes on a neutral point. He wished he didn't have to be there and he hoped he wouldn't have to stay for the duration of the trial, but he knew he would have to stick through the morning and probably that afternoon in order to demonstrate his department's solidarity.

If the taxpayers knew what they had to pay for, he thought.

Levy was asking Betty Petrucelli to resume the stand. She was wearing a white summer dress, and her hair was done neatly, Dick noticed. She was almost pretty when she looked around the room with those large eyes. But most of the time she sat with her eyes lowered, half closed, and presented that blocky, bovine face.

"May we have the reporter read back the last two questions and answers from the previous session's testimony?" Al asked.

The reporter read hurriedly:

"*Question:* And then the defendant forced himself on you sexually, even though you had repeatedly begged him not to, is that right?

"*Answer:* Yes—that's right.

"*Question:* And you struggled, trying to prevent him, and he was too strong for you?

"*Answer:* Yes. He's very strong. I couldn't make him stop."

The reporter sat down at his machine, and Al took up the direct examination from where they had left off. Betty Petrucelli sat quietly with her hands in her lap.

"Now, Betty," Al said, "I have only a few more questions. You had gone out with Robin Dexter before, hadn't you, on other dates?"

"Yes."

"Over how long a period of time had you dated the defendant?"

"Oh—about—three or four months I guess."

"You liked him, did you? Liked to be with him?"

"Well, sure, I guess I liked him all right."

"You would go to the show, have a soda or something afterward?"

"Yes, or something."

There was a titter in the room, and Judge Harris glared over his bench. The tittering stopped.

"And sometimes," Al Levy went on, "you would stop somewhere in the car and—what do you call it now—neck? Smooch? Kiss each other and so on?"

"Yes, sometimes."

"Tell me this—was it an unusual thing? This necking, kissing, and so on that you did with the defendant?"

"I don't—what do you mean, unusual?"

"I mean, do most young people your age do these things? Your friends and acquaintances?"

Gideon was on his feet with an objection as to hearsay and opinion.

"Sustained," Judge Harris said. "Stick to the facts, counselor."

"All right. Betty, in all this time you were dating the defendant, Robin Dexter, going to shows and necking and kissing sometimes, in all that time, until that night last June, did he treat you with respect and ordinary courtesy?"

"Yes, he treated me all right. He was nice to me."

"In all that time, when you were necking, did he ever try to make you go further? Try to make you do things you objected to? I mean with his hands or body?"

"Well, once in a while—he'd kind of get excited and he'd—sure, he'd try to go further."

"And would you ask him to stop?"

"Sure."

"Those other times, when you would ask him to stop he was always able to stop, was he?"

"Objection," Gideon said. "Calls for a conclusion, whether he was able—"

"It would seem to me," Al Levy said, "that the fact he could stop shows that he was able to stop—"

"Your honor—" Gideon said.

"Overruled," Judge Harris said. "It's a reasonable assumption."

"No more questions," Al Levy said and turned away abruptly.

Dick looked at his watch and saw that it was nearly ten-thirty. Gideon was saying, (...so if the court would like to take a recess at this time—"

Judge Harris looked at the clock and at the witness. "It's only ten-thirty," he said. "I think we'd better begin the cross-examination."

"Good," Dick heard Al Levy mutter to himself. "I want her to have a break in that cross."

Dick looked at him with surreptitious admiration. That was why he had terminated his direct questioning so abruptly. Al's timing was almost magic in the courtroom.

As the defense lawyer addressed the witness for the first time Dick felt a nudge and looked up to see Ida leaning over the rail, holding some papers in her hand. He turned and took them and nodded to her. She went back the way she had come.

Among the papers were some telephone messages, one from Steve Carolla, one from Evelyn that read, "Please call," and one from the City Manager. The was also a brief typewritten message from Blake O'Brien.

"Have possible lead to the Berryman killer," it read. "Name: Luke Rideout. Known user, never convicted. Never a lawyer. Sometime pimp. Also works legit, in machine shop in Crudsville. Age: 37. Known to consort with N. Berryman. Was in neighborhood of hospital early morning. Am following up. Kearney still on. B. O."

Dick folded the paper carefully and put it in his pocket. He stirred slightly in his seat but refrained from looking at his watch or the clock on the wall. He was looking at the witness, Betty Petrucelli, but it was some minutes before he could pull his mind off O'Brien's memo and pay attention to the testimony.

"But you did go out with other boys, too?" Gideon was asking insistently.

"Yes, sometimes," she said.

"You weren't going steady with Robin Dexter?"

"No. Well—I wasn't going steady with him. I don't know if he was going steady with me or not."

"But you didn't have any agreement about going steady?"

"No."

"So you went out with other boys, too."

"Sure—"

"Many others?"

"Oh—I don't know too many. When I would get a date—"

"How many would you say, during this time you were going out with Robin Dexter?"

"I don't know—maybe three or four."

"And would you neck and fool around with these boys the way you did—"

"Objection," Al Levy said. "The term 'fool around'—no grounds for that."

"Sustained."

"You would kiss these other boys and neck with them?"

"I guess so, sometimes."

"You enjoyed doing that, did you?"

"Well, sometimes, sure—everybody does."

"All right. You did then go out with other boys and kiss them and neck with them, is that right?"

"Like I said, I wasn't going steady with Robin—"

"With these other boys—when you would neck with them, did any of them try to go all the way with you?"

"They might try it—"

"But you didn't let them?"

"No, I didn't."

"How would you stop them?"

"Well, I would just tell them to stop. Once in a while I would have to slap them. One time I had to jump out of the car and run."

Dick penciled a hurried note and passed it to Al. The note read:

"She definitely intact at the time?"

Al scribbled a reply: "Med. Ex. said definitely yes. Virgin."

"Will you tell the court, please," Gideon asked, "at such times as you asked these boys to stop—not to go any further—what would be going on?"

"What—what do you mean, going on?"

"What would the boy be doing, and what would you doing at such times?"

"We would just be—well necking, smooching."

"Well, what would you be doing with your hands, for instance? What would the boy be doing?"

Betty Petrucelli squirmed in her seat and looked at Al Levy. He smiled and nodded.

"For instance," Gideon said, "would the boy have his hands on your body here and there? Feeling you?"

"Well—maybe a little—"

"Under your dress?"

Al Levy got up. "Objection, your honor. This detailed picking into her relations with other boys is irrelevant—"

"To establish her customary activities at the time in question," Gideon said, "I think it's relevant."

"I'll stipulate," Al said, "that the majority of teen-age girls indulge in necking and kissing and sometimes what we used to call petting, which involves touching or feeling of the other person's body, and that like most others, Miss Petrucelli did it too. Will that be satisfactory to defense counsel?"

"No," Gideon said. "I'm trying to establish whether or not this particular person was in the habit of permitting certain particular familiarities."

"May we approach the bench, your honor?"

"All right," Judge Harris said. "And we'll recess now for twenty minutes and resume at eleven-fifteen. The jury may step down. Witness may step down."

There was a shuffling and a buzz of conversation as court went into recess. Al Levy intercepted his witness as she stepped down from the stand.

"You're doing fine," he said. "Don't let him bug you. I'm going to talk to the judge. You go get a long, cold drink of water and sit down and relax. Everything will be all right."

"Okay," she said. "I sure hope so. Because he's getting awful personal."

"I know. Try to get a little relaxation."

She moved past the prosecutor's table, and Dick smiled at her and nodded. She nodded in return, but didn't smile.

Gideon was following Judge Harris into his chambers at the far side of the room. Al Levy caught up with them at the door. Judge Harris sat down and lit a cigarette.

"Let's thrash it out once and for all," he said. "Gideon, you first."

"There are two basic defenses to rape," Gideon said. "One—quote: 'She told me to go ahead and then when I started, she changed her mind,' and two—quote: 'She let me do everything else till I was so steamed up I couldn't stop, and I thought she really wanted me to do it.' My defense is number two. I want to establish that the Petrucelli girl was in the habit of making free with the boys and fooling around—and that my client is a normal, healthy male and was led to believe she actually wanted to have intercourse with him."

"Can't you establish it in a general way?" Harris asked.

"No, I can't, because it is well known that certain familiarities are more exciting to the male than others."

Al Levy was leaning against the wall with his hands in his pockets, tracing a random pattern on the carpet with his right shoe.

"Mr. Levy?" Judge Harris said.

"It's all right, Harry," Al said, "I'm not trying to curtail your questioning or hamstring you or anything like that. And the girl is up there on the stand and she asked for it. All right. But I think you're on shaky ground if you try to establish that it's more stimulating to a guy if a girl lets him fool around with her breasts than it is if she lets him fool around, say, with her behind, and so on and on. Because we're all different this way, and I think I can get expert testimony to prove it."

'There's more to it than that," Gideon said. "If necessary, I'll call all these other boys she was going out with, and we'll really go into detail."

"That's an objectionable remark, counselor," Judge Harris said.

"I beg your pardon, sir."

"May I say something, your honor?" Al said. "I think I know what Harry—Mr. Gideon—is working up to. Maybe I can save a little time. I'll admit there's probably a crucial gesture when a girl indicates she's willing to go ahead. A kid gets pretty well stimulated, and his tendency is to whip out his dingus. And if the girl takes note of this and grabs it and so on, then he's probably going to figure it's all right to bang-bang-bang. And your rape charge would begin to fall apart right there. But this girl never did that, I am absolutely convinced, and if Harry can prove that she did, even once, with anybody, he will be pulling off the miracle of the season."

"Suppose I said I could prove that she did and that I had pictures to prove it?" Gideon said.

Al looked at him. Judge Harris looked at the tip of his cigarette.

"Then I'd say you were duped," Al said, "by forgeries."

Gideon didn't say anything.

He's got some. He's actually got some pictures, Al was thinking. It will be interesting as hell to find out where he got 'em.

"All right, gentlemen," Judge Harris said. "I'll permit enough detailed questioning to establish the girl's habitual behavior. I won't permit the introduction of any pictures unless their authenticity is absolutely, firmly established in chambers. And if anything gets into the newspapers about any pictures, I'll decide at that time whether or not to end this trial—with prejudice to the defense. Are we clear?"

"Quite clear, your honor," Gideon said.

"Thank you, your honor," Al Levy said.

As he and Gideon crossed to their respective tables Al put one hand on Gideon's shoulder.

"Good luck, counselor," he said. "But I'll be on your back tight if you start waving your client's prong in front of that jury."

"Okay, Al," Gideon said. "Just don't provoke me."

* * * *

Dick was in his office, talking to Evelyn by telephone.

Blake O'Brien was sitting on the edge of an overstuffed chair, waiting to speak to him. Ida hovered in the doorway, trying to get a word in.

Goddam that goddam *Courier,* Dick was thinking. "Please," he said to Evelyn, "don't let yourself get depressed over it. I'm awfully rushed right now. I'll call you back around noon." He hung up.

"What is it, Ida?" he asked.

"Mr. Carolla," she said. "He's called three times."

"I'll call him back. I can't talk to him now."

Ida's eyes widened and resettled. "I'll tell him," she said. "What about this Luke Rideout?" Dick asked.

"Doesn't look good for him," Blake said. "They haven't picked him up yet because they want to check everything out and give him some rope. His errand at the hospital was legitimate on the surface—he came in emergency about six-thirty with a bad cut on his arm. He got it stitched and wrapped up, and he signed out, but nobody saw him leave—that is, actually drive away. He was around at the right time. He knew the Berryman woman well. Did business with her."

"Is he spooked?"

"Apparently not. He went to work this morning at the shop."

"Well, let's pray that nothing happens to him."

"Yeah. We're checking out his known associates. Quite a list."

"Any Mister Big among them?"

"No. Just punks, grifters, small time shits."

"All right. Thanks for keeping me up on it. I've got to be back in court."

"How long you going to sit in?"

"I don't know. Not any longer than necessary but long enough to spike this newspaper thing."

"How do you suppose that got going?"

Dick rubbed his hands over his face and got up from the desk. "I don't know," he said. "Keep me informed, will you?"

"Sure."

Blake O'Brien went out. As Dick started out, Ida popped in on him. "How about Mr. Carolla?" she asked.

"I don't have time to call Mr. Carolla. If it's so urgent with him, he can leave me a message. I don't work for Mr. Carolla."

Ida looked a little frightened, but bore up all right. Dick left the office and headed for court.

* * * *

To his own surprise Al Levy felt better when Dick Kramer got back to the table. Earlier in the day he had thought, Let him go his way, and I'll go mine and do the best I can.

"How's it going?" Dick whispered.

"Right on schedule," Al said.

Harry Gideon, with slightly more circumspection than earlier, was trying to get Betty Petrucelli to admit that she sometimes let boys touch her naked private parts while necking with them. Betty wasn't admitting it.

"No, I never did," she was saying.

"Never?"

"Never."

"Whenever you were necking, you always wore panties?"

"Whenever I was necking or any other time unless I was taking a bath or something."

"Or something?" Gideon said.

Judge Harris looked at Al Levy, who shrugged. There hadn't been any laughter this time.

"Well, on that night in June when, you say, the defendant forced himself on you—did you have your panties on then?"

"Yes, I did."

"And you didn't take them off?"

"No, I didn't take them off."

"Did the defendant take them off?"

"No—I mean—I don't know."

"Well, when it was over—whatever occurred—were your panties off?"

"No. I had them on."

"Were you fully conscious all the time?"

"I—yes, I was conscious."

"And you remember that something occurred."

"Sure I remember—"

"But you don't remember whether your panties were on or off or whether someone else took them off—"

"Your honor," Al Levy said, rising, "isn't defense counsel getting ahead of himself?"

"You run your case, and I'll run mine," Gideon snapped.

"All right," Al said. "But if we have to ask you to go back and establish the very existence of an actual pair of panties, we'll be here a long time."

"That's enough," Judge Harris said. "The court is confused as to what defense is trying to establish at the moment."

Gideon subsided, and Al sat down and smiled at Betty Petrucelli. She was tense and uneasy in the witness chair. Al glanced frequently at the wall clock. He could expect it to go on for at least another half hour before a break. He wrote Dick a note: "The kid's nervous. Shall I start heckling him?"

Dick wrote a hasty answer: "Let it go a few minutes, I'd say. You're in good odor now."

Gideon shifted his ground, easing up on Betty. Dick glanced across the room and saw Robin Dexter, slouched low in his chair, gazing at the witness. His expression was jeering, and Dick felt a sudden rush of dislike for him. The feeling was so intense he made himself turn it off by force. It left a taste in his mouth like that of burning metal.

I'll be glad when this is over, he thought.

Ida brought him another sheaf of messages. On one of the slips was written: "Grand jury brought in against Sanderson." He showed it to Al, who nodded briefly and returned his attention to the questioning. There was nothing momentous in the other messages. Everything could wait.

Gideon was bearing down again. "You're asking us to believe," he said, "that while you let the defendant and others kiss you and feel your bare legs and your exposed breasts and kiss them and talk to you freely on all kinds of sexual matters—that while you did all these things you never engaged in ultimate sexual relations with them? that on the night the defendant, as you say, forced himself on you, you had never done that? you were a virgin?"

Al Levy rose quickly. His voice was hard and low in the room. "Objection," he said. "The question is not only objectionable in a technical sense, it is socially improper and legally improper and it is irrelevant and incompetent and immaterial to the issue in this case. The question of virginity is not germane in a charge of rape."

"Your honor—" Gideon said.

"Sustained," the judge said. "Is counsel nearly finished with the cross-examination?"

"No, your honor," Gideon said.

"Then we'll recess for lunch," Judge Harris said. "Court will be in session at one-fifteen." The jury began leaving the box, and Betty Petrucelli stepped down, somewhat unsteadily.

Al Levy turned to Dick Kramer. "Listen, thanks," he said. "Last night I was pretty shook. This morning I didn't know whether it would be good or bad for you to be here. I think you were right, and I appreciate it."

"Okay," Dick said. "Just keep going the way you've been going. I'll be back after lunch. You have any plans?"

"I'd better try to rehabilitate my witness," Al said. "It's going to get rougher this afternoon."

"All right. See you then," Dick said.

"Sure, chief."

In the crowded corridor between the two departments of Superior Court Dick unexpectedly came face to face with Pete Dexter in the company of his son and Harry Gideon. Gideon nodded to him. Robin Dexter looked at his feet. Pete Dexter looked into Dick's eyes, then here and there about his face, turned away, and started down the stairs.

Funny how it gets to you, Dick thought as he walked to the elevator. I don't care about Pete Dexter or even respect him. We just happen to belong to the same club, and it hurts when he comes on with the snub. Goddam it, he thought, if you'd been a reasonably talented father, it never would have happened. When it's so easy to get without rape—why? Why?

On the way to the office he looked in on Blake O'Brien. The Assistant D.A. sat slumped in his chair, brooding.

"Hello, boss," he said. "Uh—Luke Rideout petered out on us. Kearney managed to get the deputy who was on guard duty that morning over in that plant where Rideout works to take a look at him. The deputy would swear on his mother's grave it's the wrong guy."

Dick nodded. "Well, cheer up," he said. "We'll find him."

Blake nodded, and Dick went on to his office.

CHAPTER 15

Not until late in the afternoon session did Gideon release the witness. She broke down once, and Judge Harris ordered a recess and admonished Gideon. Betty was still sniffling slightly when Al Levy took over on redirect examination in order to repair the record, but more than that, to calm and reorient his witness.

"Mr. Gideon," he said to her, "is trying to establish his client's innocence. He's fighting to do that and so he should. I am trying to set the record straight and get at the truth, and I have to do some fighting too. Witnesses kind of get caught in the middle. But I won't keep you long now. I just want the picture of exactly what happened between you and Robin Dexter to be perfectly clear. You understand that."

"Yes," she said.

"All right. Now—out of all the questioning by defense counsel, all this long day, has anything come into your mind that would change the basic picture of what happened that night in your memory, as it has been described here in court yesterday and today? Do you now remember anything that was different from the way you remembered it yesterday or three months ago?"

"No," she said. "Nothing."

"Then the truth of what happened is still clear, isn't it?" he said. "You and the defendant were sitting in the car necking, smooching, kissing. As you had done several times before?"

"Yes."

"The defendant became more excited, more urgent than usual, is that correct?"

"Yes—he was—sort of all of a sudden."

"So urgent that he opened his trousers and exposed his organ—his penis—did he not?"

"Yes—"

"And asked you to touch it?"

"Yes, he asked me—"

"And did you touch it?"

"No, I didn't. I wouldn't—"

"And you never had done that before?"

"No."

"With anyone?"

"No, never."

"You had a strong feeling against doing that?"

"Yes. I couldn't."

"And then the defendant forced himself on you?"

"Yes."

"You asked him to stop, and he wouldn't?"

"Yes."

"And he pushed you down on the back seat and held you with one hand and—you struggled with him?"

"Yes, I did. I tried to get away from him."

"But you couldn't?"

"No—he was, like I said—leaning on me, on my shoulder and—breast, and I couldn't move—"

"And he pushed your panties to one side and began to force his penis inside you, is that right?"

"Yes."

"And you tried to struggle again?"

"I never stopped—"

"And while he was holding you that way, was he talking, saying anything to you?"

"Yes—he was leaning on me so hard—it hurt—"

Gideon jumped up. "Objection, as to what the witness heard said—"

"Overruled," Judge Harris said. "It is part and parcel of the act."

"He was leaning on you so that it hurt," Al said.

"Yes, and I started to yell to make him get off, and he slapped me in the face."

"He slapped you. And he was talking?"

"Yes."

"What did he say—his exact words?"

She looked past Al momentarily toward the defense table, then her eyes fell. "He said, 'Shut up—shut up or I'll kill you—I mean really.'"

Al stepped back half a stride from the witness stand. "He said to you, 'Shut up. Shut up or I'll kill you—I mean really.' That is what he said?"

"Yes," she said.

"Prosecution rests," Al said, turning back to the table.

Dick glanced at the defense table. Robin Dexter sat very low in his seat, his eyes on the table top.

He did it, Dick thought. Exactly the way she said it.

Dick looked at Al, who was standing next to him busily thrusting papers into his brief bag. The judge had dismissed the jury and left the bench. There was the noisy shuffling as the court cleared.

"Counselor," Dick said "would you let me buy you a drink?"

Al looked down at him and after an endless, hovering moment his teeth flashed. "Yeah, chief. I'd like a drink."

"I'll stop by the office and meet you in the garage."

"Okay."

They started out. In the first row of seats behind them Betty Petrucelli sat beside her mother, her face in her hands. Al Levy paused and touched her shoulder lightly. "You're a brave girl," he said. "It's all done now."

She looked up at him dully, then looked away. "I'm glad," she said.

Al and Dick went on up the aisle and out of the courtroom.

* * * *

When Dick came off the ramp into the Sheriff's garage, Al was standing near his own car with Doris, his wife. Al grimaced. "I don't know," he said. "I picked up this broad—"

"Hello, Mr. Kramer. It's my fault. I sneaked up on him. I was in court today."

"Great," Dick said. "Let's go. I'll buy both of you a drink."

"Let her buy her own drink," Al said. "Your car or mine?"

"Yours is closer," Dick said.

"All right then."

Dick started around with Doris to the other side of the car, and Al called, "You sneak in my court again, and I'll set the bailiff on you."

"Don't feel bad," Dick said. "We both sneaked in on him. He almost threw me out this morning."

"He's sensitive," Doris said. "A nice, sensitive Jewish boy."

Al was driving a Volkswagen, and Doris got in the back seat, letting Dick ride in front.

"Hope you're not too cramped," Al said. "She runs pretty good, but it's tight. I'd like to stick a siren on it, but there's no place to attach it."

"Yes, well, you could use one," Dick said.

They were driving slowly with the downtown traffic when Doris said, "You going to let me take back something I said last night?"

Al's mouth twitched slightly. "I'll move to strike it," he said, "but the damage has been done."

There was some silence.

"I told him, Mr. Kramer," Doris said, "that he had a drive to win this case because he hated Robin Dexter."

"How do you like that?" Al said.

"Come on now," Dick said. "You've got a good marriage going here. I'm not going to monkey around with it."

"Oh, it's all right to take sides with either one of us," Doris said. "We fight like hell, but we make up pretty good."

"I'd say this," Dick said, "judging by what he did in court today, you hit him at the right time in the right place."

"Okay, Al?" Doris said.

"Okay, princess," Al said.

Al found a place to park in front of the Port Hotel, and they went into the bar of the Downtown Club. Because it was early, they had the place to themselves and could expand and carry on the good conversation they had begun in the car. Dick would remember it, sometimes wistfully, for many years to come.

He remembered it with exquisite poignancy when he got home that evening to find a note from Evelyn:

> "Dick—I can't stand it any longer. I'll be at mother's. You can make some arrangement with Edith. Good-bye. Evelyn."

Although he was shocked by its suddenness, her abrupt leave-taking didn't hit him as hard as he might have expected. It was almost a relief to be alone in the house with time to sit by himself and think his own thoughts. It was Edith's day off; Evelyn apparently had left on the spur of the moment and had left no note for Edith that he could find. He made himself a long, weak drink, went out front and picked up the evening paper, took off his jacket and tie and shoes, and settled down in the living room. The paper contained nothing startling, nothing abrasive. Its report on the Dexter trial was accurate and not excessively colorful. The details of the testimony were largely unprintable and the summary was fair enough, Dick thought. The story did not quote Robin Dexter's words by which he threatened to kill Betty Petrucelli.

By seven o'clock he had begun to feel some loneliness, but he wasn't depressed. He made himself a ham sandwich and drank some milk and did a couple of hours' homework in his study. At nine-thirty he called Mother Stevens and asked whether she thought Evelyn would care to speak to him.

"Well," she said, "I don't know. I'm sorry about this, Dick. She's very emotional about everything right now. I'm going to try to give her a sleeping pill. I don't know—I'll ask her. Just a minute."

Dick waited, and pretty soon Mother Stevens came on again. "She says she doesn't feel up to talking," she said. "Why don't you call in the morning?"

"All right, and thanks. Stay in touch with me."

"You know I will."

He went back to work until he got drowsy. He poured another glass of milk and was in the kitchen with it when Edith came in around eleven.

"Mrs. Kramer will be away for a few days," he told her, "with her mother. I'll probably take most of my meals out and I can manage quite well, if you'd like some time off."

Edith took a turn around the kitchen, moving as if lost. He felt a pang of sympathy for her. Evelyn, he thought, must be her whole existence, maybe a sister-substitute.

"I don't know," she said finally. "I might go visit my brother a few days. Shall I get your breakfast in the morning?"

"I would appreciate it very much," he said.

"All right," she said. "Good night then."

"Good night."

He had a few bad moments after he got in bed. He hadn't slept alone in the room since they had been married, twenty years before. They had been apart for brief periods, but he had always stayed with friends or in a hotel. Lying in the dark beside her empty bed, he found himself remembering the good times they had had. He was unable to think about the bad times. But underneath, though he fought against acknowledging it, he felt relief on more than one score.

Man without a wife, he thought, man going through separation, divorce, would have a slim chance running for Senator. He was content. He was a good lawyer. The day in court had stimulated and freshened his mind. There would always be work for a good lawyer.

CHAPTER 16

The next morning when he took his seat beside Al Levy, he noticed among other things that Liz Dexter was not in the room. Just as well, he thought.

"I was up half the night," Al said to him, "writing a summation. Found out Gideon's only going to call two witnesses. Might wrap it up this afternoon."

"I hope so," Dick said.

"It's still tricky. He's calling an expert psychologist we got to go around with, and I've got to handle that boy."

"Still hate him?" Dick said.

Al chuckled. "She's pretty smart, my wife," he said.

"Believe it," Dick said.

He was thinking about Evelyn when the trial got under way. Gideon's strategy was clear within a few minutes. He would try to establish mitigating circumstances and get his client off with probation.

You never could be sure, though, Dick thought. A jury is a sometime thing. If they think the girl is no better than she should be and that Robin was provoked—

(...at this age," the psychologist was saying, "the sex drive is very strong—at its peak, really—and given an opportunity, it will express itself, by force if necessary."

"You think it was given an unusual opportunity on the night in question?" Gideon asked.

Al Levy got up. "Has the witness examined the plaintiff, Miss Petrucelli?" he asked.

"No," the witness said.

"Then I don't think he is qualified to give an opinion as to the quality of the opportunity."

Judge Harris took off his glasses and scratched his nose. "Well—" he said, "let him answer the question. It's material."

"Any situation in which the partners are progressively stimulating each other provides an opportunity," the psychologist said. "Whether this one was exceptionally provocative, I couldn't say."

The testimony droned on, and Dick let his thoughts wander. He hadn't seen or heard from Blake O'Brien since early the day before. He thought he ought to call Evelyn so as not to be in a position in which he could be accused of neglecting her. He had not returned Steve Carolla's call of the day before and he no longer had any reason for putting pressure on Carolla, active or passive. He thought that his mere presence in the courtroom was unnecessary now and therefore he was—well, what he was doing, he decided, was goofing off. He was on a busman's holiday, and it was only Friday.

When court recessed a little after eleven, Ida came to him before he could rise from the table. She handed him some messages. The one on top was in large red letters: "Vince Farrell," it read, "in Washington. Please call earliest."

"You think I'm doing any real good here now?" Dick asked Al.

Al shrugged. "It's nice having you. But I know you've got other chores. I think you did it by sitting in yesterday."

"Then maybe I'll drop in this afternoon."

"Whatever you think, chief," Al said. "I feel all right about things now."

On the way to his office Dick thought about the call from Senator Morris's aide, Vince Farrell. His first thought was that something had happened to Mary Morris. He hoped not. The next worst thing would be that Vince was checking in on the narcotics thing back home, and there wasn't going to be much of anything for Dick to report.

He looked into Blake O'Brien's office, hoping vaguely that there might be some last minute news, but O'Brien was out. He placed the call to Vince on his own private line, avoiding the switchboard.

"Hello, Dick," Vince said. "How're things?"

"Not too bad. Tell me, how is Mary Morris?"

"She's going to be all right. Listen, Dick, I've got a bunch of calls to make. First—the Senator over this weekend will announce his retirement—end of this term."

"Yes?"

"On next Tuesday I'm giving a lunch for about half a dozen guys, all of whom you know, at the Greenbriar. For reasons I'll explain when I see you, we want to get some stuff hammered out right away. Can you make it?"

"On Tuesday—sure."

"Good. See you then."

Vince hung up, and Dick had a feeling as of hanging on to the tail of a kite. When he settled down, he dialed Mother Stevens' number. Evelyn answered.

"Hello," he said, "this is Dick, remember?"

"Oh—hello," she said.

"How are you feeling?"

Pause.

"I don't know. I just don't know, Dick."

"Did you get a good night's sleep?"

"Pretty good."

"I'm glad to hear it."

"Did you?"

"I slept off and on. I missed you."

Pause.

"Are you going to move into a hotel?" she asked.

"God, no," he said. "Why?"

"Well I don't know, I just thought—"

"Unless you'd rather I did."

"Oh, no, I'm quite comfortable here."

She was still firmly going away, and he decided not to put any strain on her.

"All right," he said. "I wanted to make sure you were all right. You know where to reach me."

"All right," she said. "Good-bye."

There was a message from Supervisor Floyd Cantrell, and Dick returned the call.

"Listen," Floyd boomed, "this buzzard character from city hall—Bazzard?—is still goin' on about the juvenile facilities, and somebody told him to come to today's meeting. What the hell is it about? I don't know what the score is."

"It's not complicated, but it has to go through a process," Dick said. "On account of staffing problems and so on, the city budget will have to stand part of the cost, and all that—"

"Okay, listen, Dick, can you drop in on the meeting this afternoon and help out? We need some protection from that son of a bitch. He's a regular porcupine."

"Yes, I'll come in. Around two all right?"

"Yeah, thanks."

The red light flashed on his intercom, and he lifted another phone.

"The Attorney General," Ida said. "From the capital."

"Dick Kramer," Dick said.

"Hi, Dick," the Attorney General said. "How are you making out on that narcotics thing?"

"We're working on it."

"Do you want any assistance?"

"I don't know what you could do for us right now," Dick said. "We've got a homicide to look into."

"I know. Reason I called—all right for you to talk now?"

"Yeah, go ahead."

"I just had a visit—Steve Carolla and his man, Ivo Morelli."

"Oh."

"Carolla was a little upset. Said he couldn't reach you by phone. Said the drug business hits his people especially hard, and he was concerned about it."

"His people," Dick said.

"Yeah. Well—all right, but the thing is, with his drag the papers can get to us kind of bad, and the *Courier* is already swinging. And if you're going to need help, maybe we ought to line it up in advance so we won't have any lag there."

"I appreciate your calling," Dick said. "Can I check back with you after I dig around here?"

"Sure. Couple of hours?"

"Yes, a couple of hours."

"Did you hear from Vince Farrell this morning?"

"Yes, I talked to Vince."

"Good. So did I. So long now."

Dick tried to call Sheriff Donahue, who was out. There was no answer on Blake O'Brien's phone. He sent for Ida.

"Will you try to find out where Blake O'Brien is and put me in touch with him?" he said. "And I've got a call in for Sheriff Donahue. I want very much to talk to him. And please call Floyd Cantrell and tell him I may have to back out on my visit to the meeting this afternoon."

Ida scurried out, and Dick read and signed fifteen letters that had been composed for him during the morning. He read them hastily—he was depending on Ida's accuracy—and felt guilty about it.

Ida came back. "I can't reach the Sheriff," she said, "but Mr. O'Brien is over in Department Five with three narcotics offenders at an arraignment. Judge Gorham."

"Right now?"

"Right now—just started."

"Will you call over there, please, and ask him to check in with me as soon as possible?"

Ida went away, and there began for Richard Kramer a run of days that he would remember as the most frustrating and instructive of his life.

* * * *

He was reading the transcript of the Dexter trial, Friday morning session, when Blake O'Brien came in at one-thirty. There were black circles under Blake's eyes and the shape of exhaustion in the slump of his shoulders.

I'll have to let up on him, Dick thought.

"We had these three guys for arraignment," Blake said without preliminary. "All three picked up with stuff on them, including equipment. They were picked up yesterday, late night, and four of us took turns on the interrogation until three in the morning. They didn't know anything, no names, nothing. I finally got persuaded they really didn't. So we took 'em to Judge Gorham this morning for the arraignment, and they had this Italian lawyer named Meucci, dreamy-eyed guy from a firm in Crudsville, got about six Italian names on the door. I've seen Meucci around some.

"So no problem with the arraignment. Gorham set bail at one thousand apiece. Two Italian kids and one lanky Irish fellow called Whitey, an albino I think. Cool? You never saw anything so cool—until right after that bail was set. Meucci said something to them in Italian and walked out. Then the roof fell in. Took two cops to handle them, handcuffs and all. I know a lot of dirty Italian words, and they used all of 'em.

"One of the cops was Italian, so I asked him what the trouble was. He said it was too fast for him mostly, but gathered they'd expected Meucci to come up with the bail. And Meucci had walked out. So I caught up with Meucci outside and opened a conversation. He's not very talkative. He rolled his eyes and shrugged his shoulders and was noncommittal. I asked him, 'Did they expect you to put up bail?' 'I don't know,' he said, 'but I couldn't do that. They got no credit.' And when I asked him how they came to be his clients, he said he got a call from his office to go over there and represent them, and that's all he knew.

"But I looked into Meucci's record, and in the past he has had other clients on the same type of charge. Several times he has made the bail for them, personally—I mean, not his own money, but he came up with it. On other cases we were studying, you remember, a lot of these drug cases had lawyers, and quite a few of 'em came up with bail when you'd think they couldn't raise the scratch to get weighed. So naturally you wonder why some did and some didn't. You can't go by the attorneys because some attorneys had clients who made the bail and others who didn't. Anyway, today nobody made bail for Meucci's clients. And I think I've got an idea."

Blake got up stiffly, went to the water cooler, and drew himself a drink in a paper cup. Dick waited.

"The pattern seems to be," Blake said, "that the organization got tightened up about five years ago, probably because somebody took it over. The organization is in business for profit, and they have to take care of their own customers. They lose a few—for a while anyway—but they save more. And the way they do it indicates that the organization is run by legal type brains. The man who got into Nadine Berryman's hospital room, you recall, had a Bar Association card. He didn't necessarily have to be a lawyer, but he had a card that he got somewhere."

"Mister Big—" Dick muttered.

"Yeah," Blake said, "I think, between you and me, that Mr. Big is a lawyer."

They looked at each other for a couple of minutes.

"I also think," Blake said, "that the reason these three today didn't make bail was because they don't know anything, and the organization doesn't have to invest in them. I think if we could hammer on the ones who have been picked up and booked and then bailed out, we could get some useful answers."

"How many would there be altogether?"

Blake shrugged. "Forty, fifty maybe. A few of them are doing time upstate. Most of 'em are loose, but I don't know how many are still around town."

"If we try a roundup without some evidence—I mean the stuff you can take pictures of—it can bounce all over the place. And the department would look silly."

"I know. But maybe we could schedule it. If we pick up three or four at a time and run 'em in somewhere and talk to them, they might break down faster. Word gets around, and they panic. Also, we might draw out a bunch of lawyers and we can talk to them, too. And if we scatter it out over town—different precincts—we don't have a big center ring operation and, I might add, we don't attract so much newspaper attention."

"Have you talked to Donahue about it?"

"Yeah. It's all right with him. And the city will cooperate, let us use the city stations."

Dick swung around and looked out the window for a minute, then swung back. "Let's do it," he said. "And I want to be in on it too—the questioning."

"If you say so—may get rough—odd hours—"

"I want to be in on it. When can we start?"

"Right away, as far as I know."

"Okay then. You have a good lunch—with vegetables—take a rest and go to it. I'll be with the supervisors for an hour or so, maybe longer, and after that I'll be available, either here or at home."

Blake pushed himself up from the chair and turned to the door. He managed a smile over his shoulder. "I feel pretty good about this weekend," he said. "I think the thing is cracking."

Dick raised his thumb, nodding.

* * * *

When he got back from the meeting with the supervisors, which had been a constant wrangle and had left his nerves on a fine edge, it was nearly four o'clock. There was no message from O'Brien. He went to Department Two and sat down in the back row of the courtroom. Robin Dexter was on the stand, and Gideon was questioning him on what seemed to be the redirect. That meant Al Levy was finished with him.

"Now, Robin," Gideon said, "you have never denied that you had sexual relations with Betty Petrucelli, have you?"

"No," Robin said.

"And you've told us that she might have put up some little struggle because, as you put it, she chickened out after you understood she was willing to let you go ahead."

"Yeah—that's right."

"But not too much of a struggle, is that right?"

"No, not too much."

"And you have no memory whatever of saying those words to her, 'Shut up or I'll kill you,' or anything resembling those words?"

"No, I never said anything like that."

"You never made any physical threat at all against Betty Petrucelli?"

"No."

"Defense rests," Gideon said and turned away.

Dick slipped out quietly. There wouldn't be any more time today. Summation and deliberation would have to come on Monday, maybe even run into Tuesday if Judge Harris's charge was a long one.

* * * *

The selective, staggered roundup of narcotics offenders was in progress by seven that evening. He had gone to the cafeteria in the Sheriff's building for an early dinner and was in the office when the call came from Blake O'Brien.

"Four of them," Blake said, "in a city station on the northwest side. I don't know whether it's worth your time—"

"I'll be there, but don't hold anything up for me."

"Okay."

He checked the location on his large-scale city map and was at the station in twenty minutes. It was an outlying precinct in a quiet neighborhood, and the facilities were minimum. The four who had been picked up were in a square, barely furnished room at the rear of the station. Three were young, stolid men in their early twenties; the fourth was a middle-aged man in slacks and a T-shirt, with a tic on the right side of his face and deep, apostrophic lines in his forehead. With them were Blake O'Brien and two city patrolmen. Dick went in and sat down in a corner of the room to listen. Blake was doing the questioning. The two officers were sitting with the four who had been picked up, one at either end across a long table from O'Brien.

"You shot up as late as yesterday afternoon," O'Brien said, pointing at the second of the younger men. "I can tell to look at you."

The man looked at O'Brien fixedly. "I did not," he said. "You've got nothing to hold me here. I want a lawyer."

Blake turned to the next one. "All I'm interested in is where you're getting it," he said. "You tell me that and you're free to go."

The man in the T-shirt lifted his hand like a boy in a classroom. Blake ignored him and turned to the first of the young men.

"You've been represented by a lawyer named Nat Spencer," he said. "You like me to call him?"

There was a moment of hesitation, and the young man shook his head. "No—he's out of town."

"Listen—" the middle-aged man said.

"Just take it easy," Blake said without looking at him. He shrugged in his jacket, rubbed his face with both hands, and went to get a drink at the water cooler. Back at the table he leaned on it on both hands and spoke in a casual, friendly voice.

"Look," he said, "I'm pooped and I want to go home and have some dinner. The thing is—I'm looking for a particular guy and I think you know him, and that's all I want, just the possible location of this guy at this time. He's a pusher named Rossi. They call him 'Lover.' Lover Rossi. I need to talk to him."

One of the young men glanced at the others, but they didn't move. The middle-aged man put his hand up again.

"You know Rossi?" Blake asked him.

"No, I don't know nobody like that, but I wanted to tell you something—"

"Just wait a minute," Blake said, brushing him off.

The man's forehead wrinkled violently, and the tic in his cheek squirmed spasmodically. Dick got up and walked along the table to where the older man sat, and touched his shoulder. The head jerked around, the tic momentarily suppressed.

"I'm the District Attorney," Dick said. "Would you like to talk to me?"

"Yeh—sure, I would."

Dick pointed to a small table in the corner, and they went over there. "What was it you wanted to say?" he asked.

"Well I—you the D.A.?"

"Yes."

"You fellas really squeezin', huh?"

"We're looking for someone."

"Look, I ain't been using for a long time—months. I don't know why they'd pick me up, I got a steady job, making no trouble—"

"You had something to tell us?" Dick said.

The man looked nervously toward the others at the table and lowered his voice. "Yeh—I don't know nothing about them, never seen 'em before and I don't want trouble—"

"No need to have trouble. What was it you wanted to say?"

"Well, I know there's a fella in the neighborhood, pushin'. He got onto me, and I wouldn't have none. I ain't using now. I kicked it."

"What's this fellow's name?"

The man shrugged. "I heard somebody call him Buzz. That's all, just Buzz."

"That's all you know?"

"Yeh, just Buzz."

"Can you tell me what he looks like?"

"Kind of a tall skinny fella, got a bald head. Hangs around a place called the Blue Sky, kind of a joint. In the neighborhood."

"What neighborhood is that?"

"Out around Fifteenth Street. Fifteenth and Oak."

"That's all you can tell me about him?"

"That's all. I ain't using. Look, could I go now. My wife don't know I got picked up. She'll worry."

"You'll have to check in with the officers," Dick said. "Thanks for the help."

"That's all right. I'm clean, honest I am."

"Okay," Dick said and walked away.

Blake O'Brien worked for about fifteen minutes on the three younger men, then let all four go. When he joined Dick outside the station, he looked tired but not discouraged. "Get anything out of the old man?" he asked.

"No. He mentioned a guy named Buzz. That was what he had. I think he just wanted to get out and get home."

"They all did."

"Did you get anything?"

"No. But I didn't expect to, not yet. It takes a while for it to work on them. By the time we've hauled in three or four groups, the word will be out, and they'll be nervous."

"You standing up all right?" Dick asked.

"I'm fine. I haven't had so much fun since I was on the cops in West Springfield, Missouri."

"Are you driving your own car?"

"No, I'm hitching rides with the cops. More practical that way."

"Take care of yourself," Dick said, "and call me."

"Right."

* * * *

So it went. He got another call from Blake at ten-thirty. He was still in the office, and this group had been brought into the Sheriff's Department, so he only had to go down to the ramp and up to the detective bureau on the second floor. There were three of them this time, all older men, and they had a charge against one that they could make stick. But the results of the questioning were no more productive than earlier, and Dick left them a little after twelve and drove home. He slept fitfully, waking now and then with a bad taste in his mouth and the rank, oily odor of the police world in his nostrils. Now and then he looked over at Evelyn's empty bed and wished alternately that she were there and that she wouldn't come back until this dingy project was finished. He was roused at five-thirty in the morning by a telephone call from Blake, who apologized for the early hour and said he had some promising drug users lined up in Crudsville. But it turned out to be more of what they already had, which amounted to nothing at all, and Dick went to the office at eight-thirty after a bad breakfast in a diner downtown.

At noon he met Blake for lunch in the cafeteria, and they talked about the Attorney General's call.

"I don't know," Blake said. "The state people aren't any smarter than we are. All they've got is big lab facilities and some big-time contacts, and what we want is local names. I don't see what they could do."

"I'm with you. When I called him back yesterday, he seemed relieved not to have to move."

"Have you talked to Carolla?"

"No. I don't intend to."

Blake nodded. "I think we're working the right way," he said. "If we can have a couple more days."

"We've got 'em," Dick said. "I just made the decision."

Blake grinned. "Thanks," he said. "I'll be calling you."

* * * *

Late Saturday afternoon Dick went to the Sheriff's Office and looked over the reports in the homicide investigation being carried on under the direction of Kearney. The detective himself wasn't there, but the reports were full and competent—and negative.

"It's hard to swallow," Dick said to the deputy who had got out the reports for him, "that a man could walk into County Hospital, give a patient a lethal dose, and get clean away."

The deputy shrugged. "A fluke," he said.

"Yeah. The word 'fluke' is beginning to bug the hell out of me."

"I know what you mean," the deputy said.

* * * *

By midnight Saturday the grind of the scattered interrogations was beginning to tell on Dick. The characteristic ache in his neck had settled into a chronic throb, and his legs were uncertain. He had done active police work in his younger days, but he hadn't kept in top physical condition and he regretted it. Blake O'Brien showed signs of exhaustion, but he was younger by twelve years and would be able to sleep it off. For Dick it had become a nightmare of half-sleeping and sudden rousing, starting and stopping, a cumulative depression compounded of bad smells, grinding noises and endless, worthless conversations, dribbling from sullen mouths into thin air.

When they left the precinct station at one-fifteen Sunday morning, even Blake was hedging on his optimism. "You can't win 'em all," he said, but his words had a hollow sound.

They stopped in an all-night cafe for a snack.

"Must be getting kind of tiresome for Mrs. Kramer," Blake said, "the way you've been hauled around the last two days."

"Mrs. Kramer is on a vacation with her mother," Dick said. "She doesn't know anything about all this."

"Oh," Blake said. There was no more conversation about Mrs. Kramer.

"You ever think about getting married?" Dick asked.

"I was married once," Blake said. "I was in law school in Kansas. And she was a cute kid, but she didn't like the routine—you know something about law school—and we finally broke up. Sometimes I wonder—but not very often. I'm glad I'm a lawyer."

"So am I," Dick said.

"Don't get me wrong though," Blake said. "I prefer girls."

"I'm sure of that," Dick said.

"Look, there's no more on for tonight that I know of," Blake said. "Why don't you go home and get some sleep. Outside of some big break, there won't be anything till tomorrow afternoon anyway. There's a kind of tradition about Sunday morning—you let the people go to church before you put the arm on them. Let 'em be shriven."

Dick laughed. He drove home, and went to bed, and didn't wake up till noon on Sunday.

CHAPTER 17

He made some coffee, and at about one o'clock he suddenly remembered something and he dialed Blake O'Brien's home number. Blake came on with a sleepy voice.

"Sorry to wake you," Dick said. "But I just remembered something I forgot to ask you the other night."

"Yeah? You didn't wake me. Go ahead."

"You were talking to those three fellows at the northwest station and you said you wanted to get to a man named Lover Rossi. Who in the hell is Lover Rossi?"

Blake laughed. "He's nobody," he said. "I made him up. If I'd got an answer about him, I'd have had somewhere to go. But they were too cool for me."

"Okay. Things are never what they seem, are they?"

"Hardly ever, boss."

He didn't hear from Blake again during the afternoon. He tried to call Evelyn a couple of times but there was no answer. At five he showered, and got dressed, and drove over to the club for a drink and dinner. He had chosen the club because it was nearby and on a Sunday would be uncrowded. Five paces into the cocktail and dining area he knew that his choice had been rational but uninspired. There were about twenty people in the room, half a dozen of them at the bar. He knew all of them. One said "Good evening" as he passed and two others nodded to him. The rest either ignored him or turned from him. It was a long walk to the bar, and when he reached it, the three couples lined up on stools held a brief, muttered conference, got down, and walked away to the dining room. The bartender, mercifully, seemed as cordial as always.

"What will it be, Mr. Kramer?"

He sat with his back to the room and ordered a martini. When it was served, it was the same precise, frigid, high-class martini he was used to and it comforted him. What I did, he thought, I had the bad taste to prosecute a scion of the club for banging a little dago tart and I am going to pay and pay and pay.

Pretty soon he was thinking, Maybe, too, they've got the news that Evelyn went to mother, and so I don't really belong here anymore. I married this club; I wasn't born to it. I was born downtown in a shoe store. Well—fuck you one and all, he thought.

A couple behind him were talking about the Foresters. "Is Carl at the house, or did he leave? Or did she leave? I haven't got it straight."

"I think Donna left. I think she moved into a hotel."

"Which hotel?"

"I don't know."

Donna Forester, he thought. A good-looking woman.

He ordered another martini, drank it with deliberation, then left the club. On his way home he paused in front of the Forester home and looked at it. There were no lights. A pickup truck was parked on the drive, and as he watched, a young Italian boy in clean slacks and a sport shirt came from the back of the house toward the truck. Dick drove on slowly. After a minute the pickup passed him, the motor roaring. He saw a name painted on the door in black letters: Gino Blanco—Gardener.

Trying to collect his pay, Dick thought. Nobody home.

At home he fried a couple of eggs, drank some coffee, and tried to work in the study. He called Mother Stevens and found they were home, but Evelyn had gone to bed. He said good night to his mother-in-law, drank some more coffee, and went back to work. At ten-thirty there was a call from Blake O'Brien.

"I'm over in Crudsville again," Blake said. "I don't know that it will be worth your time. I understand that these three have lawyers and the lawyers are on their way. We may not even get a chance to say hello to them."

"I'll come over," Dick said. "The Crudsville precinct station?"

"That's it."

It took him forty-five minutes to get to the station. He found Blake O'Brien half asleep, waiting in his car.

"They got sprung," Blake said. "I was afraid of it. Sorry you had the long trip."

"Anything turn up at all?"

"Nothing," Blake said. After a minute he said, "I'm sorry. You let me have it, and I you-know-whatted it up. That was the last batch, boss. I don't know what to do next."

"It's all right," Dick said. "You did well. Go get some sleep. We can talk about it tomorrow—late."

"Yeah—late," Blake said. He straightened up under the wheel, got his car started, and drove away. Dick watched till he had disappeared, then went to his own car and started the long drive home.

When he called Evelyn from the office on Monday morning, she seemed more cheerful than at any time since she had left. But she was reserved and hesitant. He had determined to leave the decision to her and to make no pleadings.

"Has Edith come back yet?" she wanted to know.

"No, I told her to take as long as she wanted."

"I see."

"Have you had any fun—any relaxation?"

"Oh—no—just rest and peace and quiet."

"That's good."

"I tried to call you a couple of times. You weren't home."

"I've been working with Blake O'Brien on this narcotics investigation. It's in and out all hours."

"Oh. How is it going?"

"Nothing yet, but it will be all right."

"Donna Forester left her husband," she said. "Did you know?"

"Yes, I overheard it last night at the club."

"Oh."

He didn't bother to say any more about the club.

"Well, thanks for calling," she said.

'Take care of yourself," he said.

At noon Ida brought the transcript of the morning session in Department Two, and he read the summations by defense and prosecution. Al Levy's had been strong and economical and, Dick thought, effective. Gideon had been more emotional, but he had hedged. He had been up against it—he had had to try to make his client appear normal and healthy enough to not be a threat to society and at the same time to be volatile enough (uncontrolled enough, maybe) to assault a girl sexually in the normal course of events. It was a tricky assignment. Judge Harris had started his charge to the jury before the noon recess, so it looked as if the case would go to the jury by mid-afternoon. It gave him a feeling of relief.

He spent the afternoon until four o'clock alternately with Blake O'Brien and on paper work at his desk. There was a Monday quiet—no big telephone calls, no alarms.

At four o'clock he went down to Blake's office and found Blake out and Al Levy curled up on a sofa in the outer office. He sat down. After a while Al blinked at him, sat up hurriedly, then groaned and lay down again.

"Good summation," Dick said.

"Thanks. They went out about an hour ago. I thought I could catch a nap."

"Go ahead, sleep."

"Don't really want to." He sat up, more slowly this time.

"I feel very funny about it," he said. "It seems to me it's in the bag, but at the same time we could lose."

"There's an old saying about that."

"Yeah, I know." Al got up and drew a drink of water, tossed the cup away, and sat down again. "How you coming among the happy hop-heads?" he asked.

"We got nowhere yet," Dick said.

"Takes time," Al said.

Dick thought he ought to go and let Al rest, but it was pleasant and relaxing to be there as a guest, at a distance from the day by day tensions that had become almost a part of his nervous system, so that he wasn't always sure whether he was happening to the environment or the environment was happening to him.

"You mind if I ask you a personal question?" Al said. "You can refuse to answer if—"

"Go ahead."

"You planning to run for the Senate?"

Dick hesitated, but not for long. "Yes," he said, "if I get any support."

"Why?" Al asked.

"I don't know that I can say. I'm pretty sure I don't want to be a prosecutor much longer. Not that I'd have much choice there; I've pretty well run my course. I'm too young for a good judgeship, and private practice in this area, I think, would be too ragged. I'd have to hook up with somebody, and there isn't much criminal business, and the other fields are not interesting to me. I like deliberation and debate."

"In other words," Al said, "you're going to run for the Senate because you don't have anywhere else to go."

"That's about it."

"How do you like that?" Al said. He grinned suddenly, frankly. "You can't win 'em all, huh?"

"You said it."

"Well, I hope you make it. I won't promise to vote for you—I'm sort of devoted to the other party. But I won't stand in your way."

"I appreciate it. It may be altogether academic. Carolla is after me, along with his boy Morelli, and I'm not popular with the country club set right at this time. I may learn tomorrow that the committee would like me to run for head janitor at the statehouse."

Al nodded soberly. "That might not be a bad job, come to think of it," he said. "I bet you come across some very magnificent bits of trash at the statehouse."

The telephone rang and Al jumped to it. "Yeah?" he said. "Yeah—? What—well why do you call me to tell me they're not in yet? I don't want to know they're still out! I want to know when they come in!—Okay, thanks." He went to the sofa shaking his head.

"I'll let you get that nap now," Dick said. "If I don't see you again before the jury comes in—good luck."

"Thanks, chief."

Dick went out, and Al stretched out on the sofa.

* * * *

At eight-thirty Dick came back to the office. There was no word from Blake O'Brien. He called Department Two, and the clerk told him the jury was still out. Al Levy will be chewing his nails, he thought.

He took the stairs down to Al's office and looked in. Al was sound asleep on the sofa, snoring. Dick sat down in a chair and waited. At nine o'clock the phone rang. Al jumped as if he had been set on fire, but Dick reached the phone first.

But it wasn't the clerk in Department Two. It was Blake O'Brien. His voice was rough and distant.

"Boss," he said, "you remember that guy named Ben that Nadine Berryman told you about?"

"Yes, I remember."

"I think we found him."

"Where is he?"

"They're bringing him into the main room. I got hold of the deputy who was on guard duty in that hospital corridor. He's coming in and we're going to throw this guy on the big lineup. You want to make it?"

"Yeah, I want to make it."

"Al's jury back yet?"

"Not yet."

"Sorry, no verdict yet," Dick said. "But Blake O'Brien found a guy we've been looking for in that homicide-narcotics thing. I'm going over to the Sheriff's Department. Maybe I can get back—"

"Forget it," Al said. "It's in the bag."

"Sure it is."

Dick went straight to the elevator, down to the ramp, and walked quickly to the garage. He didn't feel tired now and his legs worked fine. He felt expectant, with just the right amount of tension, like a well-tuned violin.

On the second floor, in the compact auditorium that was the Sheriff's lineup, a small knot of plainclothes detectives and uniformed deputies huddled near the first row of seats. Above them was a broad stage, now dark. Blake O'Brien was sitting in the next to the last row by himself. He was in his shirt-sleeves, his jacket in his lap, his tie pulled loose from his throat. Dick sat down with him.

"I haven't seen him yet," Blake said. "Kearney's in charge. They got the one that was on guard duty at the hospital there and they'll line up this Ben with three, four others and see what happens."

"Has Kearney much to go on, aside from this possible identification?"

"Quite a lot, yeah."

The lights went up suddenly, flooding the white screen that stretched across it. The screen was blank except for a height gauge at either side, marked off in feet and inches. Down front all the officers sat down except for a tall, slender man with horn-rimmed glasses and thin, sandy hair. Lieutenant Kearney, it occurred to Dick, was about as far from the movie-television portrait of a police officer as you could get.

Two uniformed deputies led four men onto the stage and lined them up in front of the screen. They were of about the same height, but their weights varied considerably. Two wore neckties and jackets; the other two were in shirtsleeves.

Lieutenant Kearney's voice was low-pitched and clearly audible in the back rows of the auditorium.

"First guy there," he said, "you—step forward, please. That's good, right there. What's your name?"

"Jackson," the man said, "Barry Jackson age 32 height like you can see. Weight, I dropped about five pounds in the last week. I take care of my old mother—"

"All right, Barry," Kearney said. "Step back."

"He's one of the favorites," O'Brien whispered to Dick. "They get him up there whenever he's around, which he usually is three, four days out of the week."

"What does he do?"

"He drinks, but he isn't very good at it."

The man next to Jackson had stepped forward. Unlike Jackson, he was not an old-timer and he was nervous. His voice didn't carry beyond the edge of the platform, so Kearney asked him to speak up. He said his name was Herman Weiss and he ran a delicatessen on the north side and he didn't mean to make a disturbance in front of his mother-in-law's house but he was provoked. Kearney cut him off. One of the officers down front had got on his feet and was standing with Kearney, speaking into his ear.

Blake sat up straighter in his chair, leaning forward.

"That's the guard," he whispered. "This might be it."

"You on the end," Kearney said, "will you step forward, please?"

The one on the end was the tallest in the group. He was dressed in jacket and tie and wore a hat. Kearney asked him to remove the hat, and after a moment he took it off.

"Your name?" Kearney asked.

"Grease," the man said.

"Grease what?" Kearney said.

"Axle Grease."

"That's pretty good," Kearney said after a pause. "Fella said that last week here and we squeezed him back into the can for about six months. What's your name?"

"Harold. Harold Smith."

"Where do you live, Harold?"

"Crudsville, Amaryllis Street."

"Sometimes go by the name of Ben?" Kearney asked.

"My full name is Harold Benjamin Smith."

"Okay, Ben—you been in any hospitals lately?"

Blake O'Brien was leaning far forward in his seat, watching. Dick managed to sit still, but his throat was going dry. The man in the lineup put one hand on his necktie, then took it away. He looked off to one side.

"You hear me all right, Ben?" Kearney asked.

"I want out of here," Ben said.

A third uniformed deputy appeared to the right of the big screen, and the two who had led in the four subjects moved in from the other side. The man named Ben turned suddenly and ran toward the left side of the platform. The two officers caught him, turned him to face Kearney, and stayed with him, one on each side.

"Don't get excited," Kearney said.

"I want out," Ben said. "I'm clean." His voice rose unexpectedly to a shout. He struggled with the officers, who had to cuff his head and bring his arms up behind to subdue him. "I want a lawyer—I got a right to call a lawyer!" he yelled.

"Sure," Kearney said. "We'll call him for you."

"Morelli!" Ben yelled. "I want Ivo Morelli."

"Take him off," Kearney said.

The lights went out and the movements on the stage were shadowy and fading. Dick looked at Blake O'Brien.

"Morelli," Dick said.

They got up together. As they left the auditorium Dick was taking a thin black address book from his jacket pocket. There were phone booths in the hall outside, and Dick went into the first one, thumbing through the book. Blake leaned on the door of the booth. Dick dialed a number, and waited.

"I'd like to speak to Mr. Morelli," he said. "Richard Kramer speaking."

"He isn't here," a woman's voice said. "This is Mrs. Morelli."

"Can you tell me how I can get in touch with him? It's urgent."

"No, Mr. Kramer. I don't know where he is. You could try the office."

"Okay. Thanks."

He dialed another number. After three rings the tone changed, and Dick knew he was getting an answering service.

"Mr. Morelli," Dick said.

"Mr. Morelli is not in," a woman said. "May I take a message?"

"This is Richard Kramer, the District Attorney. It's urgent that I speak with Mr. Morelli. Can you tell me where to find him?"

After a moment she said, "I believe he's spending the evening with Mr. Steve Carolla."

"Thank you," Dick said and hung up. "Come on," he said, leaving the booth. "My car's right downstairs."

They started away as some officers came out of the lineup room. Blake stopped, turning to them. "Couple of you guys come on, huh?"

"Sure, Mr. O'Brien."

Two deputies fell in behind Dick and O'Brien. Dick looked at Blake, who shrugged. "Are we on television?" he said.

Dick said nothing.

CHAPTER 18

They drove up the winding road beyond the country club toward Steve Carolla's big house on the hill. There were lights on Carolla's terrace.

"I'm going in alone," Dick said. "We've got too little yet to walk in with all this power."

"Whatever you say," Blake said.

Dick parked the big car on Carolla's front drive. "Just stand by," he said as he got out. "I'll be back."

"Watch it," Blake said.

"Uh-huh."

The two officers in the back seat watched him go up the steps to the front door.

"Gutsy fella," one of them said.

"Yeah," Blake O'Brien said.

* * * *

Carolla opened the front door. "Mr. Kramer," he said. "How are you? Come on in."

"Hello, Steve," Dick said. "Thought I might find Ivo Morelli here."

"Sure, he's out on the terrace. Let me fix you a little drink."

"No thanks, haven't got time. If I could speak to Morelli—"

"Why not? Private?"

"Oh, no, come along. No secrets."

On the terrace Morelli, dapper and relaxed, was sitting in a deep chair, a cigarette in one hand and a glass in the other. He waved the cigarette but didn't get up.

"Hello, Mr. Kramer."

"Ivo." Dick nodded.

"Sit down, sit down," Carolla said. "Get comfortable."

Dick sat on the stone bench at one side of the terrace. Carolla got onto a chaise longue and put his feet up. He sat with his large round head pulled down into his shoulders.

Looks like a turtle, Dick thought.

"Nice to see you," Morelli said. "You been busy lately, in and out—"

"Yeah," Dick said. "How are things with you, Ivo?"

"Can't complain."

"I tried to call you at the office," Dick said. "Your service said you were here."

"Yeah, I'm right here. Steve and I—"

"We've been on this drug thing," Dick said. "Then there was the murder of the Berryman woman in the hospital—overdose."

"I remember," Carolla said.

"We wrapped it up tonight," Dick said.

"That's great," Carolla said. "Glad to hear it."

Morelli said nothing.

"A man named Smith," Dick said, "Harold Benjamin Smith, known as 'Ben.' He's downtown with Lieutenant Kearney. It looks as if he'll stay awhile."

Morelli snuffed out his cigarette and took a drink.

"He was asking for you, Ivo."

"Me?"

Dick got on his feet. "It got to be very interesting, digging into the local drug business. Very sharp organization. Lots of lawyers."

Carolla's head was up now. He was looking at Morelli. Ivo Morelli got up lazily, finished his drink, and started across the terrace toward the bar. Carolla watched him go.

"Lawyers like you, Morelli," Dick said.

Carolla slowly straightened on the chaise and swung his legs over the side.

Morelli mixed himself a fresh drink. "That don't sound friendly, Mr. Kramer," he said. "I don't follow you."

"Then I guess we'd better go downtown together," Dick said, "and I'll try to make it clear."

Morelli started back with his drink. Carolla heaved himself off the chaise, and Morelli stopped suddenly.

"You—" Carolla said, his finger shaking at Morelli. "You—alia time—"

He even kept it from Carolla, Dick thought.

Morelli seemed to freeze as Carolla came on. Then he dropped his glass on the stone floor, turned, and ran into the living room. Carolla pounded after him, and Dick followed more slowly.

In the living room Carolla caught Morelli by the shoulder, jerking him around. His big hands went for Morelli's throat.

"You—dirty wop shit—!" Carolla yelled. Then it changed to Italian, and Dick couldn't follow the words.

Morelli was fighting for his life now. Carolla had pushed him to his knees, and Morelli clutched at the powerful hands around his throat, bleating.

"That's enough, Steve," Dick said.

Carolla, spitting Italian, paid no attention.

Dick found the porch light switch and flipped it three or four times. "Come on, Steve," he said, "knock it off now!"

He put his hands on Carolla's shoulders, trying to pull him off Morelli, but Carolla just shrugged at him. Outside there were footsteps and a pounding on the door. Dick opened it to admit Blake and the two officers.

"Break it up," Dick said.

They pulled Carolla off Morelli, who sank to the floor, holding his neck, trying to breathe again. Carolla was panting heavily; his big face was on fire. He pulled away from the officers and made his way drunkenly toward the terrace.

Dick helped Morelli to his feet and turned him over to the officers, who helped him outside. Dick went to the terrace and found Carolla sitting on the stone bench, pounding on it with both fists. Dick saw they were red and broken.

"Give me a ring in the morning, Steve," Dick said. "I've got to go now."

Carolla didn't answer. Dick went back through the living room and let himself out. At the car Blake and the two officers were putting Morelli into the back seat. Dick got under the wheel. As Blake slid onto the seat beside him he said, "Carolla didn't know anything about it?"

"I guess not," Dick said. "Funny, huh?"

Blake turned his head and looked at Morelli between the two officers. "Pretty funny," Blake said. He faced front, and they drove downtown without further conversation.

* * * *

Dick left the office at one o'clock. He and Blake O'Brien had talked to Morelli for two hours and had gotten nothing from him. Dick hadn't expected anything. There wasn't enough evidence of anything at all to hold him, even overnight. But it didn't matter. They could let him go. Morelli was on the run and he would keep on running. The organization would crumple. The rest of the investigation was mop-up.

On his way out of the building Dick stopped at Blake O'Brien's office. O'Brien was getting ready to leave.

"Just called Al," he said. "Jury came in at nine o'clock. Guilty."

Dick nodded. "Good for Al," he said.

"See you in the morning?" Blake said.

"For sure," Dick said. "Thanks, Blake."

O'Brien waved good night.

* * * *

It was a little after one-thirty when Dick got home. He was too keyed up to sleep, so he prowled around the empty house, fixed himself a night-cap, threw half of it down the sink, and tried a peanut butter sandwich. That didn't go down either. He stretched out on the couch in the living room and tried massaging the back of his neck. It only made his arms ache. He dozed off and woke to the sound of a car on the drive.

Evelyn, he thought and got up quickly. But when he looked out, it wasn't Evelyn's car or her mother's. The motor was still running, and there was a woman behind the wheel. He turned on the porch light and went out. The woman behind the wheel was Liz Dexter. She looked out at him with wide eyes as he leaned on the window.

"Liz," he said.

"Hello, Dick—I just killed Pete."

Dick reached in and switched off the ignition. "Come on, try it again," he said.

"It's true—I shot him and killed him. A little while ago."

She began to tremble. He opened the car door, put his arm around her shoulders, and helped her out. She didn't say any more till he had helped her up the steps and into the living room. He set her in a chair and put a blanket from the couch over her knees. She trembled from time to time but not violently.

"Let me get you something—a shot of something."

"No, thanks, I can't drink—my stomach—"

He sat down and looked at her drawn, white face. She was looking beyond him at nothing.

"Where's Robin?" he asked.

"I sent him to his Uncle Bob's. He'll take care of him."

He went to the kitchen and got her a glass of milk. She held it in one hand but didn't drink from it.

"After we got home—from court," she said, "Pete was in a rage. He was cursing Robin—and me, too—as if it was all Robin's fault—that Robin had humiliated him on purpose—"

"That was when you shot him?"

She moved her head and smiled slightly. "You're trying to get me to say that I shot him to protect Robin. But I didn't. I sent Robin away first." Her hand trembled, and some of the milk spilled on the floor. "I'm sorry," she said.

Dick relieved her of the glass. "Listen," he said, "if you'll feel better about it, talk to me. But you don't have to talk to me or tell me anything at all."

"I know. I have to tell somebody."

Pretty soon Dick said, "Robin's Uncle Bob—he's your brother?"

"Yes, and he's all right. He'll be a better father than Pete ever was. He's married, but they never had any children."

"I'm sorry about everything," Dick said.

"One reason," she said, speaking with difficulty as if there were something stuck in her throat, "one reason I came—I don't hold anything against you, Dick. I wanted to tell you that." She paused. "Do you think Robin will get probation?"

"I'm pretty sure of it, yes."

"He won't have to go to prison then. He'll be all right."

Dick sat still, waiting.

"After I sent Robin away, Pete was more furious than ever—yelling and carrying on as if we had betrayed him or something. If he only could have known—it was the other way around, all of our lives. And there was a gun in his den. He'd been working on it, a pistol. He'd taught me how to use it once when he was trying to teach me to shoot. I never learned much about it. But I knew enough—he was yelling at me and blaming everything on Robin and me, and I couldn't stand it any longer. I got the gun from his den and went upstairs to his room, and when he opened the door, I shot him in the face. And he's dead. I waited long enough to make sure and then I came over here. And that's all there is to it."

"All right, Liz," Dick said. "You come over here and stretch out and try to rest. I'll cover you up—"

"I can't stay here," she said. "Evelyn—"

"Evelyn's not home," he said, "and she doesn't have to know anything about it. You lie down."

She let him lead her to the couch and put her down and cover her. He waited quite a long time till he thought she was asleep. Then he went into the study and made some telephone calls.

Pete Dexter, he thought. The tough thing is, what else was there for her to do?

* * * *

Ernie Smart and Otto Mannheim were talking about Pete Dexter in the little bar off the private dining room where Dick had met Senator Morris a couple of weeks before. They broke off when Dick came in. Dick was just as glad, though Ernie and Otto were both cordial.

Everybody was cordial. Besides Ernie and Otto there were Connors and Floyd Cantrell, and the Attorney General came in with Vince Farrell about one-fifteen.

"Steve Carolla couldn't make it," Vince said. "I just talked to him."

"He'll get over it," Cantrell said. "He's a tough Italian son of a bitch and he'll get over it."

"How about lunch?" Vince Farrell said.

He led the way to the suite where Ralph the waiter and two assistants were setting up a luncheon table. They cleared the doorway, and Vince stood back to let the others go in. Dick was the last to go in. Vince smiled and bowed slightly, ironically.

"After you, Senator," he said.

I don't know, Dick was thinking as he joined the others. I just don't know. Surely it couldn't be any rougher.

* * * *

He drove down from the Greenbriar at about three o'clock and pulled into the drive at his mother-in-law's house. Evelyn was not in sight, but Mother Stevens was sitting on the front porch drinking iced tea.

"Hello. Sit down," she said. "Drink?"

"No, thanks. Just came from lunch."

After a moment she said, not looking at him, "How did it go?"

"What do you mean?"

"I heard about it. I hear everything."

"Well, the committee—this much of the committee anyway—thinks I ought to run for Senator."

"I see. Do you want to?"

"Yes. Yes, I do."

Mrs. Stevens leaned over the wrought iron, glass-topped table, picked up a pitcher, and poured herself some more iced tea. She was a large woman and she frowned as if she were annoyed at the way it kept getting harder to move than it used to be.

She drank about half the glass of tea before she spoke. Then she said, "Costly to run for a big office like that, isn't it? Takes substantial funds?"

"I guess so."

"Well, you're welcome to what I have," she said. "I'm not horribly liquid right at the moment, but I can get that way."

He shook his head once, firmly. "No," he said. "Thanks all the same. The committee can raise money. I have some resources. You've been more than generous. I appreciate it, but I think I'll swing this one my-self."

She sipped at her tea, looking at him now across the tilted rim of the glass. Then she set it down carefully. "All right, Dick," she said. "Offer withdrawn."

"Thank you," he said.

"Would you like to speak to Evelyn?"

"If I may. Thought we might take a drive."

"I'll call her."

She pushed herself out of the chair and went into the house.

* * * *

They rode up the South River Highway. Evelyn was silent most of the time.

"What did they do with Liz Dexter?" she asked.

"She's in the hospital. Got good care. Judge Harris set a reasonable bail, and she'll be all right. After all, she's not a great menace to anyone but herself."

He drove to the highest point of the highway, several miles south of the city. There was a scenic turnout where they could sit and look out over the river valley to the farmlands off to the east and as far as Crudsville northward.

"Listen, Evelyn," he said, "Liz Dexter, the Foresters, even you and I—we're not the whole world. If bad things happen to us, it doesn't mean the whole world is coming apart."

She said nothing for a long time. Then she said, "Well—?"

"I've been thinking about it. In the last few days I've seen other worlds that I never had paid much attention to before."

"What are you trying to say?"

"Matter of viewpoint. Up here on the hill"—he waved his hand broadly—"we can see a lot of our personal world all at once. Down there—by the club, in our own house—we only see a little bit of it at a time, and it's mostly scrubbed and waxed and handsome and easy—on the surface anyway. But the whole world isn't like that. And the whole world is the world I, at least, speaking for myself, have to live in."

She gestured impatiently. "I wish you'd get to the point," she said.

"All right. The committee has asked me to run for the Senate—to succeed Morris. I have a good chance to make it. I'll have a much better chance if you come home."

Her eyes filled, and she looked away quickly.

Hang on, Evelyn, he thought. Please hang on. This is the first lesson. If you can't learn this one, it's hopeless.

"That's the reason you want me to come back. So you can run for Senator?" she said.

"It's not the only reason," he said. "I'm trying to tell you the exact truth. I have a commitment to you. It's my own. I made it myself a long time ago."

"You don't have to—I mean I'm sure I can manage to get along—"

"Wait, please," he said. "These two commitments, one to you and one to the public world, are all there is of me. I speak only of myself. Other men may be different, but I don't know them. I only know myself. You are necessary to me. If I had to choose between you and the Senate of the United States, I couldn't. I wouldn't settle for a choice. I want both."

She wasn't crying anymore. She looked at him with the helpless face of a child, her eyes blinking, her red mouth begging silent questions. Dick put his arm around her. She stiffened at first, then moved to him, hesitant and uncertain.

"I'll stop talking now," he said. "I'm only a lawyer and not to be trusted. I promise I will take good care of you—feed you and buy your clothes and keep a roof over your head. I'll be kind to you and not walk out on you. And when you're lovable, I'll love you, and when you're not lovable, I won't. And that's the truth."

Pretty soon she said, "You really want me to come back?"

"Really, truthfully, I do."

She drew away from him and settled herself in the seat near the window. Her slender, white-gloved hands lay still in her lap. "All right," she said. "Could we go home now? I'm hungry."

He started the car and drove back toward town. The windows were open, and he drove slowly so as not to fan up too strong a breeze. There was a strong, rank smell from the river.

Or maybe it's Morelli, he thought. The smell of Morelli and so many others that never quite goes away.

CHAPTER 19

DONNA FORESTER

Good-bye, Gino—good-bye little Gino—

She looked with concentration into the depths of the glass on the bar in front of her. It was hard to concentrate because it was very late— almost time for the bar to close—and she had been drinking since the afternoon. It was good that there weren't any other customers around. She didn't know whether Lonnie would serve her any more if there had been others to see. Lonnie had been very nice to her. He was a nice man. Not pushy or anything, but friendly.

Good-bye, Gino—go back to Lewkie—give it to Lewkie good—oh, Jesus, what will I do?

For a moment she concentrated on staying upright on the stool. Oops, she thought.

It was pretty nice of him to tell me though, come right out and tell me, instead of just never coming back any more. He'll be all right. Gino will be just fine.

Somebody was shaking her. "Gino—?" she said.

"Time to go, baby," a voice said. Not Gino.

It was Lonnie. So all right. Lonnie was a nice guy.

"Okay," she said.

"Whoa!" he said. "You can't walk out of here like that. And you sure as hell can't drive like that."

"Okay," she said, "send for an ambulance or something—"

"Sit down over there," he said, "and I'll see that you get home." He helped her into a booth.

She clutched at his jacket. "Take me home, Lonnie. Take me home with you."

"Sure, okay, soon as I close up."

She went to sleep.

* * * *

Lonnie Kirk woke her and helped her out of the car, which was parked in front of his apartment.

I don't think this is smart, he thought, but what else can I do? I can't leave her in the car. Maybe if she sleeps it off—

"What?" she mumbled.

"Come on, we're home now."

"Okay."

He practically had to carry her to the door and hold her up while he opened it. Then there was a long, steep flight of steps to the second floor. He held her in one arm and dragged on the stair rail with his other hand, making a step at a time.

"Where we going?" she asked.

"Upstairs. I'm going to put you in bed and you're going to sleep, baby, sleep."

"Sleep, baby, sleep—that's what I need."

They got to the top of the stairs, and he started looking for his key. She was so unsteady that he didn't dare let go of her. But the key was in the other pocket, and he would have to change her from one arm to the other in order to reach it. While he was changing over she sagged suddenly, and he lost his hold on her for a moment. She fell away from him and clutched for something to hold on to, and he couldn't quite grab her in time. She fell against the stair railing, then pitched forward and fell down the stairs, heavily, all the way, rolling from side to side. He stood at the top, helpless, watching. There was a small stone planter at the bottom of the steps in the narrow foyer. He heard her head strike it, and she rolled a little way and stopped and lay still. He turned his face away, leaning hard against the door of his apartment, and managed not to get sick enough to throw up.

I'm in it now, he thought. Oh, God, I'm in deep now.

RICHARD KRAMER

Dick Kramer got the phone call about four-thirty in the morning. It was from Al Levy.

"They just brought Mrs. Donna Forester into the morgue," Al said.

Dick squeezed his stomach with his free hand. "All right," he said. "What happened?"

"She got picked up in a bar and taken home, and the story goes that she fell down the stairs and cracked her head on a planter. She's dead. She was drunk, according to the report."

"Who picked her up?"

"Remember that bartender in the Dexter case last month—the good witness I had?"

"Yeah."

"It was him. She'd been hanging around his bar."

"Donna Forester—?" Dick said.

"That's why I'm calling you," Al said, "instead of somebody from the mill. He turned himself in to me."

"Is he telling the truth?"

"I think so."

"Well, if you think so, that's good enough for me."

"You might want to talk to him yourself. Shall I put a hold on him?"

"No, I'll come down. I'll be there in a few minutes."

"Sorry—"

"All right, Al."

Richard Kramer hung up the phone, left the bedroom quietly, and began to dress to go down to the office.